Finding Sandy Stonemeyer

A ROMANTIC THRILLER SET IN NORTHERN CALIFORNIA'S SANTA CRUZ MOUNTAINS

Linda S. Gunther

A WORK OF FICTION

Acknowledgments

I would like to thank the talented people who read *Finding Sandy Stonemeyer,* chapter-by-chapter, as I wrote and edited this manuscript: Nico Swaan, Kathy Buchanan, Bill Mowatt, Jessi Kaur, and Laurel Ornitz (my editor). Your feedback was a gift, inspiring me to keep going, keep creating, keep developing, even when I didn't know where I was headed.

Additional thanks to Andy Couterier and my writing colleagues at "The Opening" for your encouragement and support throughout the final stages of the creative process.

Special thanks to Julie Tipton for another amazing cover. I always want my writing to do justice to your fine artwork.

Note to the Reader

This novel began with a dream I had one night about a year ago. The first chapter is identical to the action and characters in that dream, even the main character's name, Sandy Stonemeyer, all in my dream! I don't have a clue as to where this came from, but I do know that I am thankful for the magical forces of nature and for the spiritual energy in the universe that led me to jump-start writing this novel.

Finding Sandy Stonemeyer

A ROMANTIC THRILLER SET IN NORTHERN CALIFORNIA'S SANTA CRUZ MOUNTAINS

Linda S. Gunther

Chapter One

Ozone

Never think for one minute that your life is one-directional, still, or steady. Change hovers on the fringes of our existence, ready to strike at any given moment. My name is Sandy Stonemeyer, mother of two forever feuding children: Luke, a curious four-year-old, and Jenny, a rambunctious nine-year-old.

I can still recall most of the details about the afternoon and early evening of that day. Light was turning into darkness, the weather depressingly dismal, the clocks having just changed; time had fallen backward or was it forward? I can never remember, but night was arriving earlier. We were restless after three days of uninterrupted rain, starved for the moisture. California was in a drought.

When I suggested taking a drive to the Creamery for some ice cream, my two children were overjoyed, full of pent-up energy, ready to scratch and scream the whole twelve miles from our mountain cottage in Felton to the center of Santa Cruz, our usual destination for either animated movies or the best ice cream for miles around. Like my kids, I just needed to get out of the house, anywhere outside, although it was already 6:30 in the evening before we ventured forth on our quest.

The ice cream proved heavenly. I carried my nut-topped double scoop in a Dixie cup in one hand and held Luke's sticky little hand in the other, as the three of us scurried through the light drizzle back to our red Toyota hatchback and headed home before the skies opened up with yet another drenching.

Dammit, I thought, noticing that my gas gauge had edged into the red zone. My mint chip ice cream was overflowing the brim of the cup, some of it drizzling onto my seat, as I slurped the rim to prevent more spillage. The kids in the backseat were smacking each other, sugared up from their treat.

I spent much of that day with Jenny, Luke, and my eighty-one-year-old Aunt Sylvie in her tiny house next door, my aunt revealing hints of dementia. Luke and Jenny played for hours that afternoon with her two Siberian Huskies, Zeke and Toby. Both were sweet, usually gentle canines, but in truth I had seen each of them nip at my aunt on more than one occasion.

I drove faster than I should have back up the hill to Felton. Highway 9 was nasty that night: jolting potholes, tall trees shaking off the weight of the heavy rain, the signature mountain road with its zigzag twists and turns.

"You're a pig," I heard Jenny tease Luke, "oink, oink, oink." Then a snorting sound assaulted my ears. Glancing in the rearview mirror, I noticed Jenny wave something in Luke's face. "Mommy, he won't use his napkin. His ice cream is all over him. It's so disgusting," she said, snorting again.

Luke turned his head away and covered his ears. "Stop it! Stop bothering me," he screamed. "I don't want a napkin."

"It's okay, Jenny," I intervened. "I'll clean him up when we get home. Leave Luke alone, please." I turned my windshield wipers on faster in response to the increased downpour of the rain.

"I'm giving him a napkin to help him and he's hitting me," Jenny screeched. "Oww! Lu-uke!"

I glanced down at my gas gauge. The indicator needle had made more progress into the red zone. "Sorry kids, we need gas," I announced, hoping to put a stop to their adversarial sibling exchange.

They didn't acknowledge me. Driving another two miles, I eased the car into the Arco station on Graham Hill Road. The backseat had gone quiet at some point, while I was concentrating on my empty gas gauge, praying I'd find a station open on a Sunday night.

The rain was pelting down, but at least I'd be covered at the pump, I thought with some relief. Digging around in my cluttered brown leather purse, I found my beat-up wallet and then searched for my credit card.

At that point, I remember hearing Luke's gentle snoring. He had fallen asleep. His shirt was stained with chocolate ice cream, and his sister was slouched over him, her nose pressed up against the fabric of his car seat. She held his hand, a napkin tucked between their fingers, as they both blissfully snoozed. Like all siblings, didn't they fight like stray dogs one minute and then love each other the next? Grateful for the moment of silence, I felt content, despite the challenges I was experiencing in the role of single parent.

I recall jumping out of the car, leaving the door ajar, careful not to wake the kids. I reached back inside to pick up my ice-cream cup, thinking I'd finish it while pumping the gas. It was that good. I held the soupy cup in one hand, while I slid my Visa card through the slot, noticing that the overhead lights at the pump station were flickering on and off, producing an annoying buzzing sound. The lights flickered a second time, and then went out.

"Dammit, I need gas," I muttered to myself, having surmised that the pump action had also ceased. I could barely make out the shape of the pump head, the rain blowing in horizontally, soaking my hair and my hoodie. Placing the ice-cream cup on the roof of the car, I groped around for the nozzle, still hooked to my tank. Another sound...an electrical generator had kicked in. The pump started up again. Thank God, I thought. But the area was pitch-black and I was weary.

A pinch in my lower back—what the hell was that? I wondered. Something had crawled under my shirt, likely a mosquito, the Satan of insects, taking a bite out of me. Warm rainy nights in the mountains seemed to bring them out.

I stumbled back into the driver's seat and realized that my ice cream was still sitting on the roof. I hopped out to snatch it. More of the mint green stuff dripped onto my blouse. Sitting behind the wheel, I suddenly felt dizzy, the sight out the front window looking blurred in the rain. What...

what was happening to me? Snapshots of scenes from earlier that day raced through my clouded mind, my inner clock rewinding.

♦ ♦ ♦

Waking up in a dimly lit bedroom, which I didn't recognize, I found myself tucked in a strange queen-sized bed, a blue- and-green plaid comforter wrapped around me. A lamp sat on a bedside table to my right, and to my left was a picture window. I could hear the rain beating down on the skylight above me and in the distance the sound of people talking and children laughing. My brain was fuzzy, my head heavy.

When I looked beyond the partly ajar bedroom door, I could make out what looked like pairs of shoes lined up by the wall in the brightly lit hallway. Where the hell was I? A few people walked by the door, in the lighted hall-way, holding drinks, chuckling at some joke. God, my head hurt; it was as if a tiny person was sitting inside my skull behind my eyes turning a screw. I wanted to yell out, "Who are these people, and where are my kids?"

I heard a child's voice coming closer. "Hey Luke," the boy yelled out. "Come see this. Come on. He's got a motorcycle in his garage. It's really cool!"

Then Luke's voice: "Wait for me. I wanna see it. Hey Jenny, I'm going with Carl to see a cool motorcycle. *You* check on Mommy."

Jenny peeked her head into the semi-dark room. "Mommy, are you awake? Mom?" She teetered between the needs of a young child and the early aspirations of a teenager, flipping between "Mommy" and "Mom" from one moment to the next when addressing me. I remembered doing the same thing as a young girl, before I lost my parents.

"Jenny," I said, trying to sit up. My voice surprised me, as it was raspy, my throat bone-dry.

She rushed to my bedside. "Mom, you fell asleep in the car," she said. "We didn't know what happened to you. You were slumped over your seat and your head was down on the steering wheel. The car horn was going off."

I tried to follow and to recall the sequence of events she was describing.

"Mom, your ice cream was spilled all over. Luke and I woke up and found you like that. It was so scary. Then this man, Mr. Zachery, he saved you. He didn't know what to do, so he put all of us into his SUV and brought us here to his house."

"What? Mr. Zachery? Who? What are you talking...? Never mind, get your brother, Jen, *please*." She hesitated, but I persisted. "*Now,* Jenny."

"But Mommy, it's okay. Mr. Zachery is having a party. Kids, families are here. He took care of you. Come on Mom, you'll like him," she said in a hushed tone, but her voice also carried a stern edge. "Don't be mad at this nice man," she continued, putting her hands on her budding hips, making it clear that she was taking charge. Shaking her finger in my face, she declared, "Don't be mad, Mom!"

Another head peeked in the doorway. My focus, although still under par, allowed me to make out the tall, slim silhouette of a man with a drink in his hand. "Eh, Jenny girl, looks like your mum is awake," the man said. Then he looked over at me and asked, "Um, may I come in?"

I tried to sit up again, but the stone weight of my head pulled me back. Nauseous, I fell back onto the pillow, a sharp pain shooting through my left temple. "Oh, I...I..."

The man moved closer, turning on the bedside lamp.

Concern spread across Jenny's face. "Mommy, you want some water or a Coke?" she asked.

"No, it's just my head..."

"You're right, Jenny girl, she needs something to drink straight away," the man said. "How about getting yer mum some juice from the fridge? That will help her out with a wooly head." He smiled down at my little girl. I noticed his eyes were almost translucent. Strands of his streaked blond hair flopped down over one eye. "Just ask me friend, Sally, to give you some juice. She's in the kitchen getting the birthday cake ready for Antonio. Go now, no worry, I'll look after yer mum."

Who was this man? I was wondering. I'd never seen him before.

Jenny frowned but seemed to take pride in assuming responsibility for me. "Yes, I'll get you some juice, Mom," she said with authority, shooting me a frosty warning with her eyes and then scampering out.

"I'm sorry," the lanky man said, sitting down on the edge of the bed. "You were unconscious in yer car and yer horn was blaring. When yer little girl opened the car door and yelled out for help, well, I immediately went over to her. She tried to wake you, but with no success, I'm afraid. Then yer little boy started to cry. It was dark, very dark; the electric lights had gone out at the pump, although some auxiliary backup generator had the gas start pumping again. Any idea what happened to you?" His eyes seemed to dance as he made his inquiry, despite his apparent concern. "Honestly I was beside meself. I didn't know what to do. I was just about to call 911, but yer kids seemed scared out of their wits." He sat there, handsome in a European sort of way, speaking in an accent I couldn't quite place. With a chuckle in his voice, he continued, "As you can see, I'm having a party here tonight and I needed to get back home. People were due to arrive and it was to be a surprise for the guest of honor."

"I see," I replied. "How long was I out? I...I..."

"It's probably been about two, maybe three hours now."

I could see the wheels turning in his head, thinking that he probably shouldn't be sitting on the bed with a strange woman he just met. He eased himself up, looking down at me, going on with his story.

"Before I left home tonight, I realized that I was almost out of fuel, but that didn't stop me from comin' out in the pouring rain to pick up the birthday cake I had ordered. That's me, the just-in-time host, not an attribute I'm proud of, to be sure." He jostled his drink, rolling his eyes, trying to lighten the tricky moment. "Of course, I had to nab the cake from me favorite bakery, now didn't I? Redwood Mountain Pastries, you know of it?"

I nodded, offering a faint smile.

"And there you were at the gas station, out like a light. No pun intended." He chuckled again. "So I reassured yer kids, scooped you up in me arms, put you all into my Range Rover, and here you are. Like I said, I probably should have called 911 but..."

"No, it's fine." I shook my head. "Thank you. Listen, you don't need to defend your actions. Really, I appreciate what you did," I reassured him, trying to convince myself. If this man had not intervened, I'd have probably ended up in some hospital emergency room. "You rescued me; I...I mean us."

"Whew, I'm glad you see it that way," he said, his shoulders seeming to relax, as he sighed. "I was troubled that you'd be upset waking up in a strange house. Forgive me for repeating me question, but do you have any idea why you blacked out?"

"No not really." My mind drifted back to the rain, the dark, playing back the tape in my head. I looked up into his eyes, trying not to be distracted by their unusual color, my mind going over every detail of the scene at the gas station. "I was fine one minute," I said. "Wait, I do remember feeling some kind of pinch in my lower back, maybe a mosquito or a bug bit me. Maybe a spider? I don't know." I reached my hand behind my back to feel the likely spot where I'd been nipped, but didn't feel a bump or any noticeable itching. "God," I said, "it was so dark with the overhead lights out at the station. I remember getting into my car after pumping the gas. My soggy ice-cream cup was in one hand and—"

"Then you blacked out," he completed my sentence.

At that moment, Jenny hurried into the room holding a small glass filled with purple-red liquid. "Mom, it's cranberry, you'll like it," she said, handing me the glass like a worried mother offering a child with a fever a cold drink.

"The cake is coming now! I want to see it. I'll be out there. Okay, Mommy?" she asked, slipping back into "Mommy," no longer self-conscious in front of the stranger and wanting my permission to leave. "Mr. Zachery, come on," she said, "aren't you going to watch Antonio blow out the candles?"

I took a generous sip of the juice. It was cold and tasted sweet, soothing my scratchy throat. Jenny hesitated, looking over at me as I tried, like a sick patient, to raise my head up from the pillow, but I fell back again like a sack of grain.

"Mommy, are you okay?" she asked, then sat on the bed.

I sensed sincere worry in her voice, but I knew that as usual she yearned to engage in the social activity. My Jenny, I thought, ready for a party, anytime, anyplace. More like her dad in that regard. Me, I could take or leave the social bustle around me, especially if there was a task needing my attention.

"Yes, of course, we'll be out there for the cake. We wouldn't miss it," the man said, laughing. Then turning to me, he said, "Let me ask you, love, do you think you can manage to get up to join us for the cake or would you prefer to rest a bit more?"

"Yes, I'm getting up," I replied, hearing myself sound a bit edgy. "I'm okay, really." I bit my lip and lied for the sake of my daughter, who lingered, scolding me with her eyes, reminding me to be decent to this man, her newest hero.

The man glanced over at Jenny and said, "You go out there, love. I'll help yer mum, and we'll both be in the dining room lickety-split. No worries. You're a little momma, you are, Jenny girl."

She smiled and then raced out.

"No worries." His words resounded in my aching head. "No worries." How could I not worry? I had collapsed for no apparent reason and was lying there in a stranger's bed, although my kids were safe and happy and I was physically comfortable in a *Sunset* magazine–worthy country house.

"What happened? Where the hell are we?" I wondered out loud in a sudden panic.

The man seemed surprised by my outburst, but kept his warm smile. "You are in the Santa Cruz Mountains, love, a couple of miles off Highway 17, just south of the mountain's summit. It's a tad secluded, but I've got me quite a view of the ocean from here. When you're feeling up to it, I'll show you around."

With his help, I raised my head from the pillow, pushing myself up against the headboard. He placed a second pillow behind me. I looked down and noticed the encrusted green ice cream all over my gray hoodie.

"Oh God, I'm a mess," I said.

"Yup, looks like you have a preference for pistachio," he remarked, smiling.

I startled myself with a girlish giggle, noticing that this lean, fair-haired man had a spray of freckles running across his nose. "Let me correct you," I said, "it's actually mint chip, a weakness of mine."

He walked over to a closet opposite the bed, flicked the light on, and snatched a green-and-black checkered flannel shirt from a hanger. "Here, you can put this on," he said with a slight grin. "We don't want to miss that birthday cake. I'll meet you out there."

A second awkward moment passed between us. The idea of undressing in this strange man's room troubled me.

"Um, yes, thank you," I replied, remaining on the bed, waiting for him to leave, not quite sure what else to say or do.

With a nod, he closed the door behind him. The shirt felt soft and warm against my goose-bumped skin. The color of my favorite ice cream, I noted. Catching my reflection in the dresser mirror, I saw I was a sight and felt embarrassed by the situation I had created for this well-meaning gentleman. I downed three more slugs of cranberry juice and released the hair tie from my frizzed-up hair, unruly brown curls falling every which way around the collar of the shirt. I scrunched up the tangled mop with my hands, but failed to make it look any better. God, my eyes looked sleepy. Where was my purse? I didn't see it anywhere. I scanned the room. Where the hell was it? My nerves were on edge. Try not to panic, I told myself.

Leaving the bedroom, I spotted my shoes sitting by the front entrance along with the others. I heard laughter, shouts of oohs and ahs. The hallway leading to the living room was dark. I felt my way to the dining room and turned a corner to the left, where more than a dozen people stood watching a well-endowed blonde woman place a sheet cake on the antique dining room table. The guests stood around the seated man being honored, the candles glowing brightly in the dark. A miniature head stone on the cake read: "R.I.P. Antonio!" Black frosting—that's different, I thought.

The blonde woman announced ceremoniously, "Rest in peace, Antonio. Brilliant fortieth to ya! Happy birthday!" Then she started to sing, the adults and children chiming in, at first out of synch, then as one. Two clusters of black jumbo balloons were tied to the man's chair. Jenny and Luke sang along as if they'd known these people forever. An almost sur-real scene had materialized before me, while I felt invisible, like a ghost observing the scene from above the crowd.

"Make a wish, Antonio," a chunky, red-cheeked teenager shouted.

The bearded man closed his eyes, seemed to think hard, then blew out the candles with a single breath, everyone applauding and cheering.

The tall, attractive host headed toward me. Touching my sleeve, he looked over at the guest of honor. "That there's me older brother," he said.

His brother? I looked over at the seated man again. Antonio's eyes were large brown orbs, his beard curly and black, his body robust, his hair dark, thick, and wavy, whereas Zachery, standing beside me, had sea-blue eyes and straight blond hair. For the second time that night, I could barely take my eyes away from him. The contrast between the two men didn't add up to them being brothers. But I smiled anyway, aware that my head was finally edging into more of a normal zone.

"And that's Antonio's little girl standing to his left," Zachery continued, "Felicia."

A freckle-faced, red-haired girl, with a whimsical expression, prob-ably a bit older than Jenny, stood next to Antonio. Her eyes were as green as green gets. I couldn't help but wonder how she could be that raven-haired man's little girl.

Zachery noticed me staring at her and said, "Yeah, I know, it seems a bit strange. She's got all that fire-red hair and that kiss of freckles, the complete opposite of me brother. His dead wife was all long, wild, red hair and vivacious, I can tell you."

Zachery dropped his head down, suddenly solemn. I thought I also detected a hint of anger in his voice and was thrown off a little by his use of the word *dead,* harsh in the birthday party atmosphere.

As he spoke, Zachery's eyes seemed to travel beyond the room, beyond the house. "She's gone from us," he said, his lilt turning into a monotone. "May she rest in peace." Looking up at the ceiling, he placed his palms together and said, "Dear God, thank you for looking after her." He seemed to come back to the moment and, looking over at me, explained, "Antonio's wife was killed just thirteen months ago."

"Oh my God, I'm so sorry," I mumbled, not knowing how to respond.

A bitter expression flashed on his face. I felt flustered and wanted to change the subject.

"So, I guess your name is Zachery?" I said.

He brightened, though his voice still carried a distinct edge. "Me name is Stuart Michael Zachery," he replied, "but everyone calls me Zack or Zachery."

"Um, my purse, do you know where it is, Zachery?" I asked.

"Well, yes, I have it safely stored in the bedroom," he said, with a slight blush. "Forgive me, I should have told you earlier. It's on a shelf in the closet. Do you want it now? I can get it for you, no problem."

"No, it's fine, you can give it to me after the birthday cake," I replied. "I just need to phone my Aunt Sylvie, let her know that I'm okay, not to be rattled if she doesn't see my car in the driveway. She lives next door."

I regretted questioning him, not wanting to seem like I was doubting his trustworthiness, as he seemed more than a decent man. I was a journalist, for God's sake, and used to be full of engaging conversation, but evidently not anymore. "Forgive me for asking," I finally managed to say, "but are you Scottish or is that an Irish accent I detect?"

"The second one is right, as Irish as they come. Me brother, Antonio, is from a different father on the gypsy side of our family. You see, me mum went through a wild streak in her late teens, fell in love with a traveling gypsy." He noticed my puzzled expression. "Yes, *Irish travelers,* we call them, they're everywhere in our home country, especially in the rural areas, parking by the side of the road or out in the back fifty acres on some farm. Guess you've never been to the land of Eire?"

I shook my head. "No, but I'd like to go sometime."

"You'd love it. Ireland—the crown jewel of all Europe. Anyway, the relationship between me mum and the gypsy soured. I guess that's how you'd put it. They parted ways and then Mum married the toe-headed typical Irishman who fathered me. She had only the one child with the gypsy: Antonio," he said, tilting his head in his brother's direction. "I came along, blue-eyed and freckle-faced, and Antonio, well you can see, with the coloring of a Romanian gypsy." He gazed at the bearded man who pulled the little girl close to him. I noticed the brothers lock eyes. Antonio smirked as if decoding the essence of our conversation, then gave us a quick wink and a grin.

"A good man he is and an even better brother," Zachery said. "I owe him for helping me out many a time when I had sunk to me lowest. Hard to believe but I was a rebellious teen with dark thoughts." He closed his eyes as he spoke, seeming to battle a bad memory. "It's a long, boring story. I won't trouble you. For the past year, I've been dedicated to just one thing—caring for me brother and for little Felicia, committed to seeing them both through our terrible family tragedy. She was a good wife, a loving mother, a stunning woman, through and through, with a heart of pure gold." Zack touched his shirt, slapping his fist against his chest, with almost patriotic gusto, his eyes welling up with tears.

"Antonio's a lucky man to have you for a brother," I said. I wanted to express my sympathy, but stressed by my own nagging situation, I couldn't find the words.

"I'll introduce you after the cake is served. Everyone's already met yer Jenny and Luke," he said, waving over to Jenny, who seemed happy to see the two of us getting along.

One thing was clear: He had already captured the heart of my daughter. On that first night with Zack, I had no idea what a pivotal role he would play in our lives in the coming months.

Chapter Two

Transitioning

I was never what you'd call pretty, never, but far above average on the intelligence meter. I always looked neat, presentable, what people called pert or maybe cute. I had shoulder-length, blunt-cut, thick, brown hair, hazel eyes, clear skin, and the cheekbones of a runway model. But my nose is a little crooked and cocked a smidge to the right, the byproduct of a hard fall out of our family tree house when I was nine, a year before my parents' accident.

◆　◆　◆

I didn't share the tumble with my mother when it happened for fear she would forbid me from climbing up there again. When I was a young girl, my brother Wesley loved to sit up in this tree house for hours on his own reading Batman comics. I envied his preteen twelve-year-old freedom and wanted to be sitting up there with him, hanging out in the coolest place on our property.

One drizzly afternoon, just a few days after my ninth birthday, I climbed up the steep ladder, to find that my brother wasn't even up there. Disappointed, I rushed coming down, faltering on one of the crooked limb-crafted steps, my legs scrambling in the air, my puny body tumbling to the ground. Once I managed to pick myself up, I quickly realized that something on my face wasn't right. The area around my nose hurt, and something felt off.

Frantic to examine the damage, I dashed into the house and upstairs to my bedroom, to inspect myself in the mirror, before anyone else had the chance. Although my nose seemed to be intact, it was red, like a ripe radish on the outside, and when I probed with my finger through each nostril, on the inside, the bone didn't seem to be in its usual place, though it was in one piece, and there was a minor bruise on my left cheekbone.

For the next week or so, I hid out in my bedroom as much as I could get away with, except for evening meals with the family, where I sat quietly, my mother's foundation makeup coating my nose and cheeks, praying not to be noticed. The pain kept me awake for several nights, but I took pride in my ability to handle the adversity of the circumstances.

I never mentioned the accident to my brother or to my parents, but later that same week, Wesley unexpectedly became more tolerant of having me up in the tree house with him, actually inviting me in, where, side-by-side, we devoured comic book after comic book and snacked on untoasted English muffins covered with heaps of fluffy Cool Whip.

It was summer vacation and although our family was considered one of the more affluent in the neighborhood, my brother and I were "latchkey kids." While our parents worked all day, we hung out at home on our two-acre property. Somehow I managed to successfully hide my most likely broken nose until it healed, although I can't be sure of its precise injury because I never actually went to the doctor. The result: a permanent nose bump and the tip with the slightest tilt to the right.

◆　◆　◆

Now at five feet four inches, I have a petite frame, although my body is relatively curvy. I'm proudest of my hands, with the most slender fingers, even when compared to those tall skinny models typically featured in dishwashing soap commercials.

Why did he cheat on me? Why? I was a good wife, a loving partner, and more than a decent mother to our two children. Jenny was a little "me," nice to look at, sassy, inquisitive, verbal as hell, and academically ahead of everyone in her class, more advanced than most children even two grades up. Because we're similar in many ways, there's sometimes friction between mother and daughter, especially obvious since the separation.

Bottom line, she blames me, even though it was made crystal clear that I was the victim of an unfaithful swine of a husband, which I tried to explain to my daughter two days after I ousted Albie from our home. Inelegant with my words, I approached the subject with my usual bluntness, hitting Jenny with the ice-cold reality that Daddy had betrayed us.

"He let down the whole family," I said succinctly. I just couldn't help myself, the anger licking at me, oozing out with every word I spoke. "He's a cheat and he now has to face the music. So he's not here!"

From across the table, Jenny glared at me with accusing eyes. "What are you saying? Daddy's not coming home? What happened?" she yelled. "What did you do to him, Mommy?"

That scene between us happened nearly a year ago. At that time, she'd consistently call me "Mommy" even when angry, never resorting to the formal "Mom." I liked "Mommy," the sound of it. I hated telling her something so critical of her father, but I just couldn't bring myself to lie. It was not in my DNA, even when it might have been the best alternative for the circumstances.

Luke stared down at his plate, pushing around his peas, wishing they would disappear, and that I wouldn't pester him about how green vegetables were good for his growth.

Looking Jenny squarely in the eyes, I continued my unplugged description of her father: "I'm afraid your daddy did some unforgivable things, very bad things. He hurt Mommy." I sounded accusatory as I fought the tears welling up in my eyes, but I couldn't help it. Instantly regretting my choice of words, I blundered on further. "I mean, he didn't hurt me physically, but he did some damaging things that made Mommy upset with him, and now Mommy and Daddy have decided to live apart." I rushed the ending of the "ultimate worst news" kids can hear from their parents.

Jenny reacted with a quick swipe of her right hand against the full glass of chocolate milk, sending it spraying all over the pale-blue embroidered linen tablecloth, the one Aunt Sylvie, my guardian since I was ten years old, gave us for our fifth wedding anniversary.

Startled by the stab of my words, Jenny stiffened. At first she began to sob quietly, and then she started to scream, banging her fist down on the tabletop. Suddenly still, she stared straight ahead at the watercolor landscape hanging on the wall above my antique breakfront. Her head bent, she dropped her face down into the unfinished chicken dinner on her plate. She stayed there for a second and then abruptly stood up, throwing the chair on its side with a bang.

"You're lying," she said accusingly, wiping her face with a napkin. "Daddy wouldn't do anything really bad. He's good. I have fun with him. *You* hurt *him*, not the other way around. *You* kicked him out! Now it sounds like you hate him for no reason."

I rushed to her side. Why the hell did I use such noxious wording, and with my daughter, who adored her father? What was wrong with me? Making an attempt at tenderness, I got down on one knee and spoke sincerely to my little girl: "Jenny, I'm sorry. I'm hurting inside, and I know you're hurting, too. What happened with your father was a surprise to me." Ashamed at my earlier behavior, I gazed down at the dark-blue carpet, reining in my scattered thoughts. I held her small hands in mine. "I'm just angry, Jenny. My nerves are raw. Daddy and I love you and Luke very much. That hasn't changed. It will never change." God, I sounded like an actress on a bad TV soap opera, but what else could I say?

Flashing an unforgiving glare, she started to leave the dining room, in tears, chanting, "I hate you. I hate you."

Before she could get to her room, I was back at her side. "Look pumpkin," I said, "your daddy's coming over tomorrow afternoon. He'll be so happy to see you."

Her shouting started up again. "It's your fault... It's all your fault... I hate you."

I reached out to hold her. Wounded, her world crumbling, she smacked my hand away.

All I could think to say was, "Daddy will take you guys out for dinner tomorrow, I promise. And next weekend, he'll show you the new place where he lives. You'll see him often, as much as you want. I'm sure of it."

Still dissatisfied, she stomped down the hallway, slamming her bedroom door so hard the sign hanging from the doorknob, which read, "Princess Inside—Please Knock," crashed to the floor. Picking up the fragments of splintered wood, I turned to Luke, who had followed us, suddenly registering that he had just witnessed the whole scene. His lower lip quivered.

My almost four-year-old was confused and frightened and began to whimper, "Daddy, Daddy. I want Daddy."

Lifting him up in my arms, I asked him if he would like his box of Legos. Maybe he could build some cool cars or trucks on the living room rug. "I'll take a photo of the best one when you're finished," I said, faking a smile. "How would you like that, Luke?"

He nodded, his tears vanishing, willing to forsake thoughts of his missing daddy in favor of his favorite toy.

Entering Jenny's room, I found her huddled under the bedcovers, her mini "My Kitty" flashlight shooting its narrow beam at her Barbie pillowcase.

"Don't touch me," she yelled out. "I'm mad. Go away! You don't love Daddy anymore and you don't even love your kids. You're a mean mother."

I didn't move. A few seconds of silence, then sniffles, her body buried under the pale-pink comforter. I didn't know what to say. My automatic response was to try to physically console her, so I rubbed her back and shoulders. She wasn't coming out from under the comforter, but she had finally stopped pushing me away. I sat there on the edge of her twin bed for what felt like forever, stroking her, my weak effort to appease my impassioned little girl who was upset for good reason.

Luke came running in to show me his Lego creation, holding a lopsided red and black racecar too close to my face. Embracing him with one arm, I continued to gently make finger circles on Jenny's back. My children needed me to connect without words, without explaining away the dreaded situation. Luke brushed away a wandering tear he spotted rolling down my cheek. "It's all right Mommy," he said. With that, my heart warmed.

In bed that night, I felt lost. My mask had fallen off in front of my children, the one I wore to protect them. I stared at the shadows on the ceiling and seemed to drift between two worlds, the one I had just lost and the one that I was reluctantly entering, no longer a wife and barely what you'd call an acceptable mother.

Albie didn't show up the next day, phoning me in the morning, saying that he was unexpectedly tied up in meetings on a bitch of a new corporate case. He just couldn't get away but maybe by the weekend he'd be able to pick up the kids for an afternoon. Then he asked if I was doing okay. I didn't answer and told him I had to go.

The next time I talked to him, he inquired as to whether I thought it was a good idea to keep the house. Although suspecting he had an ulterior motive for his question, I jumped at the idea, holding a strong desire to start a new life with the kids outside of San Francisco.

"No," I replied, "I'd like to get out of the city. What if we sell the house and split the proceeds?"

"That would be best for all of us," he said, his voice solemn.

Luke adjusted well, enrolled in Felton's best preschool. His teacher, Mimi Webster, had also become my closest friend in the mountain community, my San Francisco city friends having drifted away, one-by-one, and barely making contact. Did that have anything to do with Albie? I didn't know and didn't honestly care much. Jenny made some degree of peace on the subject of her mommy and daddy, but adopted an acidic, accusatory tone with me more often than not.

About sixty miles away, Albie made his new home in a condo in Menlo Park, his employer recently having launched a second private investigations office south of San Francisco, in the hub of the high-tech world. Buried in an assortment of Silicon Valley corporate crimes, he drifted further and further away from his ex-wife and two children.

I purchased a comfortable cottage in the Santa Cruz Mountains in the old California town of Felton, known for scenic redwoods, the Roaring

Camp Railroad, and the beautiful San Lorenzo River. Aunt Sylvie had moved to this country paradise about ten years ago with her brand-new seventy-year-old husband. Then, seven months later, he accidentally tripped over the electric cord, while vacuuming their living room carpet. He hit his head on a rabbit-shaped stone doorstop, immediately falling unconscious. Her new husband died before the ambulance even arrived at the hospital.

Aunt Sylvie gradually recovered and grew to love the mountains, though lonely without her husband. The community opened their arms to her, my aunt becoming a regular at local events, like county fairs and bingo games at the senior center, where she connected with other aging folks in similar circumstances. So, after my marriage ended, I was fortunate to find a cottage right next door to the woman who had generously cared for me ever since I was orphaned at age ten. Now at eighty, she was elated to have us living on the other side of her fence.

Our new neighborhood had horses, grassy-knolled parks, hiking trails, good schools, even rodeo grounds offering cowboy shows once a month. It was a welcome change from the crazed pace of San Francisco life.

◆ ◆ ◆

My brother Wesley had moved away only a month after I told him about Albie's flagrant indiscretion. Wesley had always been obtuse, in honesty, ever since our parents died in the airplane accident. Though equally devastated, I was willing to accept Aunt Sylvie as a replacement parental figure. She and I had a kinship with our interest in writing, sharing a similar lens, seeing the world as something to shape, and full of opportunities, where we were able to make a positive impact.

My brother, three years older, never accepted my aunt as guardian, adopting a pessimistic view about life in general from the day of the accident. What bothered me most about Wesley was his unabated use of negative contractions for almost every situation—don't, won't can't, didn't, isn't, shouldn't, couldn't, haven't—unable to do otherwise. If I counted the number of contractions spewing from his mouth in a given twenty-four-hour period, I'd easily fill a blank notebook in less than an hour. As a young girl and then into my early teens, I had enjoyed the one-on-one debates with my brother about politics and social issues, and sharing our views on foreign films and literature. Despite his negativity, I missed him when he disappeared into the hills of Wyoming, saying that he was leaving to work on some obscure archeological dig with a group of UC Berkeley professors. Wesley had bounced around after graduate school, without a career goal in mind, earning money as a part-time house painter and roadway construction worker, and being a closet intellectual, reading book after book each night, but with little care or planning for his future. But perhaps that was my own distorted view of what he was doing with his life.

◆ ◆ ◆

It takes Albie a little more than an hour to get to our house in Felton when there's no traffic from his townhouse and about ninety minutes or more at peak commute time if there are no accidents on treacherous Highway 17. Moving this far away with a mountain between us was my way of punishing my ex-husband, although I recall him making the subtle suggestion that perhaps I might move closer to my Aunt Sylvie. Even though a long drive for him, he seemed pleased to have us tucked away in a distant Santa Cruz mountain cottage. Regardless, I expected some degree of reliability from him as the remote parent but instead found him often leaving town without notice on some supposed emergency investigation, this seeming to occur a few times each month.

I was trying not to hate Albie. As Mimi said, people screw up, hopefully evolving into better versions of themselves. Mimi and I agreed that it was far too late to try to repair a damaged marital relationship like ours. She said, "It's best for you to move on, create new adventures, new memories, attract new people into your life." I respected her point of view

(P.O.V.). P.O.V. is very important in all situations. I've often used that term in my journalism career. A good journalist is always looking for the inter- viewee's P.O.V. It was indeed wise advice from Mimi, but I wished that I didn't have such a negative opinion of my ex-husband. The pain in my heart should have subsided by then, but the wound felt just as fresh a year later.

What became of my "shades of gray" philosophy? I had walked around thinking that every situation, whatever it is, had two sides, but then there was the gray area in the middle. All perspectives were equally important to consider when evaluating right from wrong, especially the "gray" territory. Not on this one. For me, it was pure black-and- white, with Albie having full accountability for fucking up our good marriage.

Chapter Three

Losing Sandy

I've been lost for so long now, long before the divorce, adrift actually ever since becoming a mother. With the birth of Jenny, then Luke, I found my hopes of evolving into a serious writer had faded into the sunset. At one time, I had thought of myself as a true renaissance woman, far ahead of the social times I found myself in at college and in my early career. My only aspiration had been to become a respected journalist, travel the globe, mingle with heads of state, interviewing leaders who were changing the world. But then I had fallen for Albie Stonemeyer, impulsively trading in my dreams for romance, motherhood, and marriage.

◆ ◆ ◆

Starting out on a different track as a young girl, I pledged to myself to resist the urge to "couple up." I was focused on my future, dating boys, yes, but falling in love, no, I would not let that happen. First of all, I didn't have much confidence in my instincts when it came to boys, as my choices had proven disastrous in both high school and college.

I dated a boy named Randy Micheloff for more than a year in high school, our relationship blossoming into a steady one in my junior year. He was tall, dark, and dreamy, while I was aloof, sometimes not even calling him back after he'd leave two or three messages, or on occasion I'd even fail to show up for a scheduled date. Less than a dependable girlfriend, I preferred to spend my time catching movies with my older brother, gobbling up documentaries related to social issues, reading Margaret Mead, studying romance languages, or researching both sides of some hot school debate topic. I was a junkie for learning.

My nonchalance caught up with me in the spring of my senior year while on a dude ranch trip. Randy and my best friend Sarah seemed to be flirting with each other during the classic hayride, even though Randy held my hand tightly over the bumps and bends of the long dusty path. But I could see him make eye contact with Sarah, grin at her a few times, then nudge her in the side when we jumped off at the end. As I plucked bits of straw from my corduroy jeans, Randy turned to me, saying he needed to dash back to the boys' bunkhouse to retrieve the six-pack he had hidden under the mattress. He'd find me later, but was going to hang out with the guys for a while, if that was okay with me, or I could come with him if I wanted. I didn't mind in the least, sending him on his way without an ounce of guilt, content to see him becoming less dependent on my company.

For me, it was relaxing to be alone with my thoughts. Maybe I'd go back to my bunk and finish *Pride and Prejudice* for the second time. But I decided, first, to sit on a wooden fence and watch a cowboy who was training a muscular white stallion in the paddock. I wondered what it was like to be a cowboy, spending my days with horses and my nights twirling ropes at rodeos. I sat there daydreaming when my stomach suddenly cramped up. Feeling my period hitting me with a vengeance, I rushed to the restroom. Strolling back past the barn, I heard a familiar sound. It was Randy's voice coming from the barn. I figured the boys were drinking their treasured beer, sharing lewd stories, or who knows what. Deciding to wander inside to say hello and thinking maybe I'd have a quick beer with them, I tied my hair into a ponytail and entered the barn. I had never drunk a whole can of beer, but maybe this was the ideal time to try it.

That's when I found the two of them buck-naked, wrapped around each other like pretzels in a straw-filled horse stall. Sarah was beside herself, jumping up, the horse blanket wrapped around her skinny ass body. She ran after me, pleading with hollow apologies, offering me her promise to never talk to Randy again. Feeling like I'd been stabbed in the back, I was mostly disappointed with Sarah as my supposed best friend versus Randy as my vapid boyfriend. Was she a slut or just a girl leveraging an opportunity? My thoughts percolated.

Two days later, Randy stood by my school locker waiting for me. His eyes looked tired and pink. Had he been crying over me? I listened as he begged me to reconsider our relationship, which had so much promise.

"Come on, Sandy, you know I want only you. I strayed like an idiot, without thinking," he said. "Come on, you can't hold a grudge forever. I won't screw up again."

A grudge, I thought. He was worried about me holding a grudge. I spoke as if I were a robot. "Ran-dy Mich-e-loff," I said, "can you el-luc-i-date on the word *grudge*?"

"E-llucidate?" he repeated, seeming to be confounded by the word. Frowning, he asked, "What does that—"

"Never mind," I stopped him, putting my hand to his lips, then turned and walked away.

A week later, I found myself forgiving both of them, having realized how stupidly I'd been leading Randy on, when I didn't have any strong feelings for him. All I wanted in life was to become a world-famous journalist, and I'd do anything I could to get there, and had been only passing time with Randy. Of course, I still valued the company of boys. I liked the way their minds worked, more like mine.

My bad luck continued. I recognized that I was falling into a pattern. Not willing to bid a complete farewell to the dating scene, I also didn't plan on dedicating a lot of time or energy to it. However, it didn't stop me from complaining to my girlfriends about the dates I had accepted, including a mélange of bumbling boys who pursued me despite my tepid response to their overtures.

There was Peter, the guy who didn't call back after what I thought were two decent dates. I ran into him at the local library and he whispered in my ear, "Why didn't you call me? I was waiting for your call. I don't like being the chaser all the time. I'd rather be chased," he said. I couldn't believe my ears. I closed my textbook, stood up, and walked out. Then there was the overconfident jock Craig, who told me that he was going out to party with his football mates but instead was entangled with Audrey, the gothic girl who made her nest in the dorm room next to mine. I could hear their lustful panting through the thin plaster walls. What an imbecile he was thinking I wouldn't find out when he was in the dorm room next door. When my roommate leaked to him that I was totally aware of his cheating, like Randy, he begged me to give him one more chance.

At the hint of realizing a boy was a borderline mental inferior, I'd immediately lose interest in him as if I'd been struck by lightning, instantaneously jolted to my senses. I shook off these bad experiences, each time happy to be once again footloose, independent. Anyway, I disliked the "dance" of dating. Will he call me? Will I be alone on Saturday night? What should I wear on our next date? Should I phone *him* before he phones me? Agh. I didn't need boys to slow me down. So, cold-turkey, I stopped dating in my junior year of college and instead watched my girlfriends go through their heartaches, their roller-coaster dips and surges, their fragile hearts in shreds nearly every other week. I was free, keeping my distance from love and taking pride in my ability to remain unemotional with the opposite sex.

This restraint continued into my early twenties, when I was a grad student, working in San Francisco as a TV news intern. With a master's degree in Communications, I landed a position in Oakland as the radio station's news girl, my first paid journalism job. One year later, I competed with the "best of the best" in the Bay Area and won out, becoming a fully fledged professional news reporter. My job was to find local stories and write copy for the Channel 8 on-camera reporters. I was efficient and skilled at writing copy, eagerly working around the clock when necessary, consistently delivering much more than expected. And so when my colleague, Dalia Callaway, moved to the East Coast with her husband Rick and their two toddlers, out of the seven reporters left, I was the one selected and promoted to be the at-the-scene on-camera reporter. I knew it was partly because of my fresh college-girl looks, but even more as a reward for the high quality of my work.

However, I was still insecure. But the fire was there. My frenzy to achieve success in broadcast television soared to new heights. I was rising fast. Story after story, I was there, keenly reporting, carefully presenting myself with confidence, winning two local broadcasting awards by the time I was twenty-six. I had evolved nicely in the eyes of the station's executives and was promptly requested to interview visiting dignitaries, politicians, and even a few Silicon Valley CEOs. Additionally, I was being scouted for a possible national news show based in Washington, D.C. They hadn't directly contacted me yet, but I heard through the station grapevine that I and one other reporter were being tracked by the "big guys."

Then Albie appeared on the scene... I remember that day as if it were yesterday.

◆ ◆ ◆

I was on top of the world when he walked into the Oakland Police Station where I was interviewing the Police Chief about two high-profile murders occurring early that morning on the BART train. The bright lights of the cameras were on me and on Chief Griswold, who was responding thoughtfully and articulately to my tough questions. The killer was still out there and the public was scared. The Chief seemed to connect with their fears but at the same time exuded an unruffled confidence, sharing his updates about the search for a murderer but with an impressive calm in his voice.

In the middle of the interview, out of the corner of my eye, I noticed a nice-looking man ease himself to the front of the densely crowded room. He was wearing a gray, rain-splattered trench coat, and his hair was dark and wet. It struck me that he had an unlit cigarette hanging from his lips, an outright dare to the strict county-building no-smoking policy. With extraordinary peripheral vision even when under pressure, I would constantly scan the room for who was there and for their reactions to my delivery as a credible interviewer. A downpour must have ensued outside that day, because the man was that dripping wet. I tried to stay focused on my interview, but the man had moved even more to my right, closer to the front, now directly in my line of sight. He was distracting me, not helpful, but on the other hand, I was curious about him, a foreign sensation for me. Why was he shaking his head every time I asked the Chief a question? Every single time I spoke, he wagged his head. Then when it was Chief Griswold's turn to respond, the mysterious man would cease his disapproving gesture. The seven-minute interview ended. It was a wrap.

Although I knew the package would be edited and likely cut in half, I was feeling satisfied with my performance both as a rising television personality and as a journalist. Once I thanked Chief Griswold for his candor, the lights were dimmed and the equipment immediately disassembled by the blasé cameramen, who quibbled among themselves about the lunch options in the Oakland area. The lead man, Scott, told me that I was free to get out of there until our next gig scheduled for later in the afternoon. Craving a break from all eyes on me, I was thankful. Jamie, the other cameraman shouted over to me that he just received word that my story was first up on the Channel 8 six o'clock Bay Area news. My entire interview with Griswold was to be aired. I felt elated but apprehensive about how I might come across, my insecurities surfacing, as I questioned my journalistic abilities and myself overall. Would I appear serious enough? Would I look professional yet attractive to the hundreds of thousands of eyes on me?

As I started to leave, I passed the man who had been shaking his head at me throughout the interview. The crowd was quickly dispersing. As I moved by him, I found myself intentionally brushing up against him, and then I caught his eye. Not able to think of anything else to say, I remarked, "I guess it's still coming down out there," flashing my best TV smile. What a lame introduction that was, I chided myself and turned to flee the room.

He smiled back and said, "Yeah, no umbrella. That's me, never prepared but always ready."

I liked his gravelly voice. Polite but direct, I said, "Pardon me for asking, but I noticed you shaking your head every time I asked the Chief a question. You disliked my interview that much? Was it my choice of questions or my style in general?" I asked, nervously fidgeting with my umbrella.

"Neither," he replied, looking down at his feet as he shifted his weight from left to right and then back again. "I was trying to convince myself not to go for it, but here you are. There *is* a God!" He glanced up at the ceiling as if connecting with the Almighty. "Thank you, man. You know how to look after me."

I buttoned up my coat and chuckled. "Well, that was the best cornpone confession I've heard all week," I said. "I'm flattered. How'd you like to have coffee or maybe a light lunch with me? I have almost a three-hour break before my next assignment, which is fortunately not too far away from here."

"You like spicy?" he asked, hooking his arm in mine.

"Excuse me?"

"Not important, let's go. You'll see what I mean."

Did he mean food? Of course, what else? We're talking about lunch. I tried to keep my mind focused, as I felt myself immediately being swept off my feet.

He snatched the paisley pocket umbrella out of my hand, steering me through the exit door and speaking in a private tone, that raspy voice hooking me in. "I've seen you around, Sandy Phillips, but I'm guessing you never noticed me...until now."

"Are you a reporter?" I asked. The rain was coming down steadily, the skies transitioning into semi-darkness at only 1:15 in the afternoon, a dark-gray blanket of clouds hovering over Lake Merritt.

"Better, I'm behind the scenes. I'll tell you all about it later. Now hush up until we get there." He pulled me to him, holding me closely under my tiny umbrella, whisking me across the street, jaywalking despite the crowd patiently waiting for the light to turn green. My shoulder bag weighed me down, packed with my notebook, laptop, and notes to be studied before my next interview later that afternoon with a Superior Court Judge. "Want me to carry that?" he gallantly asked, the unlit cigarette still dangling from his mouth.

Rushing down another block, he steered me into the entrance of the Davenport Hotel, a small boutique establishment just across the street from Lake Merritt. Damn, I was hoping he didn't get the wrong idea from my forward behavior. He closed my umbrella, shaking the water all over us, and led me to the hotel reception desk, where he retrieved his wallet from the pocket of his trench coat. I gasped, unable to utter a word, but peripherally I could see that the reception clerk noticed my reaction. As Albie slapped his wallet down on the counter, he turned toward me, shooting me a "gotcha" expression. I was taken aback but steadied myself, biting my lip, searching for something to say. Snatching his wallet from the counter, he then led me away from the reception area, throwing his head back, fully satisfied with the scene he had just masterfully created.

"Did you really think...?" He laughed. "Forgive me. I was only playing with you, Sandy Phillips, star reporter. We're not getting a room. I had no intention of it. I repeat: We are *not* getting a room. Not today. Not today. Not today." He said it three times, seeming to tell himself more than me.

"Our actual destination is right this way," he said, tugging me toward an elegant archway at the end of a long corridor. "The Thai Boat," the golden sign above the entrance read. "I love spicy, don't you?" he added, leading me through the archway.

"Yes, spicy everything. The hotter, the better, don't you think?" I said, having recovered from the shock moments ago at the hotel reception desk.

Then he led me up a narrow carpeted staircase.

"Good afternoon, sir, I have the best table waiting for you," the elderly host said in greeting.

The restaurant was quiet, only one small group of businessmen left sitting at a table opposite the open kitchen, and it looked like they were getting ready to leave. Once we were seated side-by-side in a half-moon-shaped window booth facing the lake, my lunch date jumped up, taking the Asian waiter aside, out of my hearing radius. I watched the dark clouds unleash another shower outside. He came back, sat down, snuggling up close to me, seeming well aware that he was still sopping wet.

"We are set, Lois Lane. I ordered an array of 'bad ass' items for us. You don't mind, do you? Looks like you could use a little spice in your life, huh?"

I hesitated, and then nodded my head in full agreement. Taking his dare, I said, "I'm willing to try whatever you select from the menu. Just leave me able to speak with confidence and clarity this afternoon. Okay, Mr. 'know it all' psychiatrist?" I was gradually getting in synch with his humor.

At that time in my career, I was committed to looking as slender as possible for the camera. This meant that I needed to avoid ethnic food, including most carbohydrates, anything fatty, and that also meant rarely indulging in alcohol. Typically sticking to a quick salad for lunch by myself, in between bites I'd review my notes and prepare for my afternoon location shoot. But that day, I felt hypnotized, as if I were outside my life, throwing caution to the wind. Albie and I spent two hours gazing at the rain as it fell over Lake Merritt and not so accidentally touching each other whenever we had the chance, whether reaching for the one bowl of hot and sour soup or our hands coming together on the small clay teapot.

At one point, Albie reached over and untied the peach-colored silk neckerchief from around my neck. Asking me to close my eyes, he re-tied it around my eyes. "Ready?" he asked.

I had no clue as to what he was doing, but went along with it, nodding.

"Your assignment, Ms. Phillips," he said, "is to guess the name of the dish I will put in your mouth and identify the overriding spice driving its unique flavor."

I basically flunked the quiz, unable to name the precise spices in three consecutive dishes, which was extraordinary for me, since I was, at that time, continuously operating as Ms. Overachiever.

"Not very good at this game, are you?" he teased.

He kissed my lips three times while I sat blindfolded, one kiss after the Kung Pao Chicken, then again after the Four Spice Squid Curry, and then one more time after the Peppered Prawns. First it was a peck, then a long flavored kiss, and then with my head back against the cushioned leather booth.

Coming to my senses, I removed the kerchief around my eyes, glanced at the time on my cell phone, and then gulped down half of my ice water. My mouth was on fire. I finished the glass. The pitcher of water was empty.

"Sorry, but I should get ready for my shoot," I said, having recovered my senses. "I need to review my notes and go over my questions."

His face dropped, disappointed, as if the whistle had been blown in the schoolyard and playtime was over. "Your next gig is at the court-house, right?" he asked.

"That's correct, in exactly forty-five minutes, and I'm not prepared."

"You're interviewing Judge Mackey about the Juan Alvarez decision?"

"Well, yes, but how did you know?"

"Just put two and two together. It's my job. I'm a private investiga-tor, a P.I." He bowed his head, giving me a subtle grin. "Look, I'll pay the tab, have the waiter clear the table, and then leave you to make your way back. How does that sound to you?"

I nodded hesitantly at what appeared to be his curt exit line. Had I insulted him, said something wrong? The familiar insecurity had surfaced again.

"*Adios* princess," he said and then walked out.

I didn't even get his first name. Confused but wishing to push back my feelings, I pulled out the notes from my leather shoulder bag to review my list of questions for the Judge, but found it impossible to concentrate, an odd sense of loneliness overcoming me.

"More water, Miss?" the waiter asked, catching me by surprise.

"Oh, um, thank you," I replied.

Pouring the water from a pitcher, the waiter grinned, revealing uneven yellow teeth. Then reaching into his blazer pocket, he placed a roll of

Pep-O-Mint Lifesavers onto the white tablecloth in front of me, saying, "He said to tell you to enjoy these, Miss."

Mints, thank God. I didn't have any in my purse. I thought there'd be a note. No note.

"Wait, excuse me, sir," I stopped the waiter as he started to leave. "Um, the man who just left, how do you pronounce his name?" I asked, realizing that I hadn't found out his name. I felt a bit foolish, as he had probably noticed my date and I kissing at least a couple of times during our meal.

He raised his eyebrows. "His name? It's Albie Stonemeyer. He comes here a few times a month, maybe more. You don't know his name, Miss?"

"I...I...well, yes, I knew it was Stonemeyer, but I thought his first name was something else. Um, thank you," I muttered back, duly embarrassed.

Albie Stonemeyer, private investigator. Poof, and now he was gone. I tried to wrap my head around the whole quirky scenario, having no idea that he was to be my husband in less than a year's time.

He would find me just two days later, in an Oakland café, reading my notes, then pull me to my feet and ask for our first formal date. We fell in love, deeply in love, crazy in love, in less than a week. Being with Albie was an adventure, always romantic, his intensity keeping me on my toes, his sense of humor helping me to lighten up, and I liked it. I had no regrets, not once, not until a little over ten years later, when I'd be rocketed, thrown off my center, by a complete surprise.

Chapter Four

The Irishman in My Life

The day after my puzzling experience at the stranger's house, I was determined to get my life back in order, return to my daily routine. The kids went to school, while I worked in Luke's classroom in the early morning, telling Mimi, my good friend and Luke's teacher, the unbelievable tale about what happened the night before. As she prepared the easels with paint pots, she insisted on personally driving me to Urgent Care after school "just to get checked out." But I insisted that I was fine. I was telling the truth, mostly having recovered, at least physically.

At 10:30, I left Luke's classroom and drove twenty miles to cover a TV story in Seaside featuring a local high school basketball coach receiving the "Coach of the Season" award.

On the way back to pick up Luke, my cell phone rang. God, I needed to change that Disney ringtone from the annoying yet popular *Frozen* theme to anything else, I thought. Although my daughter's choice for me, it was frankly irritating, and all the more so today as my head was still fuzzy and my nerves still rattled.

"Yes," I said into the phone, "Sandy Stonemeyer."

"You're in top form, then? I'm no genius, but I can tell by the sound of yer voice."

"I'm sorry, but I'm not sure with whom I'm speaking," I replied.

The LED read: "Caller Unknown." I wondered if it was a local television associate calling or maybe a salesperson trying to build up a quick rapport. Wait, an accent, I detected, the Irish accent from last night.

"It's Zachery here, checking in on you. When I left you last night, yer kids seemed in good spirits, but well, you looked weak and honestly still a bit confused. I've been worried about you all day."

"Oh, well, my mind was jumbled. Um...about my car? I...I..."

"Nothing for you to worry about with that, I'm glad to report. The car is sitting just outside yer garage door. I hid the car keys under the flowerpot at the bottom of yer front steps."

I listened in silence.

"No worries, love, sounds like you are in the midst of something right now. I'll let you go then."

"Well, I...I..."

He cleared his throat. "So I guess you're a lucky one—you don't have to see the likes of me again. I know it was an unpleasant experience."

I chuckled nervously, thinking that I had proven once again to be a social misfit, unable to have a decent conversation, even with the man who had saved me from who knows what less than twenty-four hours ago and now seemed intimidated by me.

I replied, "Well, it's not a big problem, the car I mean. I have a second car, a Toyota Pathfinder. I'm driving it now as we speak. Listen, I'm sorry, Zachery. I was completely zoned out last night. You're right. Actually, I'm feeling a lot better now, thanks to you."

"I'm happy to hear that," he said. "I wanted you to relax about yer car being returned. That's why I phoned. My dear Irish mum always taught me to take good care of ladies in distress."

"Can you come for dinner tonight?" I asked, awkwardly shooting out the invitation.

"No, no, you don't need to repay me in any way. Think of it as—"

"But, please," I interrupted, "my kids want to see you again. They love your accent... No I mean they really liked you. You were so kind to them, and to me." I felt girlish for a moment. Hesitating, I wanted to retreat, but it was too late. Instead, I said, "Well, I hope you can make it. Around seven then? Will that work for you?"

"Me treasured mum also taught me to never refuse an invitation from a fine woman," he said, "so yes, I'll be glad to come. But would you mind if I brought along me niece, Felicia, who can surely benefit from some old-fashioned family normalcy? She hasn't had any of it since her dear momma passed away." A blanket of sadness entered the lightness of our conversation.

"Family normalcy?" I said, sighing. "Doubt if we can offer that. But of course, bring Felicia. Luke and Jenny will be over the moon."

"Perfect. Take care then."

Disconnecting, I thought, What was I going to wrestle up for dinner? Had I forgotten that I disliked cooking for guests? I'd pick up Luke, then get Jenny at her school, and head straight to Shopper's Corner market.

I buckled up my son in his car seat and took off to get Jenny. While driving, I told Luke that Mr. Zachery was coming over for dinner.

"Oh good," he responded. "I like him." Then he asked, "Mommy, are you going to have Mr. Zachery wake up in your bed?"

"What?" I said, almost illegally turning onto Mt. Hermon Road without coming to a full stop. The unfiltered responses coming from my four-year-old's mouth sometimes startled me.

He continued, "Tara's mommy met a man last week and now he sleeps in her bed every night. She told me that yesterday when we were doing finger paints. She painted the two of them in a big bed. Her mommy was red and the man was purple. After she finished the painting, she started putting fat dots all over him with black paint, almost covering him up." What Luke was saying concerned me. "Mommy, you know what *I* painted with *my* finger paints?" he then asked. Thank goodness, I thought, he was on to a new subject.

"No Luke, what did you paint?" I said, stumbling on my words.

"I painted a blue man wearing a yellow space helmet landing on the moon. It's in my backpack. You wanna see it?"

"Yes, I'd love to see it when we get home. Okay, munchkin?"

I eased the car into the school driveway, slowing my speed, but inside my head I was reeling.

Before I unbuckled Luke, I stroked his hair and looked into his large hazel eyes. "I promise you," I said, "I won't be having Mr. Zachery or any man in my bed. Got that?"

"Good Mommy, that's good," he replied as he scrambled to reach for his backpack. "Wanna see my spaceman?"

"Sure, let's see it."

I kissed his forehead. He ripped the painting out of the backpack, the top right corner catching onto the zipper. I held it up for both of us to see.

"You're such an artist, Luke. I love your choice of colors," I said, ruffling his hair. "And I love you, cowboy. Now let's get your big sister." I smiled and squinted to hold back my tears. For some reason, this moment made me think of Albie, the man I married for better and much worse, the man who was no longer *my* man.

Standing on the corner in front of her school, my daughter was chatting and laughing with her classmate, a pigtailed girl named Lola. Jenny gestured goodbye, turned, and ran past us without stopping, opening the Pathfinder's door and jumping into the front seat. I buckled Luke into his car seat and slid into the driver's seat, suddenly thinking about what happened to me behind the wheel last night.

"You were late again," Jenny said sourly, her happy face instantly having turned grim.

"What's the matter, Jenny?" I said. "You were so happy a moment ago. We weren't late at all. I could hear the dismissal bell ring as I was parking the car. Why are you saying that?"

Jenny was unconditionally down on me because I hadn't let her daddy return home to live with us, not that he asked me or ever hinted at it. She held a stubborn grudge even though I've heard Albie himself admit to her that it was entirely his fault, not her mommy's. If I remind Jenny of that fact, she immediately dismisses me and then pokes her finger in my face with her usual retort, "I know it was *your* decision, Mom." Then she'd trot off to some other activity, having once again set the record straight between us.

When I told Jenny about Mr. Zachery coming for dinner, she seemed to instantly perk up.

"Mom, really? Really? Wow," she said, starting to reach across the seat to hug me, the first time she'd given me an unsolicited hug in over a year.

"Jenny, I'm driving, honey!" I said, grinning over at her. "But I'm glad that you're happy about that. Your hero is coming to dinner."

Jenny caught herself in her sudden delight and then stared straight ahead, snapping back into her "I'm against Mom no matter what" attitude. I still sensed the excitement surging inside her little body as she put her hands in her backpack and brought out a stack of paper.

"Field trip tomorrow," she said. "You need to sign this permission slip. Seymour Ocean Center. Don't forget."

"Okay, Jenny cakes, remind me to sign it before dinner. What's that other yellow sheet of paper you got there? Looks official." I glanced over as I made the turn back onto Mt. Hermon.

"Nothing, just some stupid flyer about auditions for *Peter Pan.* I'm gonna throw it out when we get home. Mrs. Evans gave this notice to only Kelsey and me. She thinks that I'd definitely get one of the parts if I went to the audition. But I'm not interested. I just want to play softball, none of that children's theater crap for me."

"Jenny! *Crap?* Who taught you to use that word? It sounds so...so..."

"Daddy says it. I heard him say it like a bunch of times. Anyway, it's not a *bad* four-letter word. I don't say the other ones."

Why doesn't she call *him* "Dad" instead of "Daddy"? No, it's only me who gets "Mom." I swallowed hard, holding back my anger. "Hmm, your Daddy says it, does he? I must ask him about that. But listen Jenny, it doesn't sound good coming from a little girl."

She glared at me, her body language communicating, "Don't you dare start with me, Mom!"

My cell phone buzzed as I eased into the Shopper's Corner parking lot.

"Yes, this is Sandy Stonemeyer," I said.

"Jon Novak, Channel 6."

I glanced in the backseat and saw that Luke had fallen asleep. I put the phone on speaker and gave Jenny a "shush" signal.

"Hey kid," he said, "you got a story tomorrow at the County Building, the much awaited announcement from the Water Commissioner on the anticipated rationing guidelines. You up for it, or should I get someone else? It'll be at 2 p.m., second-floor auditorium."

From the front seat, Jenny turned and started to poke snoozing Luke with a plastic ruler. I whisked the ruler from her grasp, then took her hand and held it tightly, shooting her my disapproval, as I put my finger to my lips to shush her again.

"No, no, Jon, I'll be there tomorrow. Of course, I want it. Thanks, thanks for thinking of me."

"Good, our cameraman Pete will meet you in the lobby. Make sure you wear a dark blazer, pastel blouse, and your Channel 6 lapel pin, and don't forget to be there thirty minutes ahead of time. Glad you can do it."

He hung up, and I released Jenny's hand.

"God, Mom, aren't your kids more important than some stupid TV news story? How are you going to pick us up from school tomorrow? Luke gets off early and I get off at three o'clock." She shook her head, hoping to pull on my heartstrings, get back at me.

"It's not a big problem, Jenny," I said. "I'll make arrangements for you and your brother. I think Aunt Sylvie can probably do it."

Jenny was becoming more and more like the bossy parent, eager to catch me up as a bad mother or make fun of some simple mistake I made. Her behavior since the divorce infuriated me, but I accepted her feelings, though misguided. She's the child, I'd tell myself. I'm the adult.

Chapter Five

Traumatic Stumble

Our relationship was at its peak on the day of our tenth wedding anniversary. Albie gave me a sapphire and diamond pendant that dangled from a twenty-four-carat gold rope chain on the morning of our special day. Then he kissed me passionately, promising to return home from the office at five o'clock, when he would sweep me off to our celebratory dinner at some special location in our town, San Francisco.

"I've arranged for Zinnia to watch the kids for the evening," he said, while sipping his coffee. "Dress elegant; overdo it. We've never been to the venue I'm taking you to, and I think you'll be in for a surprise. I'm going to wow you," he said with a rueful smile before he closed the front door behind him.

I was impressed by his initiative, his inventive approach to our special dates. As he went off to work that day, I fell back on the bed, rereading his anniversary card. "You are my wife, and the most incredible part of my life," he had written. "You are everything to me, Jelly Bean." He liked to call me Jelly Bean, his special endearment for me. I never asked him why he chose it, but it warmed me inside every time he said it.

The kids were unusually calm the morning of our anniversary, barely presenting any hassle getting out of bed and dressed. Jenny went off to Hostetter Day School on the yellow school bus, and I dropped Luke off at his home daycare just a few blocks up the hill near Coit Tower. Luke would stay with our babysitter, Zinnia, until Albie and I picked him and Jenny up on the way back from our romantic dinner date. Zinnia welcomed Luke with a squeeze, congratulated me on our anniversary, and promised to pick up Jenny from school at three o'clock. I thanked her for being available in the evening.

"By the way, tonight's on me," she said, smiling. "No charge."

I hugged her, pecked Luke goodbye, and left, my heart brimming with appreciation.

I went off to my office, where I worked three days a week at a modest, low-budget editorial service, located near the Presidio. On that Thursday, a new college intern was coming in from San Francisco State, a girl whom I had agreed to start mentoring. Although she never showed up that morning, at about noon she left a quick voicemail to say that she was sadly dropping out of college due to a family emergency in Indiana. I can remember her name even to this day. Kate Sullivan. It's interesting how extraneous information stays buried in your mind when the day turns out to be memorable for a completely different reason, a devastating reason in this case.

Still floating from the romantic morning with Albie, I completed a textbook editing project and left the office mid-afternoon. It was my plan to rush home, take a quick shower, spray my body with Albie's favorite lavender scent, and slip on a pair of black lace panties and matching bra, over which I'd put on the lilac satin cocktail dress I set out before I left. Then I'd pour two glasses of bubbly for us in honor of ten wonderful years of marriage for a pre-dinner toast.

I would have my anniversary gift for him sitting on the coffee table, a Blu-ray collection of every James Bond movie ever made. I'd often call Albie "Mr. Bond" because there was something still mysterious about him. Sometimes this was unsettling, but it was also sexy. I'd find him suddenly standing behind me when I least expected him to be there or wake up in the middle of the night, him missing from our bed, and then find him down in the chilly garage, peering into his stand-up red metal toolbox, fiddling around with his tools. He'd go off on investigation trips usually at least once or twice a month and return unwilling to discuss the details of his destinations, jesting that if he told me, he'd have to kill me.

"I'm sorry but it's private between me and my corporate client," he'd say. "Please forgive me."

I'd pout, not accepting this chasm in our communication. Secrets were a turn-off for me. He'd feel guilty and look at me with his trademark "little boy" expression.

"Come on now, Jelly Bean," he'd say, "you know that I can't tell you." Then he'd quickly change the subject, refocusing the conversation on our children, wanting to know what mischief they'd been up to while he was gone.

Of course, I understood that he was a corporate investigator, and though I ached with emptiness whenever he was away, I had become accustomed to life the way it was and would often kid him about loving living on the edge, the spice of having my own private James Bond.

Apologetic after an absence of four or five days, he'd give special Daddy time to Luke and Jenny, inviting me to spend the afternoon shopping on my own or maybe go to the gym, free from any "kid" responsibilities. Once I had time to myself, I'd return home at least temporarily refreshed. We'd make love, and then Albie would whisper in my ear, insisting that he planned to find a new line of work because he hated leaving me and the kids for extended periods of time.

"It breaks my heart every time I go through that door with a suitcase," he'd say with what always seemed like pure sincerity and love in his words.

I'd take his hand, place it on my heart, and say, "It's okay, Mr. Bond. It's your livelihood."

I had loved him ever since I first spotted him standing there in that crowded room at the headquarters of the Oakland Police Department.

So, on Thursday, January 21st, our tenth wedding anniversary, it would be more than an understatement to say I was startled when I returned home early from the office to find him in our bed with a young Asian woman. When I glided through our bedroom door in my anniversary bliss and saw his face behind the woman who was straddled above him, I angrily pitched my purse at the two figures on the bed, hitting the shapely woman in the small of her naked back. Then I collapsed to my knees on the bedroom carpet. She swung around quickly, her long black hair swirling around her head, no distinct expression on her face. We made eye contact for an instant, the type you make when you're in the midst of a car accident, staring into the eyes of the person who's crashing their car into yours. She became flustered, frantic, hustling beneath the sheets, to hide her naked body from me...me, the stupefied, pitiful wife. Albie sat up shaking his head, pathetically speechless. The girl slid further down beneath the shelter of our pure white 1800 thread-count Egyptian cotton sheets. I was sickened as I struggled to pull myself up from the carpet.

"Get out, get the hell out my house," I screamed.

Before they could make a move from the bed, I turned and bolted from the room, out of the house, started the car engine, and screeched out of the driveway down the street. Plunging down the hill, I turned sharply into the Macy's Union Square parking lot, realizing that I left my purse with my driver's license, the one I had thrown at the girl, back in my bedroom, at the scene of the crime.

Finding a spot in the back corner of the garage structure, I slid down in my seat out of sight and cried, wailed like some injured animal, smacking the steering wheel with my fists, kicking my seat, feeling like I was going to be sick. Reclining, I curled into a fetal position and wept for hours like an abandoned orphan. Only a few hours ago, I had been convinced that my marriage was perfect, sacred to both of us. Had I been blind to the clues, those tiny giveaways inherent in our daily marital life? I stared up at the clock on the dashboard. It was 5:55 in the late afternoon and I had been barricaded in my car for almost three hours. My marriage was over, my life and the lives of my two young children instantly altered forever. I was a thirty-eight-year-old failure.

Albie left me a letter of apology, stating that he had mistakenly faltered as a husband, that he deserved whatever punishment I deemed appropriate. The Japanese woman was the office administrator where he worked, he said in the letter. Her name was Emily Kota. An affair had erupted between them while he was working for weeks into the night on his toughest case, the two of them spending hours together, him debriefing the details of the investigation and her transcribing these events into the log for the corporate client. It just happened, he wrote, without warning.

He apologized to me repeatedly in his two-page handwritten letter, but understood that I would probably never take him back. He was right. I filed for divorce within a week of finding him with the woman, with his tramp, who had to know that she was undoubtedly wrecking a ten-year marriage, the woman who was screwing my man on our wedding anniversary in our just purchased king-size Temperpedic bed. I despised her, but of course I hated Albie more.

The divorce was messy, mostly due to my uncontrollable displays of anger. And now, the worst had happened. He lied about his intent to stay in close touch with the kids after the separation. He barely saw them, hadn't taken them even once to his new residence, picking them up every third week or so, usually on a Wednesday for a quick dinner at a café down the road from my cottage in Felton. Then, once a month, he'd take Jenny and Luke to a beach hotel, each time a different place in Santa Cruz or maybe go as far as Monterey or San Luis Obispo. They would play on a deserted beach all weekend with their dad. That's what Jenny told me, anyway. Luke usually came home full of sand, his swimsuit plastered with grit, overflowing with stories of "really cool" bodysurfing and sandcastle creations. Jenny was typically sullen when returning home from visits with her father, her mouth drooped, repeating, "I miss Daddy," even before she shut the front door behind her, back to her other parent, who had become merely referred to as "Mom."

Albie was more reliable when it came to paying his child support than spending time with his children, throwing in an extra few hundred dollars every couple of weeks, his way of continuing to apologize for destroying our marriage. He must have been doing well, probably living high on the hog, and still involved with the Japanese girl, maybe sharing his new house with her.

My hatred for Emily Kota started to wane, at least somewhat, after a long, dismal thirteen months. It was Albie who had deceived me, not the woman, I reminded myself.

But why, I asked myself at least twice a day, why didn't he fight for me? His two-page confession letter was his one and only bid for forgiveness, tucked under the doormat, one corner of the envelope partially visible. I noticed it there when I dropped my keys by the front door the day after I found them in bed together. Reading the letter, I wondered why he didn't beg me to take him back. He didn't even ask when we spoke on the phone, not a word requesting anything from me, only his repetitious regrets, a full admission of his betrayal, but without any reason or excuse. I imagined that Albie had assumed that I would never forgive him. He must be in love with her, I'd think, willing to sacrifice his wife of ten years and his small children for selfish sexual fulfillment with a younger, more exotic woman.

I'd be lying if I said I didn't miss having his arms around me, didn't pine for the way he frowned in the mirror each morning, shaving cream all over his face, playfully dotting my nose with a dash of white before he washed it off, then dressing in a hurry, and rushing off for another day of corporate investigations work. I'd also be lying to myself if I didn't admit that I missed him playing Twister with Jenny, both of them falling onto the vinyl mat in fits of laughter, while Luke toddled around at their feet, then crashed atop his dad and sister, a happy trio, as I made dinner and watched them from the kitchen. Occasionally, I'd offer a suggestion to Jenny on how to outsmart her father at the game.

"Mommy, I *know* how to play. I'm beating Daddy," she'd discipline me for breaking into their fun.

That was me, eager to offer my daughter advice even when she didn't need it. Was I jealous of their special connection, the connection that she now craved, the absent bond that she held over my head on any given day?

Chapter Six

Zack's Irish Wit

With Zack joining us for dinner, Jenny was initially quiet at the table. It was the first time a man had shared a meal with us since her dad left. Her smile encouraged my positive thinking. She couldn't take her eyes off Zack. It had been a long time since I'd seen her eat the main course I served up without some kind of an argument. And that night it was my famous quick lasagna and garlic bread.

Zack's niece, Felicia, sat upright, a broad smile on her rosy face, taking big bites of lasagna, but not saying much, being cautiously polite. Her eyes were like saucers of emeralds, her cheeks freckled, her lips a natural crimson. She was lovable, her curly red hair framing her face, curious, and quick.

"Do you have any pets?" Felicia asked.

Jenny jumped in. "No, Mom won't let us. She wants Luke to turn five before we have a dog. When we get one, I'm going to name her Grouch after you know who." She looked over at me and rolled her eyes, while stuffing a forkful of lasagna into her mouth. Felicia seemed uncomfortable, glancing over at her uncle across the table. Jenny continued as if her words weren't lined with bad intentions. "I've wanted a dog since we moved here, but Mom just won't budge."

Zack reached across the table to take Jenny's hand. "Jenny, your mum has a good point. Actually, she's a wise woman, wiser than you think. It's better to wait until the youngest child in the house is at least five, otherwise the pet may be accidentally abused by the toddler. Yes, I think it's actually a very good point yer mum makes. You don't want yer pet to be hurt or yer little brother to be harmed, now do you?" he said, seeming to exaggerate his Irish lilt.

"Nope," Jenny replied, shaking her head. "Well, Luke turns five in two months. I want a white, shaggy dog, a big one, a girl dog... I guess I wouldn't name her Grouch. Sorry Mom, just kidding about that," she said. It was her way of apologizing to me. "I'd name my dog Matilda. She'll be a *good* dog named after a *bad* girl."

Felicia hesitated but then burst out laughing. Luke spit out a noodle onto his plate, amused by his sister. From that point on, the evening was coated in an upbeat sheen. It was nice to see that my daughter still had a whimsical sense of humor, I admitted to myself, even if side-swiping me was her first-pass approach.

Zack commented, showing versatility, "Jenny, do you know what the name Matilda means?"

She shook her head. "Nope."

"Well, it actually means 'battle-mighty, ready for a fight.' Sounds like you have a bit of that fire in you, little Miss Jenny Stonemeyer. You sure do."

Jenny chuckled, taking a nibble of the store-bought crispy garlic bread. "I like the name Matilda," she said.

Zack and Felicia both nodded their heads.

"Here's the main idea of the story," Jenny continued, having read the children's novel with that name the year before. "You see, Matilda is a trouble-maker at school. She gets in all kinds of trouble. Her teacher goes crazy."

Laughter erupted from all of us, Luke banging his fork on the table in delight. The lighthearted dinner conversation had returned to our dinner table. Zack then told a story about the dog he had in Ireland when he was a boy.

"I was a young lad growing up in Dublin and me dog was me best friend. I'd take me dog, Casey, down to the River Liffey and throw a stick in the water for him to fetch. We'd both get all muddy after a good rain, and blessed me, there's a lot of soak in Ireland, I can sure tell you." Zack had Jenny and Luke's undivided attention. "One afternoon down by the river, Casey came running up to me with something white and mucky in his chops. You know what he waved in my face?"

The kids shook their heads.

"No, what was it?" Jenny asked.

"It was a pair of underpants."

"Yuck," said Luke. "Ick."

"Well, I was horrified, and I threw those undies back into the river and watched them float away," Zachery said. "Can you imagine the scene?"

For a few moments, it felt like a typical family dinner, like the atmosphere Albie knew how to create with the kids. Zack asked Felicia to sing an Irish children's song as we ate our apple pie and ice cream.

She sang gently in her Irish soprano voice: "A long time ago, when the Earth was green, there were more kinds of animals than you've ever seen. They'd run around and play while the Earth was born, and the loveliest of all was the unicorn. The loveliest of all was the unicorn."

We clapped and cheered.

"That's 'The Unicorn Song.' We sang it all the time back in Ireland," Felicia said.

Jenny wanted to learn the song right away. So the girls hurtled off to Jenny's bedroom. I cleaned up from dinner, and when I walked into the living room fifteen minutes later, Luke was fast asleep on Zack's lap.

"Well, that's some Irish charm you have there, Mr. Zachery," I said. "Can I get me some?" I asked, and then became flustered, realizing how those words might have sounded to this man I met only twenty-four hours before.

Zack looked over with a questioning yet hopeful expression. "Well, for a start, can you make me a cup of tea, love?" he asked.

"Tea? Um, well, yes, I think I have some Earl Grey. Will that do?" I said, fumbling my words.

I could sense that he was covering for me, knowing that I was embarrassed. The last thing I wanted was some new complicated relationship.

Here I was freshly divorced with two young children, a tiny glimmer of a possible budding local TV career, and still a broken heart from a bad marital split. How could I possibly consider a romantic linkup at that time? I wanted to hide.

When I returned with the tea, Zack was speaking into his cell phone, his voice hushed, seeming to be mindful of not waking Luke. "Antonio, no worries," he was saying, "I'll have her home in about an hour. Take off your rubber dollies and get to sleep. I'll tuck her in. 'Night, brother."

Zack carefully slid out from under Luke, gently lowering his head to the couch, then tiptoed over and sat beside me at the dining room table.

"Rubber dollies? Hmm, sounds interesting. What are those?" I asked.

"Ah, yes, that's Irish lingo again, I'm afraid," he replied, his dimples indented and his floppy blond mop falling into his eyes as he shook his head. "Antonio was just out for a run before I called. Rubber dollies are what you, in America, call sneakers or running shoes. My brother likes to have his run in the evening, his favorite pastime, a champion sprinter in secondary school and also then at university. He jumped hurdles at record speed—many a medal on me mother's mantle. Can I use your restroom, love?"

I pointed behind him. "Sure, it's right there."

He went in. I started to clean up, but I could hear him speaking quickly, seeming to be back on his cell phone. The words were muffled. The toilet never flushed. The sink water never ran. Zack emerged, no phone in sight. About to say something to me, he was interrupted by the girls as they came running down the stairs.

"Mommy, you gotta hear this," Jenny called out.

I was grateful to hear the endearing "Mommy" come out of my daughter's mouth again. The two girls sang "The Unicorn Song" with great gusto, all the way through, like sisters. They squirmed and giggled as they belted it out, proud, happy nine-year-olds, eager to entertain, ending the tune with their arms stretched out. And Luke slept right through it.

"Mommy, Felicia's in a children's theater class in Scotts Valley," Jenny said. "Isn't that cool? Same place I got the flyer from."

For an instant, I recalled that Jenny had referred to it as the "stupid flyer" just hours ago.

Zack stood up. Bending down, he looked into Felicia's eyes and said, "Time to say good night, little niece."

He then turned to me. "Thank you for your fine hospitality. It was a delicious meal indeed." He kissed me on the cheek and affectionately hugged Felicia to him. "Good night, ladies." He looked into my eyes. "Looks like you're well mended from last night. Stay safe, love."

"Yes, thank you. Bye Jenny," Felicia said shyly.

Jenny pulled at me. "Felicia asked me to come and see her drama group perform on Saturday. Can we go? Can we?" She was enchanted with her new friend, Felicia, and couldn't stop beaming at Zack. "I want to go. Can we? Please Mom!"

I peered at Jenny, my eyes wide, hoping to calm her down, signaling that she should lower her voice, not wake her brother.

"But Jenny," I said, "Dad is supposed to pick you up on Saturday morning."

"I really hope she can come," Felicia chimed in. "We're performing three of Grimm's fairytales."

Jenny cut in. "Mommy, Daddy will understand. I can call him. He can see us next weekend or he can take me there on Saturday if you can't."

Zack came to the rescue. "Let's have Jenny and her mum catch their breath, shall we, Felicia?" He touched my shoulder. "These young girls, they can be quite exuberant. I'll give you a call in a day or two and you can let us know if Saturday afternoon will work. If not, *Aon imni*."

I was puzzled.

"That's Gaelic for 'no worries,'" he said, with a wink.

Felicia graciously said goodbye, offering a slight wave. It was true—I needed to catch my breath.

Chapter Seven

Years of Service

Spitfire, that's what they called him. He earned the title over his last ten years at the Agency. They had his back—at least that's what the chief of his region repeated to him time after time. Thanks to them, he felt confident that his recently estranged family would remain safe, escape the crosshairs of his worst enemies. He did a bad thing, or at minimum, his wife perceived that he had committed the most heinous of marital crimes, infidelity, not just with another woman, but with the most beautiful young Asian woman one could imagine. One problem and one problem only, he didn't really do it—it was merely a manufactured scenario, courtesy of the CIA.

It was the first time in Albie's career that he had truly feared his nemesis. His closest family members were in serious physical danger. The "hunted" had become the "hunter," this gang, a relentless bunch of gunrunning criminals, dealing in "hot" automatic weaponry up to and including a variety of nuclear arms capable of mass destruction. Their key customers, a network of terrorists linked from the United States to three locations, in Turkey, Afghanistan, and Lebanon. This gang boasted a brutal track record and was known for taking aim at their hunters' immediate family members, wreaking havoc on innocent people, often killing them under the guise of a random home break-in or an ambiguous accidental death. They showed no mercy and were experts at staging with purpose.

One fellow agent's father had already been taken down and murdered by the gang's bloodied hands immediately following the Agency's last big weapons deal raid. The CIA called the division's mission "Project

Retired," which equated to rubbing out the entire squad known as "the Brethren." It was a gang of fifty or so gunrunners and agitators who traversed the globe causing violence and then selling weapons to whomever would buy. They traded hefty quantities of top-of-the-line weaponry for high price tags. Their signature was to eliminate those CIA agents who crossed their path. To them, they were giving a warning: Get out of our way or suffer the casualty of your next closest relative.

In his gut, Albie knew that the Brethren's intent with him went far beyond the warning stage. They were out for the simplicity of revenge targeted at him and his family, their philosophy always an eye for an eye. Thus, the Agency's senior team devised a plan to separate Albie from his wife and kids in an effort to protect the immediate family. Their formula to achieve this goal was to have the agent fake his adultery and purposely get caught doing it. It had to be realistic, made to look authentic to the innocent singular audience known as his wife. To him, his superiors were hardcore assholes on the "right side" of the law with a plan to destroy his family life, and the beautiful Emily Kota was to be the bait for this deed.

Ashcroft, the Agency director, had sat her down and convinced the young single mother that it was her duty to take on this brief assignment, especially if she aspired to move forward in her budding CIA career and go beyond her desk job. Albie sat there witnessing Ashcroft delineate the plan to her, first broaching the touchy subject, checking her loyalty, and then making the insane request, selling it as an honorable mission. Ashcroft, he was a true bastard, Albie thought.

"Emily," Ashcroft said, "we called you in because we think you can help us with a task of immediate importance to the Agency, an unusual activity to be sure, and a choice assignment for a rising agent. We think you have the skills and attributes to pull off this assignment. The good news is that you will help save lives here, the lives of this agent's immediate family."

Yeah, Albie thought, she had the skills and physical attributes to make it believable, but Ashcroft was an imbecile!

Staring at Emily, Ashcroft waited for her to digest the whole meal he had just put on the table. "Do you understand how crucial this is for the team, Emily?"

She nodded. Her eyes widened as Ashcroft laid out the plan and explained her role in greater detail. Emily's body grew rigid, her face twisted in disbelief, her fingers gripping the sides of the straight-backed chair. Then she quietly accepted the assignment. Albie could see her body resisting at first, as she ached to scream out her refusal to participate in such an unethical deed, but she didn't say a word. The plan was finalized all in a matter of twenty minutes.

Albie and Emily had two awkward rehearsals over the next two days, and on the third day the ruthless deed was scheduled to happen. The timing couldn't be worse, or more brutal, the target date being his tenth wedding anniversary.

He had little choice. It was either this rocky road or the possibility of Sandy, Luke, and Jenny not seeing the end of the year. In a bust, Albie had shot and killed Cassandra, the wife of Wendall Stuart McKinney, the Brethren's leader, herself a notorious arms trader. It had been a challenging sting, their targeted purpose to interrupt a major arms deal, which had turned into an event that would alter his life forever. Once that night went down, the Brethren would be out for the blood of his family first and then for his. In circumstances like this, the gang would want him fully aware of just how they took care of his family before they came after him.

Being an undercover agent was dangerous—that was the undeniable bottom line. His family had no idea of his true occupation as far as he knew, as he took pride in his success at keeping it a secret from Sandy for more than eleven years. He had taken an unconditional oath and he wasn't going to break it, but he needed to get his family out of the impending danger as fast as he could.

◆ ◆ ◆

When he thought back to the beginning, how it all came together, he had to admit that he had enjoyed the rise to becoming the highest ranked undercover agent on the West Coast. Before being recruited by the CIA, he had good success for five years at Carmichael and Clarkson, a top-tier private investigation firm in San Francisco. It was his arms background that had attracted his prospective employer, as he had served three tours in Afghanistan, developing a unique expertise in high-end weaponry and a keen ability to assess the best arms choice for any given scenario. The result: He became a trusted, valued advisor to arms manufacturers regarding the features and functionality of the most competitive weapons of tomorrow.

The Army had been good to him, but he felt the magnetic pull of the world outside the military, an attraction to the private sector, where he imagined he could make a lot more money, have more freedom, and gain the ability to be more creative outside the stifling restrictions of the formal military environment.

Before he landed his first private corporate gig, he was recruited to be Staff Advisor to the San Francisco Bay Area Special Investigations Team, becoming a lynchpin for coordinating various local police departments, reporting to the State of California's head office. Somehow they found him. He eagerly took the job, absorbing a cavalcade of knowledge, while contributing in many ways, and was duly respected for his military experience and arms expertise.

Full of testosterone and a cynic after only three years of police work, he already felt the need to spread his wings yet again, seeking to transition into the field of private investigations work. It was a surprise though when the CIA came knocking on his door, urging him to hop over to undercover work at the Agency. It was a tough decision for Albie in terms of what direction he should take in his career, what lifestyle he preferred to embrace. But the CIA was successful in its seduction.

That was about the time he ran into her. He fondly recalled the first moment he caught her eye. He had just finished his meetings and found himself pulled to the main conference room in the same building where a pretty young woman was interviewing the Police Chief. He prayed that she would notice him, finding her incredibly attractive. But how could he get her attention? Ironically, she noticed him and asked him to lunch, and their romance was kicked off.

He hadn't expected it to turn into a blazing hot love affair and then to make a proposal of marriage just eleven months later. He had fallen in love with Sandy Lee Phillips, ace reporter for Oakland's Channel 8 news, and made her his wife, Sandy Stonemeyer.

◆ ◆ ◆

One year later, when she mentioned the idea of children, even while on the verge of becoming a nationally known TV reporter, he knew that he needed to convey his concerns. But Sandy had been full of fantasy, full of dreams, chattering about how wonderful having children could be, that she'd even be willing to step back in her own career, at least for a few years, and fully understood that his line of work was bound to be unpredictable.

He listened to her passionate argument for introducing offspring into their already fine life together. But he argued against it, questioning whether she was willing to forfeit the rising career she had carefully culti-vated in exchange for starting a family. Was the trade-off worth it to her? If it was what she wanted, he said, he'd back her decision all the way and become a good father, but he also reinforced the fact that his job was in-tense, that he could be gone unexpectedly for chunks of time, and she'd have to live with that. Once they had a child, there would be no turning back. Of course, her understanding was that he was working for a private investigations firm, not for the CIA.

"No more talk," she insisted that night, turning off the bedside lamp. She sat up, raised her arms in the air, and slipped off her satin nightgown. "Time to embark on this mission, Mr. Bond," she said. "Would you like to begin the investigation, or should I?"

Chapter Eight

Tamakichi Kota

Emily suffered for months after the sting was done, the debacle having turned her into a damaged woman. It was an overcast Sunday afternoon and Emily's daughter, five-year-old Miyoko, was sitting beside her, drawing stick figures in her sketchbook. She drew a crescent moon above the two figures, one short with cropped silver hair, wearing a black shawl and eyeglasses, and the other taller woman with long flowing black hair. Emily sat upright in an upholstered chair, a book on her lap, a *New York Times* bestseller she had already started three times but could somehow never get beyond the first forty pages. Tamakichi Kota was sitting in a bleached cane rocking chair, staring out the window, worried for her daughter and grandchild.

Tamakichi looked over at her daughter, both of them feeling the sadness hanging in the room. Now in America for more than a month, Tamakichi longed for the serene nights back in Kyoto, where she'd happily sit in her garden and take in the scent of the flowers she grew with great care from tiny seeds, like the daughter she had nurtured from sapling to beautiful blossom. But those days were past. My daughter is in pain, she thought, and I don't know how to tend this damaged rose.

Just four days ago, by accident, Tamakichi overheard Emily speaking English in hushed tones on her cell phone. It was late at night and little Miyoko was fast asleep in her mother's bed. Tamakichi was ascending the stairs to the guest bedroom, stepping lightly up the carpeted staircase. She could hear her daughter speaking in an intense, fast-paced manner, as she stood on the landing outside the bedroom Emily was sharing with little Miyoko since she arrived from Japan. Tamakichi listened to Emily's description of her regrets, her recounting of the details of the "faked infidelity."

"I never should have agreed to this deception," Emily was saying, sobbing into the phone. "Never. Every day for these past several months, the memory of what we did haunts me. Albie, you must understand, I cannot live with this. What can we do to right this wrong?" After a pause, she went on. "Yes, I know, and you're right, I don't want to lose my job. I've worked so hard, but I...I..."

Tamakichi stood at the top of the stairs, looking at her daughter's body bent over, distressed. Emily dropped down to her knees, sniffing back her tears, when she suddenly noticed her mother standing a few feet away in the shadows. Knowing that Tamakichi's English language skills were quite limited, she was sure that her mother would not have been able to comprehend the content of the conversation with Albie.

She knew her mother had a stubborn resistance to all things "America," including its language and customs, although Tamakichi had made two extended visits to California in the past three years. Her mother's refusal to accept the United States puzzled Emily. At some point in her life, Emily thought, my mother must have embraced Western culture, having named me, her only daughter, Emily, a popular American first name. But it was also true that ever since Emily had announced interest in leaving Japan for America, her mother's distaste for America had increased exponentially, becoming more apparent in her disapproving attitudes and disparaging comments.

"I must go," Emily hastily said into the phone. She immediately disconnected, placing her focus on her mother and escorting her to the bedroom.

"I thought you had already gone to bed, Mother," she said. In Japanese, Emily explained that a friend's mother had unexpectedly passed away and she had been consoling the girlfriend on the phone, and that's why her eyes were filled with tears. Shifting subjects, Emily asked her mother if she needed more green tea or other food items from the Japanese market tomorrow. "Perhaps you'd like to go with me and do some shopping for the things you like," Emily offered.

Realizing that her daughter had made an excuse for her tears, Tamakichi responded in Japanese. "Yes, child, I would like to go with you. It would be good for me to get out."

Saying nothing about the conversation she had just overheard and fully understood, Tamakichi struggled with how to help her troubled daughter, perhaps persuade her to return to Kyoto. Emily's steadfast intent on climbing the career ladder with her American employer was clear to her mother, although her daughter did not offer much detail about her position or her specific duties at the American company. Despite her knowledge of Emily's high ambitions, Tamakichi was determined to influence Emily's plans for the future, and this included whether or not she should stay in America.

She could not understand why, after so many years, Emily had been unable to find another man to love. She was young, beautiful, and intelligent, though admittedly an emotional island in many ways, still a rose to be appreciated, far from a dried-up cactus. It was true that her years of youth were slipping away, but at least the girl's marital tragedy was now far behind her.

Emily's husband of a mere two years had died in a fatal airplane crash just after takeoff, the commuter plane hitting a flock of birds, the engine clogging, forcing it to slam down onto a crowded freeway just outside Kyoto. That was over five years ago, just one week after Emily had received the news that she was three months pregnant. The seed inside Emily's belly would enter the world as an infant fatherless and at a great disadvantage. Emily had retreated into herself, showing little outward emotion for anything, and closing herself off from her mother, the disconnection a painful experience for Tamakichi.

Her head on little Miyoko's "My Kitty" pillowcase, Tamakichi stared at the glowing cat-shaped clock wagging its tail on the wall opposite the bed. The image of Miyoko's sweet dimpled face crept into her mind. She was hopeful for the child's future. Closing her weary eyes, she drifted back to her own years as a young girl growing up in Kyoto, where she had been a geisha in training, a fact of her life she had never shared with Emily. It was her shame to bear alone.

◆ ◆ ◆

When she was sixteen, Tamakichi fell in love with a boy who worked as a servant at the geisha house, taking orders from the head geisha, Aneko, and from the chief housekeeper, Mai. He was a slender boy close to Tamakichi's age named Sato-san, and he seemed to keep one eye on her while he cleaned, assisted with meal preparations, ran errands, and did chores. Sato-san also had a knack for asking obscure questions of his superiors without seeming to insult them, occasionally offering a clever anecdote or entertaining joke in conversation, even in front of Aneko, who just laughed it off, sometimes actually praising him. Tamakichi quietly observed the young boy, admiring the finesse he showed in everything he did. She caught him at least once or twice gazing at her, thinking him a handsome boy, admiring his positive energy and touch of mischief.

One stormy afternoon, Tamakichi badly damaged her shoe, having stepped into a pothole on the street. She was on her way back to the boarding house from the training annex just steps away from the main geisha house. The heel of the shoe had cracked, causing her to fall to the ground. From the sitting room window, Aneko observed the young trainee's accident and directed Sato-san to quickly go to the girl, help her up the iron staircase to the boarding house, and see if he could mend the shoe without having to take it to the repair shop. Eager to help, Sato-san ran to Tamakichi's rescue, inviting her to lean on him as he helped her up the five slippery steps and then up the winding staircase to her room. He was so taken with her that he forgot to take the shoe to be mended. Embarrassed, he later knocked on her door. When she opened it, she beamed, feeling a sudden joy rise inside her.

Over the next several weeks, she secretly wished that she could speak with him, even if only for a few brief minutes. But a geisha in training needed to focus on nothing but learning how to please potential clients, the men who she would fully service in less than a year, if things went as planned. The head geisha took pride in Tamakichi's progress and had already informally presented the girl to a few of her high-powered clients, treating the men to just a peek at the budding geisha developing under her wing, artfully being groomed to become the epitome of Japanese grace and beauty.

Sato-san lingered a moment as his hand touched Tamakichi's when she gave him the damaged shoe. Thirty minutes later, he returned, the shoe sparkling clean, polished, its broken heel fixed like new. Within twenty-four hours, the two were in each other's arms, and after that, they met night after night in the back garden by the lavender agapanthus. He was gentle and open, sharing his vision for the future. He would stroke her soft hands as he talked about his dream to own and run an elegant tourist hotel perhaps in Tokyo or Yokohama.

One evening, he invited Tamakichi to have a dip with him in the koi pond, promising that the fish would not bother them, and because it was the warmest night of the summer thus far, they could savor their time together with a soak in the cool water. He thought ahead, bringing along a soft white towel to help them dry off before separating back to their individual rooms. At first, Tamakichi hesitated about taking a dip with the boy, but after he ran his fingertips up and down the back of her neck, and kissed her tenderly on her shoulder, she slid off her white cotton dress. Sato-san stood at the water's edge watching her glide down, a small koi splashing at her side as if greeting the girl.

"I cleaned out the pond today, hoping we would do this," he confided.

The water was refreshing, and once Tamakichi shed her dress, she felt relaxed, releasing all inhibitions. His skin was smooth, the light of the half moon exposing a childlike yet adult twinkle in his dark eyes. It was her first night of ecstasy.

When her belly began to swell just two months later, following more than a dozen clandestine meetings under the stars, she immediately shared the news of her probable pregnancy with the young man she had quickly grown to love. He seemed sad, almost melancholy that night, as though his favorite ship had sailed away. But his gentle words gave her hope. Touching her silky hair by the light of the moon, as they dangled their feet in the pond, Sato-san reassured Tamakichi that everything would be fine. He kissed her good night and told her that he needed to think on this news for one more night and construct a plan for them to be together to start their family.

"You are a smart, sweet girl, Tamakichi," he said, "a person who I deeply respect. I am cunning and will figure this out for us."

The next day, he vanished from the house. Numbed and with child, Tamakichi felt humiliated and betrayed, her life instantly in ruins. The only action that made sense to her was to end her life, she thought, as she stared at the beautiful silk kimonos hanging in her closet. How could she possibly tell the head geisha of her plight or admit what happened to the other geishas? She could not bear the indignity.

Sneaking into the house kitchen late one night, she took a long knife from the cook's wooden rack and went out to the koi pond. She would plunge the knife into her stomach, fall into the water, the same water that had taken her future, making no mess. But she could not muster the strength to follow through with her plan. The seed inside was longing to sprout and already had begun to console her. She could feel it alive, her baby to be born. Dropping the knife into the pond, she watched it sink out of sight, then quietly rushed back into the house to pack a small bundle, a jar of homemade kimchi, a box of green tea, two casual dresses, a hairbrush, a few undergarments, a nightgown, and a towel, rolling everything up in a tablecloth that she found in the linen closet.

Melting into the early morning, two hours before sunrise, she left behind her life as a promising concubine. It is for the best, she told herself. The geisha life was not meant to be my fate. Terrified, yet feeling a tinge of confidence with the growth inside her belly, she secured a position as an apprentice seamstress in a small suburban factory just thirty miles away. It was the only talent she had acquired thus far in her sixteen years of life, having been raised as an orphan in institutional care until the day she had been taken in by the geisha house. Her baby was born seven months later: an alert, lively little girl. Having watched many American movies in her childhood, she had a favorite name picked out for her baby. I'll name her Emily, she thought, as the beautiful baby nuzzled her breast.

Tamakichi never married, opened her own seamstress storefront, and became a small business owner in the city of Kyoto, quietly raising her daughter in a suburb not far away on the edge of the Bamboo Forest. The rhythm of the sewing machine and the envied designs she produced made her feel proud and secure in her future.

As Emily grew into a gifted and beautiful young woman, she began to outgrow many of the traditional Japanese customs, becoming Internet-savvy, well educated, and hungry for faraway adventures. She studied English outside the traditional classroom, spending hours at night reading American playwrights and popular novels, hungry for stories about New York and California. Upon graduating from university with a degree in Economics and Western Studies, she jumped at the chance to have an interview with an American company. Just ten days later, she crawled into her mother's bed and expressed her deep sorrow as well as excitement in announcing her impending departure from Japan. Two weeks later, Emily Kota boarded her first airplane bound for San Francisco.

Tamakichi felt devastated, but at the same time, happy for her daughter's success in achieving her dream to work abroad. She didn't know the precise name of the company where Emily would be employed but understood that the job would be interesting for her and that was most important. Tamakichi adhered to the proverb, "Affinity is a mysterious thing, but it is spicy!" Emily had enthusiasm for everything American, wanting to plant her seeds in a new land where there was boundless opportunity. Tamakichi felt she would be a fool to thwart her daughter's growth and dreams. It would be up to Emily to make her cake rise or fall. What will happen to my daughter will happen by her own hand without my interference, she thought. I must embrace this principle, support my daughter, and should the need arise, be there for her.

◆ ◆ ◆

Now, sitting across from Emily in her tasteful modern California home, Tamakichi felt powerless. How could she rescue Emily? What could she do for her when she had wandered so far off the path of acceptable behavior?

It was time for Emily to return to Japan, where she could introduce her young daughter to a world of simplicity and balance. Comprehending the extent to which Emily had veered off the path of decency, having contributed to deceiving an innocent wife and mother, Tamakichi felt shaken to her core. Her daughter had conspired to lead a woman, Sandy Stonemeyer, to believe that her husband had committed an act of flagrant adultery when in fact he hadn't. How could Emily bear to go on in her present life with this weighing so heavily on her? It was only a job, a thankless job in a thankless country, Tamakichi thought.

She felt ashamed and responsible as Emily's mother. Somehow she needed to break through and influence her daughter to do the right thing, steer her in a better direction, and rescue her from this untenable situation. Have I been beaten with my own rod? Tamakichi asked herself. Is my daughter's destiny rooted in my own mistakes as a young girl?

Chapter Nine

Late Night for the Irish

It was late and Felicia had fallen asleep in the backseat of the Land Rover. A tough little girl and a fine actress, he thought, my cunning little ten-year-old. He had carefully coached her to call him Uncle Zachery, his cover name in California, and never to call him by his real name, Wendall, or Dad when referring to him or talking to him in front of others. In fact, it was best not to call him Wendell or Dad even when they were home, he told her, "since you never know when one of our enemies might somehow be listening." Felicia had easily agreed, and because of her worldly nature, Wendall felt comfortable with her promise to consistently call him Uncle Zachery or Uncle Zack. She's a smart little lass, he thought; there's no doubt about that.

His cell phone rang out with the river dance theme. "Yeah?" he answered.

"How did it go tonight?" It was Antonio. "Was Felicia convincing with her prey?" he inquired. "So, *Uncle Zachery*," he said, exaggerating the phony name, "did your girl manage to lure the American lass into her sticky web?"

"She's asleep in the backseat, Antonio, tired out from her performance. I was tempted to waste the woman tonight. But we must do this deed carefully. I want to slowly sink the knife into the gut of Albie Stonemeyer. We'll take his wife, then his kids, like he took my wife. Your sister will be avenged; that's a promise. That fucking CIA agent will get everything he deserves for killing our Cassie, and we'll do it in our own sweet bloody way."

"So, I guess your Felicia did good work then?"

"Me little girl is well on her way to claiming the 'Best Actress' award."

"Good to hear. So, when are you getting back here? Don't ferget our appointment tonight. We're meeting Farat to make the deal. Olivia's here to watch Felicia."

"On my way... Should be there in fifteen minutes. Get the samples loaded into the van, will ya? They're expecting us to show two of everything, every firearm we propose for trading."

"I'm on it, brother. Lots of foliage and debris atop the bunker. I'll need time to clear it away to get the guns out. Better start now."

Zack clicked off the phone and turned on the car radio. Boring country music, he thought, American rubbish. He raced through the stations, looking for something better.

"Dad," the sleepy voice came from behind, "Dad, are we almost home?"

"Felicia, you're awake, love. Bloody exhausted, are ya? All that acting! You were spectacular tonight."

"She's a dumb arse, that one, she sure is," Felicia said, yawning.

"You mean the girl or the mum?"

"Jenny, the girl. She thinks she's so smart and that her mum is the dumb one, but I see it the other way around. Jenny's the stupid one."

"Bless the Lord you're a hard-ass yerself, love...maybe even more than yer dad," he said, chuckling.

"It was fun, Dad, reeling her in like that. To be sure, she'll join my theater group. And then, snap." Felicia clapped her hands two times, very loud, behind his left ear. "She'll get what's coming. Right, Dad?"

"Agh. Don't clap in my ears. You're going to make me deaf. Don't do it again. But I must admit I like yer gumption."

"Dad, I was reading the dictionary again this morning. You know how much I like studying it. I've found me a new word. Know what it is?"

"Nope, not a clue, Fel. Tell me."

"*Supercilious*. That's my new word for today. Another way of saying it is 'super silly arse.'" She giggled.

"Very funny," he said, grinning. "What does the word mean?"

"It's like that Jenny girl, Dad. She thinks she's superior to others. She's so full of herself. She's a 'super silly arse,' that's fer sure. Supercilious," she repeated as if a contestant in a spelling bee. "The precise meaning describing Jenny Stonemeyer, a super silly arse."

He was proud of his daughter for many reasons and chuckled to himself.

"A word a day, Dad. That's what I'm learning now, like I told you I would."

"You're a little wonder. Acquiring quite the vocabulary, aren't ya?"

"Do you like pretending to be my Uncle Zack instead of my real dad?" she asked.

"No, but you know we need to keep it like that for that 'silly arse' and her naïve mum, right?"

"Yes Dad, I know," she said, looking out at the dark road, secretly fearing where the lies would take her.

He pulled into the winding driveway of their mountain retreat, a hard place to find either in the light of day or in the darkness of night, the fog often hanging at the entrance to the private road. As he turned in, he could make out his brother, Antonio, loading a gun into the white van. He stopped the Range Rover close to the redwood stairs that led up to the front door.

"Night Dad," Felicia said, yawning. "I'm going to bed. Pretending is hard work." Then after a pause, she asked, "Where's my Fred?"

"I think he's in the back, Fel. Let me get him fer ya." He opened the hatchback and tossed her the worn, faded, gray stuffed rabbit. Her mum had given it to her on her sixth birthday. At ten years old, she still carried it with her around the house. When Felicia held Fred in her arms, she felt the spirit of her mum keeping her safe. "Good night, love," he called to her.

She rushed up and kissed him on the cheek and then held Fred close to his face and mimicked a nibbling sound. "Fred and Mum are both smooching you good night, Dad," she told her father.

The reminder of his dead wife startled him. He missed Cassie's scent, the essence of lavender surrounding her, her crooked grin, her fingertip massages on his neck when he was stressed. He also missed her sharpshooter skills, the concentrated expression on her face, the way her left eyebrow curled up whenever she held a pistol ready to take a shot. He still couldn't imagine how she took the bullet instead of Antonio or even Garrett or McCormick at the warehouse that night. She was a far better shot than any of them. This puzzle surrounding her death continued to torment him. The CIA agent had purposely taken out the only woman there. He's a bastard and he will pay for it, he vowed to himself.

"Ready to go?" Antonio said, interrupting his thoughts.

"In a minute," he replied. "I just have to change my clothes."

"Question mate: Why take so long to snuff out the wife and kids? Just get it over with, man."

"Antonio, you know the answer," he said. "We've got a bundle of trades to do with the Turks and Egyptians over the next couple of months. Big money. I don't want CIA scum hunting us down because someone in the Stonemeyer family ends up injured or dead."

Seething within, his hands trembling, Wendall gazed up at the night sky. An ocean of stars enveloped him, reminding him of the twinkle in his wife's green eyes. "For Cassie, I want that piece of shit to know that it's me who's twisting the rope as I bring down each member of the Stonemeyer family, one at a time," he said to his brother.

"It's your choice, brother. We're both on the same page. Look, we're on for eleven o'clock at that storage place by Lexington Reservoir. Better get going... We don't want to be late."

"Give me five minutes. Just need to change. We're early anyway," Wendall replied.

He walked into the house, up to his bedroom, dropped his car keys on the dresser, and stared down at his dead wife's photograph in the silver picture frame.

She smiled up at him, her arms around Felicia, the two of them standing in front of a Christmas tree yet to be decorated. The picture was taken a couple of years ago. Cassie wore a crimson-colored wool cap and a red and black tartan scarf, the three of them having just arrived home from cutting down a blue spruce in Grass Valley, north of their home in Pleasanton. It had been a long drive that had included a quick detour at an arms trader's warehouse to pick up a few items for an exchange scheduled the next day.

As Wendall gazed at the photograph, he took in the watercolor green of Cassie's eyes, like sea glass, he recalled. Her hair was as red as her hat, her Irish cheeks ruddy, a smattering of light-brown freckles was sprinkled across her straight, regal nose. The Kelly green windbreaker accentuated her radiance. Wherever she went, she was the center of attention. Maybe that's why she took the bullet in the end, Albie Stonemeyer's bullet, he mused.

His anger rising, he sat down on the bed, looking back at the eyes in the photograph, the magical eyes of his beautiful wife. My grief will be my fuel, he promised himself. "I love you, Cassie," he whispered.

Turning from the photo, he saw his red-haired little girl, the image of her stunning mother, standing in the doorway to his bedroom, the shabby stuffed rabbit tucked under her arm.

Tears erupted in her eyes as she stood witnessing her dad's anguish. Moving to him, she spoke with confidence, like a warrior preparing for battle. "We're going to get even, Dad," she said. "Those nasty people will get what's coming to 'em."

"You've got spirit, Fel. I love you for that. Listen, I'm going out with Antonio for a bit tonight. Olivia will be staying with you until we get home. She'll be downstairs if you need anything."

"Okay, Dad," she replied, kissing her father's cheek. "Good night *Uncle Zack*," she corrected herself and winked.

Holding Fred in her hand by a threadbare paw, Felicia left his room. She could hear Antonio downstairs greeting Olivia, who seemed to be a hundred years old, always grouchy, never listening when Felicia spoke, and usually wearing headphones, her attention on political news from Ireland.

In her bed later, Felicia stared up at the vaulted ceiling, which her father had decorated with dozens of small neon stars, like diamonds in the darkness. I wish he'd tuck me in like he did in the old days, she thought, remembering her mum and dad together on either side of her, while she gazed up at these same stars. She was aware that her father had been avoiding being close to her lately. Maybe he's afraid I'll just up and die like Mum, she thought.

"I promise I won't die. Don't you worry, I'll help you get even, Dad," she whispered before drifting off to sleep. "I'll help you get even for Mum."

◆ ◆ ◆

Albie sat impatiently behind the steering wheel, ready to take down the three targets, thankless scavengers who he knew were sitting in the paint-peeled blue house preparing for their late-night raid on a local disk drive company. Their plan was to snatch 4,000 high-end disk drives, having no idea that the Agency was on to them.

"But why was the CIA involved and not the FBI?" his rookie partner had asked him earlier that evening.

"Simple, because the disk drives were targeted to be routed to the Middle East within the next twenty-four hours," Albie reminded him, annoyed at the young man's obvious inexperience.

The tip had come from an anonymous source directly into the Agency's hotline. It would probably be awhile until the thieves would emerge from the dilapidated house just down the street in front of them.

Albie hated waiting around. Pulling a soggy ham sandwich out of some tin foil, he looked over at his temporary partner, Brian Wu, who appeared efficient, scratching notes in his logbook with his mechanical pencil, but nervous as well. I need to help increase the rookie's confidence, he thought. "Want half?" he asked, extending the sandwich.

Brian nodded. "Yeah, hey, thanks man. Waiting makes me hungry."

"Me too." As he passed half of the soggy ham on wheat to Brian, his cell phone beeped, and he clicked to answer it.

"Hey *amigo*," the voice filled the car. "You arrest that scum yet?" It was Manny, his regular partner, checking in.

"Nope, those two are taking their time, Manny. Waiting for the graveyard-shift security force to get good and sleepy. Sorry, I won't make it to your Irish jig tonight," Albie kidded, wishing he were with Manny instead of doing this low-level crap job. "Anyway, who's taking my place with you to bust the Irish?"

"Gordie Corcorran."

"Shit, Gordie? Yeah, well, he's a good guy. Don't start making out with him and cheating on me. Got that? The poor guy might catch something from you."

Brian took another bite of the sandwich, looked over at Albie, raised his eyebrows, and grinned. The rookie appreciated Albie's openness in allowing him to hear the dialogue between the division's two most esteemed agents.

"The man's got two years on me and hundreds of take-downs, Manny. He's a cracker. You're in good hands."

"Yeah, I know. I'm going to get those buggers before they fucking get you, jefe," Manny insisted. "Those Irish have it in for you, Albie. You may have saved your family, got them out of harm's way with that bogus infidelity shenanigans, but your ass is still on the line. Those fucking misfits are ruthless killers. Don't forget it. Part of me is glad you're not here. You're their number-one target, man. They'll be looking for you tonight when I show up with Gordie."

Discomfort overtook Albie as he realized that he was having this conversation in front of the rookie. Although he was on the Brethren's hunted list, he didn't relish sharing that fact with the unknown quantity sitting next to him. Then he thought, Why should I worry about him? He's an operative like me. Edgy, I'm too damn edgy.

He wished his regular partner good luck, adding, "Give my regards to Gordie. *Hasta la vista,* Manny. See you in the morning, *amigo.*"

Disconnecting, Albie spotted the two thugs exiting the blue house. "Let's follow," he said to the rookie, throwing his half-eaten ham sandwich in the backseat and pulling out behind the gray van.

The bust went down just after the two thieves disarmed the building's security system and broke into Kramer Enterprise Disk Drives, located a half mile away in the town of Mountain View. At that moment, Albie signaled for Agent Wu to take the lead.

The rookie proved to be professional, ordering, "Drop your weapons and kneel down on the floor, hands above your heads. Now! Drop!"

The men complied, first letting go of the huge wheelbarrow they were rolling in, each slowly taking their firearm out of a pocket and placing it on the carpeted floor, then obediently dropping to their knees, almost in unison. "Shit," one of them said.

Brian handled the bust calmly and with unexpected confidence. He handcuffed them and gestured for the men to get in the back of the unmarked Agency's dark-blue SUV.

"Wait, we're checking their pockets first," Albie said. "You never know, partner. They could maneuver something out into their hands before you blink." Albie gave them each a pat-down from behind, recovering a switchblade from one and another small pistol from the other.

◆ ◆ ◆

Antonio and Wendall spotted the black SUV's dimmed headlights just outside Locker #42 at the back of King's Storage as they passed through the chain-link gate that was already ajar.

"Don't forget to call me Zachery, okay Antonio? Remember, when in California, I'm using only Zachery with everyone. No slip-ups."

"Yes mate, you don't have to remind me. I don't have me head in the sand, ya know."

"Okay, good, I just want to be consistent. Maybe we shoulda changed your name too," Wendall said, chuckling. "We'll all be going back to Ireland in a few months. As soon as we do these deals and get our revenge we're gone."

"I'm with ya, mate. We've got that Libya deal three months away, so a couple of months at home would be a blessing. Tonight's trade should help Brethren finances. We need to get this revenge thing over with, then just focus on the gun deals."

"Yeah, I know, I know," Wendall said. "Don't keep bugging me about it. I'm working on it."

Wendall slowed the vehicle as he pulled up to the back of the storage structure. "I think you just want to get back to Ireland with your girlfriend in tow. That's why you're in such a hurry, isn't it, mate?"

Antonio shook his head. "Screw you. Everything's not just about women or sex, ya know."

Three men stood in front of a locker, all of them wearing dark leather jackets. Wendall and Antonio noted the two dead German shepherds down on the blood-stained cement as they approached the trio.

Looking over at Wendall, the tallest Turk said, "You got the goods, Zachery?"

"Yes! Farat, who are these other guys?"

"Cool your Irish ass. These are my colleagues, Amir and Dharva. You think I'd come here alone?"

Wendall glanced over at Antonio. Under his breath, he muttered to his brother, "I hate these fucking Turks, so shifty."

Farat continued, "I'm opening up the locker first and we'll all drive in, so we're out of sight."

Dharva got back into the black SUV. Amir popped the lock and raised the door, which opened to a large storage space. The other Turks walked inside as Wendall drove in. Hopping out, Antonio moved fast, opened the back of the van, grabbed two army green blankets, spreading them out on the stone floor, and then pulled out the first firearm from the hatchback, placing it down on the blanket.

"No, not here, in the back," Farat ordered. "Put them out in the back room for us to examine."

"Back room?" Wendall echoed, puzzled. "There's a back room?"

"Yes, there's a back room," Farat barked.

He nodded to Amir, who unlocked the camouflaged door, which looked like part of the back wall, but opened into another space about twice the size of the front section of the storage locker and fully insulated on all four walls. The floor was a polished wood, and there were metal shelves along three sides, stacked with large storage boxes, designed for stockpiling firearms.

"Well, fuck me, this is some highfalutin locker space," Antonio remarked. "Never seen this before."

"Yes, it is highfalutin," quipped Farat, mocking him. "Very fancy. Lay the goods out back here. We want no lights visible."

Antonio nodded, reached inside the van, and started to unload, passing the firearms, one-by-one, through to his brother. The buyers watched carefully, speaking to one another in their Turkish tongue, picking up each weapon, examining it closely, and then passing it back and forth between them. Twelve different samples were laid out on the two green blankets. Farat gestured for Antonio to move into the back room and then closed the false wall behind him after flicking off the front locker light switch. The Turks grinned.

"Looking good," Amir said. "I think we have a deal if you're keeping your word on the price I quoted. You got all 144 of them, twelve of each type?"

"Sweet Jesus," Wendall replied, "you have yerself a deal if you've got the $350K in cash."

Chapter Ten

Sacrifice

As Senior Agent, Manny Villanova took the lead that night. There was no guarantee that a trade was going down between the Turks and the Irish, but the tip had been registered by a top operative, a highly reliable Agency source. The exchange originally planned for Friday night at midnight as described on a call earlier this week had switched to Thursday at 11 p.m. Manny and Albie were initially scheduled to work the job together, partnered as usual, Albie, having a vested interest in finishing off the Irish Brethren for the safety of his family. But when the update was called in two hours before on the hotline, there had to be some quick re-partnering of agents. The bad news was that Albie was already scheduled to work another case as a substitute, partnered for only one night with a rookie named Brian Wu. Despite the update on the Brethren trade, Ashcroft refused to change the pairings, quietly satisfied that Albie wouldn't be working the Irish case, thinking him too personally involved.

It was no damn time for a toothache, but Manny had a volcano brewing in his mouth. Gordie Corcorran, his partner for the night, was at the wheel. As he drove down Frontage Road to the reservoir shoreline where Stanley's Storage Lockers was located, Manny was examining his inflamed red gums in the dashboard mirror. About a half mile before they approached the target location, Gordie cut the headlights, stopping the Ford Taurus 200 yards away from the chain metal gate.

"We'll park here, all right?" he said, turning to Manny.

"Yeah, this is fine."

"What's up with your mouth, my friend?" Gordie inquired.

"Damn toothache, three days now. I'll need to call a dentist in the morning. I hate dentists," he said, shaking his head in annoyance. Then putting on his night vision glasses, he remarked, "I can't make out any vehicles with this damn thing on." Ripping it off and throwing it down into the backseat, he told Gordie, "I'm getting out so I can get a closer look on foot."

"Right. I'll put my vest on. Be out in a sec," Gordie replied, reaching his arm to the back of the van to retrieve a bullet-proof vest. "Hey, two of 'em back here, Manny," he said, dropping the hint.

Manny ignored him as he opened the car door, his weapon drawn before his feet hit the ground. Once outside, there would be limited dialogue between them, mostly signaling to one another.

Bad night for Manny, Gordie thought, with the guy's usual partner assigned to another case, his mother recently buried, and now with a major dental problem.

Moving ten yards or so, Manny stepped closer to the storage structure. Rounding the corner, he spotted two dead dogs just inside the unlatched gate at the side of the building. The storage lockers here were narrow and long. Manny had meant to review the layout earlier in the day, but didn't have a chance, as the tooth pain had set in and he thought a quick nap would take care of it, but it didn't. The place seemed deserted. The shits must have already made their trade, Manny surmised, another sharp pain shooting through his upper gum. Crap.

Both men walked stealthily, canvassing the entire site, but saw no lights, no vehicles, no action.

Thinking of his mother, Manny recalled her warm sweet voice: "You need to take care of your body. Your health is all you got, *niño,* all everyone of us got." Damn doctors, he thought, catching the cancer too late in the game. Within twenty-eight days she was gone. That was the longest month of his life...his mother drugged up to dull the sharp pains in her abdomen, practically comatose until the end.

A low beam of light flashed behind Gordie, two swings sideways, one vertical flash, the signal for an agent approaching another in the dark. Glancing back at Gordie, Manny shook his head in disgust. "We were given the wrong time, *amigo;* the deal's been done," he said with annoyance.

"How d'ya know that?" Gordie asked, not convinced.

"No vehicles, *amigo.* Two dead dogs," Manny replied, pointing with his flashlight to one of the expired canines.

Gordie nodded. "Looks like you're right. What now?"

"Survey the place for any clues or maybe find some incriminating debris left behind."

"Your vest, Manny, you should get it from the car, just in case."

"No need, man. Geez, my mouth is freaking killing me!"

"Your call. I'm your partner, man, so I have an obligation to point it out, protocol."

"Thanks man. Appreciate it," Manny said as he walked along the periphery of the storage lockers, his flashlight pointed down along the base of the paint-peeled walls. "No lights inside anywhere. Wrong time, dammit. It's a bitch," he muttered to himself.

Gordie followed close behind, then vectored off to the left, hearing a faint shrill sound coming from the line of lockers just opposite from where Manny stood. He walked a little further, edging closer to the locker door, the high-pitched noise more audible.

Tripping on something, his ankle gave way, his body dropping to the tarmac. A third German shepherd lay there, only this beast wasn't dead yet, but lay in a fetal position, yelping in pain. Landing on the pavement a few inches from the animal, he moaned, "Agh," knowing he had injured his ankle.

The flashing signal came from Manny as he approached. "Gordie, shit, man, what the hell happened?" he said. "Crap, another dead dog. Are you okay?" Placing his gun back in his jacket pocket, Manny put the flashlight down on the ground and attempted to lift his partner. "How much you weigh, man? 275? 300?"

"Fuck you," Gordie said, managing a chuckle. "Ain't we a useless pair of invalids? It's embarrassing," he said, and then moaned in pain.

"You can't walk, man, and I can't lift you to get you back to the car," Manny said, assessing the situation. "No worry, Corcorran. You stay here. I'll bring the car closer. There's nobody here anyway."

The dog whined on the blood-stained pavement. "But first," Manny said, "this dog needs to meet his maker." His mother's velvet dark eyes flashed before him. With a single shot to the head, Manny ended the dog's suffering.

Two tears drizzled down Manny's cheeks just before the bullet hit him in the back, as the image of his mother beckoned him. "Come *niño*," he could hear her say. "It's your time to join me."

Chapter Eleven

Critical Thinking

Anxious to see his kids, Albie pushed down on the pedal, doing seventy on Highway 17, taking the turn-off for Mount Hermon Road. Would Sandy be angry? It wasn't his scheduled weekend, but then he had purposely stayed away for the last three months, cutting off communication with his family. The Irish had been hot on his ass. He had been warned by his superiors. Disassociation from his ex-wife and kids had been a wise prescription from Ashcroft, but Albie now felt worn down, desperate for some connection with his kids, even if brief. At a breaking point, he had called Sandy's cell, but left no message.

His phone twittered as he took the exit onto Scotts Valley Drive, the ringtone indicating that it was Ashcroft.

"Yeah, Stonemeyer here," he answered.

"Albie, where are you?"

"Taking a drive. It's my day off, remember?" he said, not wanting to flag the intended visit to see his kids, having pledged to lay low on the family horizon for everyone's safety.

"You alone?"

"Totally. Why? Wanna wine and dine me, Ashcroft?"

♦ ♦ ♦

After a sting worthy of whiskey and cigars went down, Manny and Albie would typically commiserate about Agency politics.

"Ashcroft, what an ass-kisser," Manny would complain after spitting out a kernel of tobacco as he slugged down the whiskey. "The guy's got no heart, *amigo*. If we were wasted on a case, he'd have a dial-tone reaction, then replace us in an instant."

Albie remembered Manny saying those words just a week ago, the last time they indulged in a celebratory night out. When they had made the toast, Albie remembered being hit with a sudden sting of guilt, having just been informed that he was named to take Ashcroft's place within the next two months and would become the Bay Area Agency director, while Ashcroft would be transferred to Minneapolis to run the Midwest division. Just yesterday, however, Albie had decided to pass on the promotion. He wanted none of it, preferring to stay behind the scenes if he continued with the CIA at all. But before he made any noise about it, his first priority was to rid the world of the Brethren, namely the two Irish brothers and their cutthroat gang.

◆ ◆ ◆

Ashcroft's voice sounded stressed, broken. "Albie, as of late last night, we're down two men," he said. "A wet job, looks like targeted assassinations."

"Down two agents? What area?" He was avoiding the direct question, feeling a sense of terror creep in under his skin.

"Manny, he's gone. I...I'm sorry," Ashcroft stumbled on the words.

What? Albie couldn't believe it. "Manny?"

"Yes," his boss replied. "Manny."

Albie didn't know what to say. Disconnecting, he picked up his speed. "Fuck," he said, hitting the steering wheel, causing the car to veer off to the right, as he took a left on Graham Hill Road, just missing the red stop sign in front of him, almost taking out a scantily clad female crossing the street. For a split second, the two had locked eyes, the girl, evidently in her teens, flashing him an accusatory glance. She passed in front of him, swinging her hips. Beating on the steering wheel again, he yelled, "Three kids, dammit." Manny was a dedicated father. Was it a bullet, a knife from the Irish? What? He hadn't stayed on the phone with Ashcroft long enough to get any more information.

Stopping the car about a quarter of a mile from Sandy's cottage, he hit the button on his phone, his return call going straight through to Ashcroft.

"Again, I'm sorry, Albie," Ashcroft said. "Manny was a good agent. By the way, Corcorran also went down."

"Shit! Bullets or what?"

"Manny was shot in the back and it looks like Gordie took one in the head. Hard to give any more details at this time, but based on the bullet type, it was the work of the Irish. We know that much."

"Yeah, well in the meantime, fuck me..." Albie said, hanging up and throwing the cell phone down.

Ashcroft didn't get the chance to say two things to Albie before the call ended: one, that he had genuinely admired Manny's sense of humor and his usually cool head under stress, and two, awhile ago, the Irish had moved locations from Pleasanton to the Santa Cruz Mountains. But Stonemeyer was just too heated to hear this, which led him to intentionally hold it back. He knew that Albie would likely go off like a rocket if he knew the Irish were within less than fifteen miles of his estranged wife and kids.

Sitting in his car, Albie stared out at the tall trees around him, thumbing through his thoughts, replaying the events that had gone down over the last twenty-four hours. His mind shifted to Manny. At least his ex-wife, Natalie, had recently remarried a stable Silicon Valley type of guy, but Manny's absence would be sorely felt by those three young boys who had idolized him. Natalie would be crushed knowing that Manny would never see any of his kids reach high school. She had struggled with Manny's career, even though she had been in the dark throughout their marriage, Manny covering his secret agent life with that of a corporate Safety and Facilities Management job, which provided him free reign to travel the world working an array of bogus site building projects. Instead, he was traversing the globe with Albie from Glasgow, to Lima, to Odessa, hunting down bad ass gunrunners, busting arms deals wide open, and nabbing renegade gangs in the midst of trading weapons for money with arch enemies of the United States.

◆ ◆ ◆

There had been quite a few close calls. Sometimes Albie had the feeling that Manny was his long-lost half-brother from another father. Time after time, he'd anticipate Albie's moves. Whenever they got separated in the middle of a sting, Manny was able to sense the moment when his partner's life was in jeopardy. His intuitive abilities had saved Albie on a number of occasions. It was as if a GPS had been implanted in Manny's brain signaling Albie's exact location, enabling him to sneak up on the danger and waste the perp before Albie's eyes.

The smirk he saw on his partner's face just after that motivated Manny to share something with him at one of their whiskey binges the night his partner's divorce was officially final. Down in the dumps, Albie was getting as drunk as possible, reminiscing about Sandy and their life together.

Changing the subject, Manny burst out laughing and said, "Hey *amigo,* you know what turns me on, besides hearing about your friggin' divorce and your sexy ex-wife?"

Taking a long sip of the smooth Oban, Albie was annoyed at his partner. The only guy he could talk to about the faked infidelity, the devastating blow to his wife, and the purposeful separation from his kids was Manny. And now Manny was shutting him down. Albie grumbled, "What are you snickering about, you cockroach?"

Manny held his grin and said, "I'm thinking about the expression I see planted on your face every time I save your butt, that's what. You know what pushes me to do it even though you're a splinter in my ass?" He slugged down the last drops in his whiskey glass.

"No, what?"

"That smirk on your face *amigo* when you first realize that you're not gonna die. I can see it on your ugly mug each and every time. You look like goddamn Jack Nicholson, with your cocky expression, having just skirted death. Such a wise-ass you are, man."

"Yeah, well, maybe next time you won't do me such a kindness," Albie retorted with sarcasm, slamming down his glass. "I've got nothing left now, anyway, except this fucking CIA job."

Manny retreated, regretting that he had provoked his friend, even though in jest. He looked down at the marble bar counter, feeling ashamed. Then he glanced over at Albie, ready to apologize for his awkward jesting, and there it was, that cocky smirk sitting on his partner's face. Rolling his eyes, Manny mumbled, "You cocksucker, you got me."

They both roared with laughter, Albie falling back on the rickety bar stool, Manny shouting over to the bartender, ordering another bottle of the premium whiskey.

While Albie's overconfident nature had somehow propelled him to be viewed as leadership material, in contrast, Manny demonstrated a quiet air of loyalty, refusing to be moved in at least two instances when Agency superiors proposed an alternative partner. The CIA preferred to change up the pairings, discouraging agents from becoming too attached. But Manny had vehemently protested, and the second time a change-up was suggested, he laid his job on the line to stay by Albie's side. This caught the attention of the CIA's West Coast leadership team.

"Albie Stonemeyer, he's got magnetism, charisma, and leadership skills," Ashcroft once told to Albie, repeating a conversation he overheard at the top. "That's what they're saying about you, Stonemeyer, whether it's reality or not."

What also helped pedestal Albie in the eyes of Agency leaders was the pair's track record. The duo's success rate thwarting numerous hefty arms deal threats was unmatched, keeping local CIA decision-makers from mandating any separation of the two men.

◆ ◆ ◆

As he sat in his car, torn up about losing Manny, Albie's eyes filled with tears, his mind flooded with vengeful thoughts. "I'm going to kill those assholes," he vowed, looking down the road, through his dusty windshield, at Sandy's A-frame house.

She called it a cottage, but it was more of an artsy bungalow, he thought, reflecting on the style of his ex-wife, who was beautiful, in a no-frills sort of way, but always bringing her unique zest to everything she did. He hadn't noticed before but there was a lot of land at the side and back of the house, with two large oak trees on the far perimeter of the fenced-in yard. He spotted a large picnic table flanked by two long wooden benches on a patio outside the kitchen area. Luke's outdoor toys were stacked up on the table and a colorful mini jungle gym was set up close by.

Tilting the rearview mirror, he peered at his reddened eyes. Looking back at him was a weary middle-aged man, a man he barely recognized. He would ring Sandy's doorbell, then start apologizing for his unexplained estrangement. It had been three months since he'd seen his ex-wife and kids. What could he possibly say to make it up to them? To her?

He hit the steering wheel, beating it this time with his fists, then remembered that he'd buried a half pack of Camels under the driver's seat sometime ago when he swore to himself to quit the habit, his third attempt. The divorce had re-triggered his desire for nicotine, but he had successfully resisted, mostly because of Manny's encouragement. It was now twelve months since his last smoke. He thought about how Manny had unconditionally supported him in so many ways over the years. Shoving the cigarette pack back under the car seat, protecting his health one more time, Albie flashed on the connection between this action with the cigarette pack and the way he had shoved Sandy and the kids out of his life to protect them. Shit, he thought, I need a smoke, and even more, I want to hold my ex-wife in my arms.

Releasing the catch on the glove compartment, he foraged around, locating a sticky matchbook. "Falafel House," it read, "707 The Alameda,

San Jose." This had been Manny's favorite hangout for lunch, a place he dragged Albie to at least once a week whenever they were south of San Francisco. Manny, a Mexican, who preferred Middle-Eastern cuisine to burritos or enchiladas, was addicted to the texture and taste of deep-fried chickpeas. He was also a man who had a penchant for astronomy and would spend much of his free time at the Lick Observatory or buried in a book about the planets while gobbling down his falafel. He'd share his stargazing bytes of knowledge with Albie, what he had seen or learned the night before at the observatory, highlighting the incredible marvels in the night skies. Manny was a man full of surprises, with many colorful layers to him.

Albie's fingers hunted again, under the car seat, for the pack of Camels. Lighting an almost flattened cigarette, he toasted Manny with his first puff. "Quality, my friend, you had it on all counts," he said, looking into the smudged mirror. Taking a second drag, his body stiffened, as he felt disgusted with himself. "What the hell am I doing?" Flinging the car door open, he snapped up the cigarette pack, removed the five remaining cigarettes, and, one-by-one, crumbled each into small bits, watching the particles of tobacco catch the wind like scattered ashes. Then resuming driving, he wondered what it would feel like to put his hands around the Irishman's throat.

For a quick moment, he had an irrational image of his ex-wife welcoming him, embracing him the way she used to when they were together, with a quick hello at the door, then rushing back into the kitchen to finish cutting up the vegetables for dinner, and then presenting him with some sparkling water in an iced martini glass. She'd whisper in his ear: "For you Mr. Bond, shaken, not stirred, just the way you prefer it." Occasionally, maybe one out of ten times, she'd hand him an actual loaded martini. "Olives?" she'd inquire. He'd hold up two fingers. She'd grin, and within a few seconds, two toothpick-speared olives were dropped into his glass. Upon realizing that Dad had just arrived home, the kids would emerge, surround him, Jenny spilling spirited tales of her day at school and little Luke trying to add something in his simple language.

His head down on the steering wheel, Albie mourned, thinking, Those days are over, you fool. Should I knock on her door, or just turn around, drive home, and drink my way to tomorrow?

Chapter Twelve

Unavailable

"Mom, what do you think? Does this costume fit okay? It feels too big and I'll be flying across the stage on wires. I don't want this thing to fall off," Jenny said, panicking, as she examined herself in the wall mirror.

"You look like a star, Jenny. Honestly, that green costume shows off your hazel eyes. They shine!"

"Mom, I'm supposed to look like a boy, not like Tinker Bell. Thanks a lot."

I smiled... Jenny, never satisfied with anything I say. In a few hours, we'd be at the theater, my nine-year-old daughter about to make her stage debut. Felicia had been a gift for Jenny, connecting her with the Scotts Valley children's theater, and now my rambunctious daughter was starring in their fall production. It had been a surprise to me that she could pull it off—auditioning, then being selected for any role, let alone the lead. But Jenny was quite remarkable when she wanted something badly enough. It had been Felicia who had ignited her theatrical flame, coaching her on how to compete for the part.

"I better take this thing off so I don't ruin it," Jenny said as she did an arabesque across the living room as if already performing Peter Pan, stopping every other leap to scrutinize her ballet pose in the mirror.

"Good idea, sweetheart. Just don't wake your brother from his nap. If he doesn't sleep now, he'll be finicky during your show, and we don't want that."

"Oh no! Mom, there's a rip under the arm. Look!" she screeched.

"Let me see. Yep, but it's only a tiny tear on the seam, Jenny. Take it off and I'll mend it. It'll take me two minutes. You go take your shower while I'm doing this."

Jenny peeled off her glittery green costume. She was already growing into a young woman, I thought, as I watched her disappear down the hallway in her underwear, yes, definitely racing through her childhood years. In some ways the divorce has seemed to have accelerated her maturation, yet in other ways her emotional growth seemed to be stunted, a byproduct of a broken home, I thought. Reaching for my sewing kit and glancing up out the window at the day, one minute gray and the next streaked with sun, I felt a sense of melancholy overtake me.

◆ ◆ ◆

Is that Albie? What the heck is he doing here? I wondered. After being who knows where for the past three months, wham, he shows up. I felt agitated as I watched him climb the porch steps to my front door, Luke's three-wheeler laying across the bottom steps, a hazard for visitors. I watched Albie as he picked up the bike and placed it carefully down on the front lawn. My heart still fluttered at the sight of him despite how I felt about him as a father and a husband.

He's got the worst timing, I thought. Zack and Felicia were scheduled to be here within the hour. God, I didn't want some ridiculously awkward scene.

Scrambling to the door, I opened it and stepped outside, not wanting to alert Jenny or napping Luke. With my hands folded across my chest, I stood firmly blocking him from entering the house. "No," I commanded, having instantly fallen back into angry "jilted wife" mode.

Damn him, I was finally feeling attractive again, especially during the last few months. I felt desirable, even sexy, with Zack in my life. Now Albie had appeared out of the blue after a record-breaking hiatus, probably just back from a long trip with his Japanese protégé, the woman who was likely his steady girlfriend or who knows maybe his fiancée at the speed I recall him working our romance.

Ready to crush him with words, I looked into his eyes, noticing a grave sadness, his usual cocky light having dimmed, his vulnerability revealed. Like some schoolboy mischief-maker who'd been scolded once too often, he lacked the spirit of playful sarcasm I always associated with him. Dropping my defenses, I took his hand and leaned back against the screen door.

"You look like hell, Albie. Did something happen?" I said. My concern grew as I gazed at him. It didn't take long for our old familiarity to kick in. I squeezed his hand. "Is it bad?" I inquired.

"Hmm. My best friend, a close colleague, was killed. Gone. Fucking gone for no good reason."

"Oh God. How?"

He stared off behind me, his eyes vacant.

"An accident. It was a car crash, happened late last night. Drunk driver, showed no mercy."

I felt my body stiffen, realizing that the reason for his three-month absence wasn't connected to his friend's death. The warmth that had just surfaced for the man I loved for so many years cooled as I was soberly reminded that he was a cheat and most recently a deserter to his family. "I'm sorry about your friend," I said, "truly sorry, but why are you here like this unannounced?"

He was stoic, unable to make eye contact or respond with words. I was lying to myself. I knew why he was standing in front of me.

"Albie, you've literally abandoned your children. Have you even registered that fact? You couldn't spare two minutes of your time to make one lousy phone call to say hello to your own kids? What kind of father... Look, you can't just show up and expect..."

"I expect nothing, Sandy. I can go. I'll leave right now."

Though infuriated, I had the urge to invite him in, maybe make him some lunch, let him visit with the kids. They missed him. But Zack and Felicia were due to arrive in less than thirty minutes. Anxious thoughts swirled in my head. I still had to mend Jenny's costume, get the kids ready to go to the theater, and my ex-husband is in love with a beautiful woman at least twenty years my junior.

"We have plans today, Albie," I said. Damn, he looked terrible. "You can call me tomorrow and we'll schedule a day for you with the kids. I'm...I'm sorry about your friend." I felt the tears surface and focused down at the wooden porch. He cupped his hands around mine.

Then, touching my cheek, he said, "It's okay, Jelly Bean." More conflicting emotions welled up inside of me. "I'm probably in no shape to see them, anyway," he continued. "I'll phone you in the morning." He turned to go, then looked back at me and gestured, his index finger first pointing to his eye, then to his heart, and then at me. Then he mimed, "I love you."

The lump inside my throat had become a boulder. I rushed inside the house, gently closing the door, stepping back to the sofa, where the Peter Pan costume and sewing kit waited for me to resume my mending. Should I have let him go? I wondered.

Albie got into his car, feeling the layers of loss, his wife, his kids, slipping further away, his best friend now dead. But there was something, something major, that Sandy wasn't sharing with him. He sensed it even through his grief. There was a significant change in her. She seemed younger. A light he hadn't seen in her eyes for far too long had returned. And then he saw the SUV drive up, a dark-blue Range Rover. A little red-haired girl jumped out from the passenger side. A man emerged from the driver's seat. Albie couldn't bear to see any more of it. He started the ignition. His tires screeching, he made a sharp U-turn, flying down the street, the wind rustling the trees, the skies gray again, the mountain drizzle beginning to fall. She's in love; that's what's changed, he thought. Maybe that'a her new guy in the Range Rover.

Chapter Thirteen

Peak Performer

The girls chatted with each other most of the way to the theater, practicing lines from the play, discussing their costumes, singing their finale number, Jenny excited to be Peter Pan and Felicia enchanted with her role as Wendy. Luke sat between them in his car seat, envious and equally animated. As we were about to turn off Mount Hermon Road, a half-mile from the theater, I noticed that it was only Jenny who had been talking for the last ten minutes, Felicia having become quiet. I wondered if perhaps she was getting the jitters, maybe experiencing some stage fright. Once again, her dad wasn't here, and neither Zack nor Felicia had mentioned he'd be showing up later.

"Two fine little artists we have here," Zack said, smiling over at me. "You okay, love? Seems like yer mind is full of serious thoughts on the brink of yer little Jenny taking the stage for her debut, flying on a high wire, to boot."

At first his words didn't register for me. I thought maybe he was talking to the girls. I had been staring out the window, detached, preoccupied, my mind having traveled back to the earlier scene with Albie.

"Um, no, no, I'm fine Zack, just nervous for Jenny, I guess. I'm so proud of her." Glancing back at the girls, I noticed that Felicia was staring pensively out the window while Jenny was taking another look at her script.

Zack touched my hand, as he made the right turn onto Kings Valley Road, saying, "She's a lot like you, Sandy, a fighter, a fierce competitor, going after what she wants and taking it. You have every right to be proud."

A flash of guilt swept through me. He ran his finger in circles in the palm of my hand, something he did lately to show his affection. Last night, he had whispered in the dark, "I love you," and then kissed me good night. It was the second time Zack said those three words to me. I was falling in love with this Irishman, although today I noticed a slight retreat in my feelings for him. Damn you, Albie!

Arriving at the theater, we saw kids in costumes rushing in through the backstage entrance. Jenny was anxious to scoot out of the Land Rover. Felicia seemed more hesitant and was still quiet. The show's director stood at the stage door to greet the young thespians. She graciously welcomed them, one-by-one, clearly excited herself about tonight's performance.

Zack jumped out of the car to hug Felicia before she disappeared with Jenny. Looking down at his niece, he said, "I'm sorry your dad didn't make it here today, Red, but he's on his way to Killarney to take care of your mum's property. You've got 150 percent of me to cheer you on. Don't forget that."

Felicia looked up at him. "Thanks, Uncle Zack. I'll do everything as planned," she said, narrowing her eyes and nodding up at him. I detected some discomfort from Felicia, as though she seemed skittish about going inside. "Um, um," she said, "what I mean, Uncle, is that I'll be the best Wendy I can be."

Zack nodded, flashing his Irish smile, and then focused on Jenny. "And you, little Miss Jenny Stonemeyer," he said, "my advice for you is to fly as high as you possibly can, especially in your Mister Crocodile solo."

My daughter blushed, thankful to have the attention from this magical man.

I bent down and looked into my daughter's shining eyes. "I'm so proud of you, Jenny," I said. "Have fun out there—that's more important than anything."

She reacted with a dimpled smile, a quick hug, and a rushed "Thanks Mom." She was already moving, pulling Felicia from Zack, and pointing to Miss Lucy, the director, who gestured for both of them to hustle inside.

I found myself wishing that Albie were there to participate in our little girl's big debut. Maybe I should have invited him to attend despite the awkward scene it certainly would have created. Then I turned to Luke to give him my full attention.

He tugged at my skirt, whining, "Mommy, I'm hungry. Can we eat before the show?"

Zack broke in, picking my son up in his arms. "How about we get a pizza next door? We don't have to be in our seats for an hour yet. What do you say, lad?"

They were good together, I thought, Zack consistently knowing how to save the day almost like clockwork when Luke made his four-year-old little-boy demands. With his flair for anticipating my son's needs, he seemed to consistently respond with ease. Occasionally I felt that he was a little too ready, maybe overeager, to impress me. But why would I question his motives? I wondered.

The auditorium was packed with kids, parents, seniors, even a sprinkling of reviewers I recognized from the local paper. We snagged three seats in the first row that was reserved for immediate family members of the cast. And here she was, the star of the *Peter Pan* classic, my daughter, starring back at me from the front of the theater program, sitting on my seat. I ran my fingers over the cover, over Jenny's photo, and then tucked it into my purse. Maybe I'll show it to Albie the next time I see him, I mused.

I sat back and watched my daughter command the stage, performing her role with confidence and skill, not missing one line. I was enthralled, wondering which parent had passed on this talent to her, thinking maybe it was me.

Offstage, Felicia stood in the wings, waiting for Jenny's entrance for her solo number, "Never Smile at a Crocodile." It was already the middle of Act II, the "lost boys" had just left the stage, and there were only three scenes left until the end of the show.

At that point, Jenny came flying out, suspended on thin, almost invisible metal wires, gliding across the stage, while an eight-year-old boy named Stephen, in a green crocodile costume, swam below, snapping his jaws as he moved back and forth, following Jenny's lead.

Between costume changes, Felicia wore only her black leotard and tights. She wasn't scheduled to be back on stage for another fifteen minutes, enough time to complete her mission. Stuffing the mini wire-cutters into the waistband of her tights, she started the climb up the metal ladder leading to the catwalk high above the stage. Once at the top, she crept along the railing, looking down at Jenny, who was flying, toes pointed in the air, moving from left to right and back again.

Tonight was the perfect opportunity to take revenge, Felicia and her Dad had agreed, having planned this incident for weeks. Eager to avenge the death of her mother, Felicia thought about Jenny's father, the hateful man who killed her mum. The Stonemeyers stood to rightfully suffer, everyone in her Irish clan agreed.

Her stomach fluttered and her heart pounded in her chest. As she moved closer to the position where she'd be able to reach down to cut the wires, the vocabulary word she learned today drifted into her head: *Psychoneurology*, defined in the dictionary as "the study of emotional disturbance." She had forgotten to share the new word with her father this morning, her usual routine, having been so focused on the deed planned for today. Tugging the wire cutters from her waistband, she laid low in the dark on the metal grid so the man operating the movement of the wires on the other end wouldn't see her. He sat on a metal chair, his eyes glued to the scene below, carefully sweeping Jenny across the stage, electronically controlling her moves, raising and lowering her in time to the music, with a keypad mounted on the wall. Felicia reached down about to snip the wires, as she had been coached to do, but the vocabulary word she learned today nagged at her, and she just couldn't do it. *Psychoneurology*. Am I emotionally disturbed because me mum died? she couldn't help but wonder.

"Snip swiftly girl, and get out of there." She could hear her dad's voice instructing her in her head. I can't do it, she admitted to herself, tears trickling down her cheeks. I just can't! I like Jenny—she's become my friend. Stuffing the cutters back in her waistband, she turned and crawled back to the ladder and descended.

Zack sat in his seat, holding the squirmy Luke on his lap, waiting, looking forward to the sound of the thud when Jenny would hit the stage. Maybe it would kill her—at the very least, she'd suffer a severe injury, exactly what the Stonemeyer family deserved. His grip on Luke tightened as his anticipation grew.

"Oww," Luke yelled out, reacting to the intensity of the clutch. Catching himself, Zack tickled the boy, Luke letting out a loud giggle in the middle of his sister's solo.

Jenny ended her song with a hearty declaration: "Clear the aisle, but never, never smile at Mister Crocodile. No, never, never smile at Mister Crocodile!"

Lowered by the wires to the stage floor, Jenny unhitched herself from the mechanism and joined Felicia, who had just entered from stage right ready to perform their last two scenes together.

Felicia seemed to hesitate with her first line: "Hello...Peter. Are you safe now? I'm so happy you survived Mister Crocodile and that horrid Captain Hook."

Bloody hell, Zack thought. The little bugger didn't do it. What in God's name went wrong? I should have done the deed myself. He looked over at Sandy, who sat there, tears of joy streaming down her face. His impulse was to grab the proud mother and tell her that her precious little girl was actually supposed to die this afternoon, or at the very least, be injured for life. He resisted and instead reached out to hold his lover's hand.

At the end of the performance, the young actors took their bows. Jenny jumped off the stage to join her family to start enjoying the afterglow of being the star of the show. Dozens of people in the audience stood up to give the cast a standing ovation. More people rose from their seats, clapping enthusiastically. The show's director looked over at Jenny, signaling her to return to the stage for another bow. After two more bows from the cast, Jenny ran back to her mother and brother, filled with pride and happiness.

I reached under my seat and pulled out a bouquet of red roses tied up with a giant red-and-black polka-dotted ribbon. "These are for you, Jenny," I said, extending the flowers.

Felicia trailed behind Jenny, avoiding eye contact with her dad, who was likely furious at her failure to deliver the results he expected. I nudged Zack, moving my eyes to the floor behind him, gesturing for him to pick up his bouquet of flowers to hand to Felicia. But he continued to hesitate, wanting nothing to do with rewarding his daughter for what he assessed as a poor performance. Bewildered by his lack of enthusiasm, I reached down for Zack and presented the roses to Felicia myself.

"Congratulations, Felicia," he mustered up the words. "You were the best Wendy imaginable, absolutely lovely." He gathered himself together, pressing Felicia to him, offering her his hollow embrace.

At that moment, the cell phone vibrated in his pocket, probably Antonio checking in, he surmised.

"Well, let's go celebrate," I said. "Stone Cold Creamery anyone?"

Luke and Jenny replied in unison, "Yes!"

Zack grimaced while Felicia stood at his side, silent. "Sorry love, but I'm afraid that pizza did me in. I'm not feeling so well. We'll be going home instead, but see you soon. Enjoy the ice cream."

"Of course, no problem," I replied.

Zack was silent as we drove up Mount Hermon Road, Jenny gabbing away about the performance, smelling her roses, Felicia listening quietly, and Luke napping. Zack didn't look over at me, which was unusual for him, when I recall that day. I couldn't help but question whether he was faking not feeling good to get away from me.

Chapter Fourteen

His Irish Eyes

The drive home was excruciating for Felicia. She could feel her dad's disappointment with every jarring turn of the car. Wendall sat fuming with anger. Felicia felt guilty and fearful of the words that would follow once they got home. She made herself as small as possible in the backseat, pretending to be asleep, cloaked under a fleece blanket.

When the car stopped, without a word, she fled, running up the stairs headed for her bedroom.

Expecting Antonio to be home, Wendall headed to the kitchen, but his brother seemed to be out. He grabbed a beer and headed upstairs to his room, slamming the door shut. Dropping his brown leather jacket on the chair, his blood began to boil again. Slinging his car keys across the room, he bared his teeth, as he grabbed the photo of his dead wife, staring into Cassandra's green eyes.

A knock on the door.

"What?" he grumbled.

"Can I come in, Dad?"

"Your choice," he barked back.

A weepy Felicia sat down beside him. "I...I don't know what happened, Dad. I just couldn't do it. Something inside stopped me."

She slid off the bed and stood in front of him. He put the photo down and sat upright on the bed, still, like a stone, his Irish eyes staring off into the mirror on the wall behind his little girl.

Felicia mumbled, "I...I learned a new word this morning, Dad. That's what stopped me today. The word is... *compassion*," she lied, "and it means..."

Grabbing her arm, he exploded, "Screw the 'compassion' girl. Didn't you love your mum? Didn't you?" He shook the silver-framed photo close to her face. "Don't you still love her, think about her? Do you understand how she suffered?"

Felicia started to cry, not knowing what to say. Of course, she missed her mum, but hurting Jenny Stonemeyer would not change things, would not bring her mum back.

"You failed, Felicia! What's your explanation, girl? Compassion, is it? Do you think Jenny's dad had an iota of compassion when he brutally murdered yer mum?" He pulled her toward him, dismissing her sobs. "We agreed as a team to avenge yer mum's death and hurt that family, one-by-one, make them pay. You were our number-one weapon."

"I know, Dad," she whimpered. "I...I know. I'm sorry."

He pushed her away, Felicia falling to the wood floor. Scared, she lifted herself, getting onto her knees. She wanted to please him. "I...I could try again if that's—"

"Quiet, Felicia! We had the perfect setup, but you..." He sat back down on the bed, his body trembling with fury, shaking his head back and forth, wringing his hands together. Then he barked, "Forget the girl. I'll find another way to get our revenge. Just keep yer cover and keep wooing Jenny as yer best friend. Can you do that?"

"Yes, Dad. Okay," she murmured, trying to hold back her tears, still down on the floor.

Antonio appeared in the doorway. "So, no win tonight then? Ya can't depend on yer little girl for this, man?"

"Shut the fuck up, Antonio," he shouted. He looked over at his daughter, whose tears covered her face. "Get to bed, and stop reading the damn dictionary, will ya?"

She nodded, feeling like a complete failure, and crept out of the room.

"So, what's your fucking plan?" she heard Antonio say as he slammed the door behind her.

In her bedroom, there he was, her tattered stuffed rabbit, Fred, crumpled up on the carpet by her bed. She slid down next to him and held him in her arms, her body shaking. One of his eyes came loose in her hand, a fractured black button. Who would sew it back on?

Mum, I wish you were here with me," she cried, looking up at the ceiling, connecting with the heavens above. "I need you, Mum. I can't do this. I can't."

Chapter Fifteen

The Left Bank

The day following Jenny's performance, Albie contacted me as planned. We agreed that he'd pick the kids up on Tuesday, a school holiday, him assuring me that he'd be free from work, and if I were okay with it, he'd like to take them overnight, maybe down to Monterey. He could then drop them off at school on Wednesday morning.

Since I didn't have a scheduled news shoot, Mimi invited me out for lunch at a trendy French restaurant called the Left Bank located over the hill in Silicon Valley.

Mimi and I started our lunch with a glass of pinot noir, both ordering the French onion soup and Nicoise salad.

"So, it sounds like your romance with the Irishman is going gang-busters, although today I'm detecting you a bit on edge. What's up, girl-friend?" she asked.

"Nothing much, I'm good. My life is just complicated. Zachery's been total magic for me...and for the kids, quite honestly."

"So then what's the problem?"

"I'm falling in love with Zack, but I still feel attached to Albie, despite him freezing out the kids for the last three months, despite what he did to us, despite everything. It makes it difficult to fully open up to Zack."

I took another sip of wine, commenting, "This is good stuff."

"Tell me more, Sandy. Maybe I can help. Look, that barrier between you and Zack—it might be your instincts kicking in. I'm not sure he's all that he says he is."

"You mean you think he's some kind of fraud?"

"Maybe, I also have the feeling that you're not ready for a big romance."

"Yeah, it's me, not unusual. I've always had a problem letting someone into my life, exposing the raw me. It scares me. Albie was my only exception. I guess it goes back to losing my mother and father."

"It was an accident, wasn't it? You mentioned it once, but I didn't want to pry."

"Yes, they died together in a plane crash on their way back from Tahoe. It was a rainy day in November. I was lucky to have Aunt Sylvie rescue my brother and I, raise us with all the comforts. She encouraged my writing, my studies. I owe her so much for her relentless devotion. That's why I moved to Felton, not just to get away from everything Albie but also to be close to Aunt Sylvie."

"You're certainly a blessing for her, as well as for me."

The waiter placed the bill on our table.

"I'm getting this," Mimi said, picking up the check.

"No, no, I should get it after bending your ear with my troubles," I said.

"It's on me, I'm insisting, but first let's have coffee and split a French dessert."

"I can't say no to that," I replied, laughing. "Thanks for being such a good..."

Oh God, I thought, as an Asian woman passed in front of us, the one who I caught in bed with Albie. I would have known her face anywhere. The hostess escorted her, a pigtailed little girl and an older woman following just behind, to the table adjacent to our booth, all three of them well dressed.

"Sandy, what's wrong? You're as pale as a ghost," Mimi said, patting my hand.

I leaned close to her, feeling like I could faint any moment. "It's the woman, the one I found in bed with Albie," I muttered. "Oh my God, it's definitely her."

I tilted my head a couple of times to make sure. Mimi glanced across the aisle. The older woman looked in our direction. I quickly turned, shielding my face.

"Well," Mimi whispered, "they look like a family—a mom, a grandmother, and a little girl, about five or maybe six years old. The young woman is quite beautiful, but she doesn't look like the type who'd lure a married man to cheat on his wife. Hmm, well, she's not wearing a wedding ring."

I could hear the little girl reading the menu aloud, excited. "Mom, they have escargot on the menu!" she exclaimed. "I really like it. Can I have that? Can I?"

"Mimi, I feel sick. I need to go to the restroom," I said in a panic.

"Do you want me to come with you?"

"No, please, just order me some coffee. I think I've had too much wine. Sorry, I'm not used to drinking during the day. I'll be right back."

"All right, honey. I'll order the cheesecake for us to share. Are you sure you don't want to leave right now?"

"I'm fine. Be right back," I said before rushing away.

I steadied myself in the restroom, holding onto the counter, taking deep breaths. I was curious about the woman who had taken my place in Albie's heart, I admitted to myself, as I stared with distress at my pale, drawn face in the mirror.

Taking out the compact from my handbag, I brushed some color into my cheeks. Frazzled, I dropped my handbag on the black-and-white checkered tile floor, the contents spilling out: my wallet, a hairbrush, mascara, my coin purse, a notepad, my checkbook—all of it. I noted that the designer handbag on the floor was the same one I had thrown at the young woman when I saw her in bed with my ex-husband less than a year ago.

As I bent down to gather the items and shove them back into my handbag, the restroom door swung open and in walked the older Asian woman. She smiled, politely acknowledged me, then hurriedly turned on the faucet and splashed her face with water, patting it dry with a paper towel. Looking down at me, she said, "Hot," waving her hand, "too hot in restaurant. You think too?"

Kneeling down on the floor beside me, she began to help me pick up the items that had tumbled across the floor in every direction, a couple of them sliding under an empty bathroom stall.

Flustered, I gathered the rest of the contents and nervously said, "Thank you. Thank you." I knew it was the beautiful woman's mother. "You are very kind to help me," I added, managing a half-smile.

Fleeing the restroom, I hurried past the Asian woman's table, as the little girl looked up from her menu. Her mother made eye contact with me as I walked by, the look on her face telling me that she also recognized me, but only at that very moment. Her mouth gaped open. She immediately looked down at the table, seeming to be stricken with shame.

Returning to the booth, where the coffee sat waiting for me, I could see Mimi's concern for me on her face.

"You okay? Drink some coffee," she said, lowering her voice. "It's not the end of the world running into 'the other woman.' Trust me. Maybe it's actually a good thing. No, maybe not. Look, I already paid the check, so we can leave any time you'd like. But have a bite of this cheesecake first."

"No thanks Mimi. Listen, I...I wanted to buy lunch. I feel responsible for having ruined this wonderful outing you so graciously planned."

She smiled, coaxing me out of the booth. Minutes later, out on the street in front of the restaurant, I embraced my friend.

"That woman's mother was in the restroom. She actually seemed very sweet, caring," I said, tears welling up in my eyes.

Just then the older woman came running out of the Left Bank's turnstile exit. "Wait, wait," she called out, heading toward me. "This yours? I think it yours," she said, holding up my silver-plated business card case. "You drop this in restroom."

As she handed it to me, the case sprung open, more than a dozen of my TV news business cards escaping, being caught up in the wind. The older woman reacted quickly, picking up the cards, one-by-one, from the pavement. I watched her in silence. Because she moved so quickly, I didn't attempt to help. Mimi stood at my side watching her with equal fascination. Rushing back to us, the aging, yet physically agile, petite woman suddenly stopped, holding a business card close to her face so she could read it. Her face seemed to drop as if in shock. As she approached us, I could see that her dark eyes were moist. She fumbled, placing the business cards back in the silver case, handing it to me. A single tear slid down her cheek, her mouth was open, but she seemed unable to speak.

Taking my hand, she led me away from Mimi, closer to the restaurant, cupped her hands around mine, and looked down at the ground. Speaking softly, she said, "Your pain, my pain." She shook her head from side to side, and then peered deep into my eyes. Her face was filled with emotion, her voice shaky, as she said, "What you see not real, not real, Sandy Stonemeyer. You understand?"

I held my breath, feeling her torment, finding myself wanting to help make it all better for her, for myself. Then she was gone, running back inside the restaurant to join her daughter and granddaughter.

She knew my name. She knew who I was once she read my business card, which meant that she must know about the affair, what happened between her daughter and my husband.

Mimi walked over to console me, draping her arm around my shoulder. "What did that woman say?" she asked.

"I...I'm not sure. Something about 'not real.' I...I didn't really understand what she was saying."

"Sandy, it's over, that whole uncomfortable episode. Come on, let's head back over the hill. It's a beautiful day, and it's not over yet. It's been a bit bizarre, yes," she said, rolling her eyes, "but there's still time left to turn this into a nice day out. Hell, it's my day off!"

In the car, Mimi treated us to an Edith Piaf CD, an early collection of songs, ballad after ballad playing as we climbed the Santa Cruz Mountains. Piaf was called "The Little Sparrow," a wounded bird like me, I thought. I then found myself drifting into thoughts of my mother and father, who loved to slow dance in our living room to old-time French songs, anything European.

◆ ◆ ◆

Two days after my twelfth birthday, the morning of their fifteenth wedding anniversary, I lay there in bed in a lazy slumber. My older brother had spent the night at his best friend's house. I could hear my parents getting ready for their special brunch at Llewelyn's Restaurant at the top of Harveys Hotel. My father was to fly his single engine Cessna to Lake Tahoe, something they did every few months or so, sometimes taking us with them.

When my mom was in the bathroom starting up her shower, I heard my dad call out, "Patsy, it's already 7:30. I'm off to the airport to get the plane ready. Can you meet me there in an hour? Just park the car off to the left, outside the hangar. We don't want to be late for our reservation."

Noticing me standing at their bedroom door, he scooped me up and whispered, "Aunt Sylvie will be here in a few minutes."

"Okay, Mark," my mother called back. "See you at the airport. I'll hurry, I promise... Wait, honey, what should I wear?"

My father looked puzzled. "You're kidding, right?" he said, mussing my hair, teasing me. "Since when do you take fashion advice from your husband? I'm off, okay sweetheart?"

"All right, I'll do what I can to look my best...if you're lucky," my mother replied.

Smirking at me, he put me down and gathered up his keys and wallet, gave me a hurried hug, and closed the front door behind him. Still half asleep, I walked back to my bedroom, crawled into bed, snuggled up to my Cinderella body pillow, and fell back to sleep.

Awaking again maybe a couple of hours later, I tiptoed downstairs to find my Aunt Sylvie in the kitchen singing to herself as she poured pancake batter onto Mom's griddle.

"Someone's got banana flapjacks coming up in about four minutes," she announced.

I giggled in response and gave her a big hug as she poured orange juice for me into one of my mother's antique teacups.

"Your brother's already come home and gone out again with some friends to play basketball."

I remember noticing Aunt Sylvie's journal sitting on the kitchen table, the one she wrote in every day. She had two published romance novels and was working on a third. We ate together as she explained her latest plot, sharing with me some of the notes from her journal, wanting my opinion about the two little girl characters she was in the process of developing. I remember feeling important, thrilled that my talented aunt valued my ten-year-old thoughts.

We were eating our pancakes, chattering away, when the telephone rang. My mother had collected antiques for many years and even our landline telephone was an old-fashioned royal blue police phone mounted to the kitchen wall.

Aunt Sylvie picked up the receiver and sang out, "Yes, hello." Listening for a few seconds, I watched her face suddenly transform. She dropped the phone, looking horrified, the cord swinging like a pendulum, twisting this way and that. She appeared to be in shock, glaring at the dangling phone for a moment. She hesitated and then picked it up and said, "Yes, I'm here... How did it happen?" She listened, gasping for air, almost losing her balance. She turned off the griddle, and said, "Oh God, Oh God, I'm here with their young daughter."

"I'm here with their young daughter." I remember those words as if it were yesterday. I remember thoughts speeding through my mind, dreading the sentence I would likely hear next. She sat down, put her head down on the table, the spine of her journal touching her gray-flecked hair. The house was very quiet. The only audible sound I remember in those moments was the ticking of the antique clock in our living room and Aunt Sylvie's fractured breathing.

After hanging up the phone, she bent down by the chair I was sitting on and embraced me like a treasured doll. "I'm so sorry, sweet child. Your mom and dad—they're gone," she said. "Their plane crashed, sweetheart, on the way back from Tahoe." Her voice sounded far away, as if in a tunnel, a dark musty tunnel. Grabbing the chair next to me, she sat me down on her lap and rocked me like a baby. "How can it be? Your father was a good pilot," she said, "a professional. Such a tragedy! I'll be here for you Sandy, for you and for your brother, always here for both of you."

Sitting on my aunt's lap at the kitchen table, the smell of flapjacks and maple syrup in the air, I cried, hiding my face in the warm crevice where her arm met her breast. Her robe was soft.

"Aunt Sylvie," I said, "I can't believe it." I was overwhelmed, but the horror of what happened would take a long time to fully register.

She continued rocking me, holding me tight. "You will recover from this," she said. "But it's hard, so hard when something pointless like this happens to people we love."

Aunt Sylvie kept her promise, raising my brother and I, encouraging us at every turn, making sure we had the best education, and above all, blessing us with her unconditional love.

◆ ◆ ◆

Mimi eased the car into a parking space. For a few seconds, I was disoriented, but then returned back to the here and now. We're at the beach in Santa Cruz on West Cliff Drive, I realized. Mimi cut the engine and the great Edith Piaf stopped singing.

"I'm sorry," I said to Mimi, surfacing from my thoughts. "Hearing Edith Piaf, I couldn't help but think of my parents. I'm such bad company."

"You've had a shock, my friend, running into the woman who broke up your marriage. How about we take a stroll along the ocean for a little bit before going back to Felton?"

A strong black woman with a huge heart, Mimi was a wonderful teacher for my son and a caring friend, having taken me under her wing since the day I met her.

We walked a little and sat down on a wooden bench facing the ocean when Mimi's phone suddenly chimed.

"I'll get it later," she said.

"No, no, please take it. Might be important."

She smiled, apologizing with her eyes. "Mimi."

I watched her face light up, pleased to have taken the call.

"Yes? Yes, I will be there," she said.

I pretended not to listen, but noticed my friend's eyes widen as she listened to the voice on the other end.

"Ahh, I understand. I must go now," Mimi said as she stood up from the bench, moved a couple of feet away, and whispered, "*Uh roon shark. See you later.*"

Was she talking about sharks? I wondered. Or was that some other language she was speaking?

Just then my cell phone rang.

"Your turn," Mimi said, laughing. "Take it, it's only fair."

Reluctantly I answered the call. "Sandy Stonemeyer."

Unable to hear well, I put the phone on speaker.

"Sandy, it's Jon here at Channel 6. Tomorrow at 3 p.m., can you be at the Old Carmel Mission? They're going to make Junipero Serra a saint and I'd like you to cover this story. There are three people to be interviewed. Important coverage for our station. Can you do it?"

Mimi nudged me, nodding, mouthing that she would take care of the kids.

"Yes, sure, I can make it, Jon."

"Great, meet me at 9:30 in the morning at the station, and then tomorrow afternoon at the mission," Jon said, sounding pleased. "You'll find Gabe the cameraman will be there looking for you thirty minutes before the shoot. Get your interview questions ready, Ms. Stonemeyer. I know you'll be well prepared. We'll nail down the final content in the morning."

"Both times work, and thanks for thinking of me, Jon," I said, disconnecting, still staring at my phone.

"Wow, you're becoming quite the local TV news celebrity," Mimi said, hugging my arm, as we got up and walked along the stone path, looking down at the surfers in the waves down below.

"You're my biggest fan, you know. Not sure there are many others out there."

We both smiled.

"And who was that on the phone with you before I got my call? Hmm? Your eyes lit up when you were speaking. Someone special?"

"Just a friend," Mimi replied, shaking her head and rolling her eyes. "Well, kind of someone I'm sort of dating."

"Well now. Hmm, my close friend is keeping secrets I see." I threaded my arm through hers and hugged her close. "And...were you talking about sharks or something with your friend? I thought I heard you say a ruined shark? I don't see any sharks out there, just surfers."

Mimi threw her head back, laughing. "No, we already share this silly secret language between us, kind of like Pig Latin. He's totally a casual friend, but with a few benefits." She raised her eyebrows. "Anyway, forget about him. Let's talk about you. Look, I think you'd be wise to put the brakes on with this Zachery guy." It was a curve ball I wasn't expecting from Mimi. "It's up to you, Sandy, but I have some reservations about him. Maybe I just need to get to know him better. I only met him once for a couple of minutes."

I nodded. "I understand what you're saying, I do, but well, I think I'm falling in love with him."

"Oh, I see," Mimi said, nodding. "Well, you'll do what's best for you. It's your life that you're rebuilding, and I think you're doing an impressive job of it. Look, you're stuck with me no matter what your decisions are about Zack or anything else. He could be 'the guy,' but I have veto power."

"Indeed you do. How about if I planned a little dinner Saturday night at my house with Zack, and what if you came and brought someone with you like what's his name?"

"You mean, bring my casual friend as my date?"

We both smiled again.

"Yes, bring the guy on the phone. You seemed smitten. Your own secret language?"

"Actually, I think I'd prefer to come alone. Then I won't feel obligated to entertain the date plus get to know your heartthrob."

"Good point. You're so logical, like some sort of teacher or something."

We smirked at each other.

With a sigh, Mimi waved her arms in the air. "God, what a day we've had, huh?"

I rolled my eyes, nodding in agreement, giving her arm another squeeze. "Yeah," I concurred.

"Life," Mimi quipped, "it takes no prisoners."

Chapter Sixteen

Tamakichi's Dilemma

Five-year-old Miyoko peered down at the white butcher paper place setting at the restaurant, and using her purple crayon, added a geometric border around the stick-figure family she had drawn. Then she looked up to see her grandmother return from the restroom and sit back down in her chair, looking troubled.

♦ ♦ ♦

Miyoko had hoped that her grandmother wouldn't speak that much Japanese, because she didn't like it and didn't know that many words. She wanted to eat, breathe, write, and speak only in English. Nobody else outside her family spoke Japanese. Some kids in her class spoke Chinese, or Korean or Tagalog, but none spoke Japanese. Her teacher insisted that all the children speak just English in the classroom.

Her mom had prepared her for her grandmother's visit, saying, "Miyoko, she might speak often in Japanese, and I will in turn speak back to her in our mother tongue. I know you don't like it when I speak Japanese, but you will need to respect your grandmother's needs. Anyway, you know many words and phrases. Maybe you can take this opportunity to practice while she's here."

"But Mom, I...I don't want—"

"That's enough," her mother interrupted. "This is not your choice, Miyoko. I want your grandmother to be comfortable in our home. You understand what I mean? She is my mother like I am your mother. But let us see how much English your grandmother speaks and understands. She may surprise us both."

Glum about the prospect of having to listen to a constant foreign language but obeying her mother's wish, Miyoko muttered back, "Okay Mom, okay."

Her mother had become moody over the last several months, often tearful. She seemed to be carrying some big weight on her shoulders. Miyoko missed the way her mom used to be, how happy she was, how her beautiful face used to shine. But those days were gone.

The first night Tamakichi was there, she offered to tuck Miyoko in bed.

Miyoko looked into her grandmother's eyes and asked, "Grandmother, do you speak much English?"

"Speak English? Me?" replied Tamakichi.

"Yes, I'm hoping you speak English so I can talk to you."

"Sweet grandchild, I try best. Yes."

Miyoko smiled and kissed her grandmother's cheek, saying, "Don't worry, Grandmother, if you have to speak Japanese, it will be okay... Can I call you Grandma, and not have to say Grandmother all the time?"

"Yes, you call me Grandma."

◆ ◆ ◆

Miyoko finished her drawing and looked over at her grandmother, who seemed to be upset. Tamakichi sat there with her hands clasped together on the table. Emily poured her mother a cup of tea from the short white stone pot. She then reached over, placing one arm around her mother's shoulders, and moved her chair around the table to caress her with both arms.

Emily spoke gently, first a few words in Japanese, and then in English she asked, "What's wrong, Mother?"

"I know what happened, child. I understand on phone that night. You did bad thing with colleague but not as it seem to Sandy Stonemeyer."

Shaken, Emily dropped her face, her mouth open in disbelief. Looking over at Miyoko, she said, "Miyoko, please go to the restroom, you know where it is in the back of the restaurant. We're going shopping and there will be no good opportunity. Okay, sweetie?"

"Okay Mommy. I have to go, yes." Miyoko jumped up and left the table.

Emily followed with her eyes, and then looked at her mother, feeling shamed.

"You understood about the work thing—the shame of the staged infidelity?"

Tamakichi nodded, staring down at her plate, and then looked hard into her daughter's eyes, nodding again.

Swallowing hard, Emily gathered herself together. "Mother, please understand," she began, "this is my own ugly beast to tame, the beast *I* created. Please, you can see that I have great guilt about this deception. I will deal with it in my own way." Then she said in Japanese, "I appreciate your intentions, but the action you are thinking about, I can see it in your face, can do great harm."

With those words, Tamakichi lowered her head in her hands for a moment, and then looked up, feeling an ache in her heart and conflicted in her principles. Returning from the restroom, Miyoko sat down to continue her drawing, but could feel her grandmother's distress. Tamakichi stared out the restaurant window, and then closed her tired eyes, searching for how she could help her misguided daughter.

Miyoko put down her crayons. She said nothing but placed the finished drawing down on the table in front of her grandmother. Opening her eyes, Tamakichi instantly warmed to the beautiful colors, the imaginative shapes and figures depicted on the butcher paper, admiring the brown and white spotted dog standing next to the likeness of Miyoko. Her granddaughter had been given a gift with art, not something prevalent in their family line. Perhaps it came from my lover's side, handed down generationally to little Miyoko, Tamakichi thought as she focused on every detail of the drawing.

She touched her granddaughter's hand, kissed the drawing, and gently said, "I very much like, very much. Thank you... Move chair close to me, please Miyoko." She made space for the young girl, who scooted over as requested. "I ask you question. This is beautiful drawing. How you know that I was hoping something of beauty appear before my eyes...as if you knew that I needed this to lift my spirit when I did not even know I needed it myself?"

Miyoko beamed. "I made it just for you, Grandma. You seemed unhappy so...I...I..." Miyoko pointed at the figures she created in the drawing. "See, that's you walking with me and my doggie friend on the beach. We are enjoying the sunny day."

"I see. I see. What impress me is you go inside my head, know I need something to lift spirits. In Japanese culture, we call it *amae*. Miyoko, *amae*. Yes, word say?"

Emily smiled.

"*Amae?* What does that mean, Grandma? I don't know that word," Miyoko replied.

"It mean 'pretty petal' or to do something from heart before someone aware they need or want. You give beautiful art to me before I know it will make my day bright. Understand?"

Miyoko gazed at the picture and nodded. "Hmmm. I understand Grandma. *Amae*—it's a nice word."

Emily observed the interaction in silence, and then stood up behind their chairs to caress both of them on their shoulders, whispering, "I love you, Mother. I respect you, and am happy to have you here. We both love you." Emily sat back down across from her mother and reached for her small hands. Her voice became more emphatic and direct as she said, "But I need your promise not to interfere in my personal business or in my work. My bosses would be very upset if they knew that I was talking about this with anyone. Mother, can you give me your word? Please, I am begging you."

Tamakichi nodded solemnly and looked down at her granddaughter, who had already started on another drawing. Emily's pleading words put Tamakichi to shame. She had already betrayed her daughter with her counsel to Sandy Stonemeyer just minutes ago, though it appeared that the woman failed to understand her true intention, probably a blessing in disguise. In an outburst of raw emotion, Tamakichi had spilled the words out to the poor woman: "What you see not real, not real, Sandy Stonemeyer." She regretted the provocative statement she had made, but could not bear to confess this mistake to her daughter.

While Emily paid the check and Miyoko finished her second drawing, Tamakichi's thoughts grew darker. The worst thing for a mother is when the child loses trust in the parent. This is bad karma that must be coming back to me, she thought, as she gazed out the window at the passing shoppers, Sandy Stonemeyer's business card sitting in the breast pocket of her green velvet jacket.

Chapter Seventeen

Corned Beef and Cabbage

I studied up on Junipero Serra, the focus of the next day's interview, surfing the Internet and learning more about this man and why the Catholic Church had identified him as their prime candidate for sainthood. Reviewing the history of his accomplishments in the 1760s, I gathered that after coming from Spain to America, Serra had successfully established over thirteen missions in the state of California, converting thousands of people to Christianity, including scads of Indians. But there was controversy among several interest groups over the Pope's recommendation to canonize the man. Some considered Serra to have operated with brutal force, having used imprisonment and even torture to convert many Indians to Catholicism. I was poised to interview representatives from both sides—those in favor and those opposed. I wanted to be as well versed as possible on the thinking behind each perspective.

I took in screen after screen of content, crafting straightforward and tricky questions, working late into the night. Wanting to avoid creating a puffed piece of TV journalism, I yearned to instead offer a balanced view. Engrossed in my professional playground, I was fully enjoying my fact-finding mission while I slowly sipped a glass of merlot, Beethoven's "Moonlight Sonata" on Pandora. On a journalistic high, I considered the possibility that this story could potentially turn out to be the break I needed to get noticed for bigger assignments.

I felt free, having been blessed that night with not having to deal with the challenges of getting Luke and Jenny off to bed. Both were spending the night with Albie at the beach, and he was dropping them off at school the next morning. I tried calling Albie twice to let him know that Mimi was going to be with the kids after school the next day while I did the Channel 6 interviews at the mission. I wanted Luke and Jenny to be aware of this without being surprised tomorrow, but Albie's phone went straight to voicemail both times. Instead, I left Mimi a quick message, letting her know that the kids may not know what's happening until she tells Luke in the morning during preschool and then shows up to collect Jenny from her school later in the day. Regardless, I knew Jenny would have never-ending complaints about this and would likely chastise me about it as soon as we were together. Although our relationship felt less troubled than before Felicia and Zack came into our lives, Jenny couldn't resist an opportunity to jab at me, pointing out any evidence of my inadequacies as a parent.

It was 10:30 at night when the phone rang while I was in the midst of drawing up my questions, doing a final round of edits. Ahh good, it was likely Albie responding to my messages. Snatching the phone from its cradle, I answered it, recognizing the accent.

"Sandy, my love, is it too late for me to be calling? I could easily hang up if you're already off to sleep. I just wanted to hear your voice before I went to bed."

"Zack, no, no, it's good that you rang. Really. Actually, I have a big story tomorrow for Channel 6 and I'm in the middle of doing my prep."

"Fancy you, Miss Stonemeyer! Stupendous news, I'll let you go then. I was just checking in and wondering how your date with your friend Mimi went."

"Um, well, there's the good news and the bad news," I said, taking a deep breath and another sip of merlot, feeling my throat tighten, thinking about seeing the beautiful Asian woman and her family at the restaurant. "It's a long story, Zack. I'll tell you about it another time when we have more time."

"My interest is piqued. Sounds like you got into some dandy shenanigans." He laughed a hearty laugh. "Well, I'll leave you to your work. You are one busy lady. Your work, your ex-husband, your kids, it's grueling. Just ring me back then when you have a free moment tomorrow."

"No Zack, wait before you go, I wanted to ask you what you're doing Saturday afternoon. How about coming over for a barbecue? I'm inviting Mimi and my Aunt Sylvie, and maybe two of my aunt's friends. I'd love for you to come. Just a small get-together."

"Intriguing, all those beautiful women in one place," he said, chuckling. "I'd jump at it, love, except that Saturday is St. Patrick's Day, and you know what that means for an Irishman."

"Oh God, I completely forgot. Well, how about you come over and I rustle up some corned beef and cabbage? I've actually done it once before, and well if I've forgotten, I'm a quick study. Hell, if I can become an overnight expert in Junipero Serra, then I can certainly concoct an authentic Irish meal."

"Junipero who? Sorry love, I'm not following."

"Oh, never mind about that. It's TV interview talk. How about Saturday, Zack?"

"Well, I'd be honored if you don't mind me bringing the Guinness ale and how about me brother, Antonio, and little Felicia? Can you handle the extra crowd? If not, I can come another night but..."

"Of course, bring them both. We'd love it but only if you're ready to share more of your childhood stories with the kids and my Aunt Sylvie."

"Game on, love."

I stared at the photo I took of Jenny and Felicia after *Peter Pan* a week ago, listening to the rhythm of his voice.

"Zack, you'll love getting to know Mimi. She's quite engaging, funny, and holds nothing back."

"Well good. I hope to see you a dozen times before Saturday." His voice changed to a throaty whisper. "I'm dying to touch you. Maybe tomorrow night?"

I took another sip, seeing my face blush in the mirror.

"I'll ring you in the morning to make a plan then. Break a leg tomorrow with Channel 6, and keep me posted as to when the story will air. I don't want to miss it. I'll record it, watch it in slow motion, oh, I don't know, maybe ten or twenty times, then send copies to all my Irish relatives."

I laughed. "Right, sure you will."

"Ta-ra sweet one." His voice softened to a whisper. *"Uh roon shark."* Then he disconnected.

Had I heard that expression from Zack before? It sounded familiar. I had no idea what it meant, but I knew I liked the timbre of it. Then I thought of Albie's endearment for me, "Jelly Bean." His voice echoed in my head. As my mind wandered, I took another sip of wine.

Chapter Eighteen

Tamakichi's Discovery

Her daughter was on her way to work, her granddaughter off on the school bus, as Tamakichi sat in the morning light on the upholstered chair gazing out at the back garden. She was reading the Japanese newspaper Emily had picked up for her yesterday at the international bookstore. Her eyes wandered from the small typeface to the white **calla lilies** just beyond the picture window. It was a cool yet sunny spring day, the blooms dancing with a slight flutter in the breeze. She planned to go out into the backyard to do her morning tai chi as soon as she finished reading the week-old news from Tokyo.

She scanned a few more headlines, put down the paper, and noticed how tall the flowers had grown since she had first arrived in California. The badly needed, late-winter rains had produced a sudden spurt for the trees, plants, and flowers, which now all looked happy and strong. If only my daughter could regain her spirit like these flowers had done, she mused. Ahh, but those roses could use some trimming. Growth is good but better with the gardener's care and control. She recalled seeing some hedge cutters in the garage when little Miyoko had fetched her bicycle two days ago. Slipping on her outdoor shoes, Tamakichi smoothed the bedspread, folded the newspaper, and headed down to the garage.

Sitting on the wicker cabinet shelf were a pair of rusted hedge cutters. But where were the garden gloves? Wasn't her daughter personally caring for her beautiful flowers or was it left solely to the gardener who came twice a month to tend to them? The gloves must be around here near the tools, she thought, but she didn't see them anywhere. She then spotted a large, dusty, plastic bin pushed into a corner near the side door that led out to the garden. Opening it, she found a collection of small house and garden tools. A gray metal box was also inside the bin.

Removing the lid, she was confronted with a small black pistol and noticed several bullets rattling around the metal container. She immediately closed the small box holding the gun, her hands trembling.

A large unmarked manila envelope was tucked at the bottom of the plastic bin beneath the paperwork. Curious yet shaken, she unraveled the string to open the envelope. Three words hit her, "Central Intelligence Agency," printed in boldface on the front page. Tamakichi had forgotten to bring down her reading glasses, which sat upstairs in the crease of the easy chair. "Agent Emily Kota," she read, squinting to read the business card stapled to the front of the paperwork. Looking more closely at the card, she read the boldface print: "Not to be carried on person except when directed." She read it twice to make sure she understood the English words. A black-and-white digital photo of Emily was imprinted in the upper left-hand corner. A ripped sheet of yellow lined paper with scribbles was at the bottom of the package of paper. Tamakichi recognized her daughter's familiar handwriting. A San Francisco address was written in longhand: "426 Olivia, San Francisco." And a numbered list appeared below a heading:

Mission Requirements

1) *4 p.m. at the San Francisco house*
2) *Albie in bed, we fake the infidelity*
3) *Ready for target wife to see in plain sight*
4) *Wear lingerie, hair loose*
5) *Practice mistress role*
6) *Goal: Convince the wife that husband is cheating*
7) *Phone number—Albie: 415-206-4464*

Piecing together the meaning of the notes on the page, she noticed another sheet of yellow paper in the box with more handwritten notes:

Debrief from Ashcroft

1) ***Protect staged infidelity***
2) ***Keep out of sight from ex-wife, Sandy Stonemeyer***
3) ***Steer clear wife's new address and surrounding areas in Santa Cruz Mountains: 404 Pine Hill Road, Felton, California***

Like the lens of a Japanese camera, the tempest that must be brewing inside her daughter's troubled soul crystallized for Tamakichi. My daughter, she worried, what fate is she creating?

The paper slipped from her hand, floating to the garage floor like a bird's feather. As she dropped to her knees, the shock of the cold cement sent shivers through her weary body. With her head lowered to her lap, she sobbed, feeling the canyon of broken intimacy between mother and daughter. Once so close, now they each stood on different patches of the same earth.

A lie, she registered. Emily doesn't work for a corporation but is employed by the CIA. Tamakichi knew little of this agency but was aware that it involved danger. The faked infidelity looks to have been some kind of assignment for Emily, one where she was instructed to participate in a sham designed by her superiors. Sandy Stonemeyer's husband must also be some type of CIA agent. Tamakichi wondered if Sandy knew this about him. The American woman had been, not once, but maybe twice, fooled.

Emotions rose within her body, as a sense of responsibility enveloped her, fueling an increasing desire to fix things for her daughter. The woman must have recognized Emily at the restaurant, she thought. That's why she seemed so flustered when I entered the restroom, knowing I was connected to the woman who had ruined her marriage. In her eyes, I was the enemy.

A black spider moved across the garage door. Tamakichi could sense the insect's acute awareness that it was being watched, it's short life suddenly in jeopardy. The hair-thin legs froze in their tracks, as the creature attempted to blend into the gray of the garage door. She moved to get something to scoop up the spider, but then noticed the spider scurry away through a crack, escaping its human predator. If she could only help her daughter do the same, escape this terrible situation she found herself in, convince her to return to Japan, flee this strange country of tricks and lies.

Gathering up the papers, Tamakichi shoved them back into the plastic bin, making sure the metal gun box was carefully closed and replaced atop the package of official documents. She pushed the bin back into the corner of the garage where she found it. Turning to retrieve the hedge cutters, her eye caught the printed fabric of the garden gloves, which were folded neatly next to the cutters, the gloves she had failed to see earlier. The obvious can be so easily missed, she thought.

Sandy Stonemeyer's innocent eyes then flashed before her. I have information that would help this woman and help relieve Emily's guilt, she thought. I must see her again, right a wrong for my daughter, and inform Sandy that the two actors are both connected to the CIA. Emily would not choose this option for herself, but there's little stopping me, except the promise Emily insisted I make when we were sitting in the restaurant, but I cannot compromise what I know is right. My action will help to untangle a wicked web of deceit, begin the cleansing of our karma. With these thoughts, Tamakichi stepped out into the garden, her face raised to the sun, ready to begin her morning tai chi.

Chapter Nineteen

The Cheater and the Delinquents

Eighteen children would clamor into the room in about thirty minutes. Craft tables were set up, easels prepared with paper and paints, today's featured story-time book, *Where the Wild Things Are,* sitting on the chair, everything just about ready.

Oh, I forgot to put the shamrocks up before the kids arrive, Mimi thought. She stood on a wooden chair and started to tape the first green cutout to the windowpane when she spotted Luke outside in the playground, his father down on one knee, tying the boy's shoe, then rising to hug him close, both of them laughing at something private between them. Luke then ran off to climb the metal ladder up to the slide and slid down, his dad meeting him at the bottom with open arms.

They were here early, at least twenty-five minutes before class would begin. She watched the two of them for some minutes, as she taped three more shamrocks onto the window. Opening the classroom door, she gestured for them to come in.

"Mr. Stonemeyer, Luke," she called out, "it's starting to rain. Come inside."

Luke responded by running toward her, Albie following. "Miss Webster, Miss Webster, this is my dad," he said with excitement in his voice.

"Yes," she said, smiling, "I think we've seen each other a few times, but I don't think we've ever spoken to one another. Nice to meet you, Mr. Stonemeyer."

"You got the shamrocks up. Wow, Miss Webster, they look great," Luke said. Then turning to his dad, he said, "I gotta go bad, Dad. I'll be right back."

"Okay, I'll stay here with Miss Webster until you get back, buddy," Albie replied, as Luke shot through the classroom door and raced down the hallway to the bathrooms.

Mimi taped another shamrock up on the bulletin board. "So, you seem like a good father, but I guess you disappeared for awhile. Luke and Jenny sure missed you." She was up on the chair, her back to him, her voice raised.

Albie raised his eyebrows in surprise, resisting his visceral reaction to her sharp words. He strolled around the classroom, noticing how small the chairs and tables were, something he had forgotten about the world of preschool, still feeling uncomfortable with this woman judging him.

"I'm happy to be here *now* with my kids" was all he managed to say.

"Was it the young woman, the one you cheated with, or was it the job that kept you away?" she said, as she got down from the chair. She now spoke in a low tone in case the boy returned too quickly. "You catch the bad guys? That is what you do, Mr. Stonemeyer?"

"I...I...yes, my business is catching corporate criminals. At least that's been my work, but recently I've been rethinking my career path."

"I see." She moved closer to him, fixing the books on the shelf. "Your ex-wife is in a good place now." Mimi reached up and pushed a corner of a bent green shamrock, pressing it back to the window so it was flush. "If you care about her at all, Mr. Stonemeyer, you'll leave her alone. Let her be. She has someone new in her life. Why confuse her, distract her?"

"And now you're giving me advice because...you know so much?"

"Hey Dad, can we go to that same place next time?" Luke said as he burst into the classroom, interrupting his dad and teacher. "Can we, Dad? That was such a cool beach."

"Sure buddy. Sure, we can go back there." Albie glanced out the window and noticed a little girl arriving with her mom. "Look, I better go now. School's about to begin. I see a pretty little girl about to come through that door," Albie said, giving his son a grin.

Mimi stood facing Albie, behind Luke, her hands set like bricks on the boy's shoulders.

Albie bent down and gave Luke a peck on the cheek. "See you soon. I love you, buddy," he said, getting up to leave, catching the iciness of the teacher's stare.

"Oh, by the way, Mr. Stonemeyer, I'll have Luke and Jenny this afternoon while Sandy is on a news story. She wanted you to know, so I'm telling you now."

He nodded and held his thumb up in response. As he opened the door to exit, the little girl walked in.

"Good morning, Katie," Mimi said in a welcoming voice, and then gave Albie a chilly nod goodbye. "Drive safely, Mr. Stonemeyer. Don't let those bad guys get the better of you." Turning her attention back to Luke and Katie, she said, "Get those wet coats off and sit down in the reading circle. The others will be here any minute."

As Albie walked back to his car, he registered the short but intense interchange he just had with Luke's teacher. I know that she's also Sandy's close friend and she cares about her, he thought, but hell, was our personal life really any of her business? Probably the woman's protective nature, but I wasn't quite expecting the snake venom.

Hmm, Mimi thought, Sandy had described him as passionate, confident, and intelligent. I just don't see it. Hollow, she judged, watching him walk through the school gate, back to his parked car. She felt disgust for him rise as she watched him drive down the street.

Mimi's thoughts went to Cassandra, her best friend, slain by the scumbag who just left her classroom, the classroom she wanted to leave behind as soon as possible.

She was too angry now to read a story aloud to four- and five-year-olds. She looked over at the half-circle of children sitting in the reading corner on the rug ready for their morning story.

"Children," she said, "instead of starting today with story time, we're going to do some drawing. Please get up and get some drawing paper from the paper tray and a basket of crayons to share with a partner. I'd like you to create a picture showing what you'd like to do on your next family vacation. What's that one special activity you'd like to do? Draw yourself doing it. You might include some family members too."

The kids stared up at their teacher, surprised by her change in their schedule. Then, one-by-one, they scurried off to grab drawing paper and crayons. While the children were busy drawing, Mimi stared out her classroom window, which was now covered in shamrocks, recalling how she met Cassandra many years ago in Dublin.

◆ ◆ ◆

They were both twelve years old and incarcerated in a summer camp where delinquent girls were sent for rehabilitation. Mimi had moved from the United States to Ireland two years before with her father, who was born in Ireland, her mother having gone off with another man. Mimi had led a rebellious life with few restrictions in a low-income neighborhood in the city. In contrast, Cassandra was born into an upper-class, educated family and lived on the other side of the river. Since Mimi arrived in Dublin, she was involved in petty theft activities almost daily with a small gang she formed in the inner city.

The stern-looking head camp counselor was named Libby. She had the girls stand in line in front of her where she could see every set of eyes. Wearing a gray, almost military-looking uniform and Coke bottle eyeglasses, the hefty head counselor got the girls' attention.

"Now all of you stand straight, your feet together and hands at your sides," she barked to the fifteen or so reluctant eleven- and twelve-year-olds. "You are all at a critical point in your lives and seem to be going down the wrong track. Every girl will leave this camp at the end of the next four weeks headed down the *right* track, if I have any say in the matter. Yes, even if this has to be accomplished by brute force by me and the five junior counselors standing around you. We are here to keep you in line. *We* are in charge here! You are slabs of clay to be molded into respectable young ladies by us. Got that?"

There was silence, not a girl moved. Libby stared each girl down individually for three or four seconds, going down the line, one-by-one.

"I want to hear you all respond with 'Yes, Captain.' I want to hear that every time I make a request. Let me hear it."

The girls responded, some weakly: "Yes, Captain."

"No, that's not what I want to hear. All together, *yes Captain!*"

"Yes, Captain!" they all said.

That's when Mimi saw a girl take something from her pocket and thrust the object, snapping Libby in the right ankle just above the end of her gray sock, where her pale white flesh was bare.

"Ouch!" Libby yelled out. "Shit!" Her jaw clenched in anger. "Who the fuck did that? You're going to pay!"

Mimi noticed the girl staring down at the ground, making faces, as the head counselor continued to rant and rave. Mimi struggled not to burst out laughing, in awe of what she just saw the red-haired girl do, without regard for possible repercussions. When the girl looked up, she stepped forward with an amazing belligerence, thought Mimi, confronting Libby's fiery rage.

The girl turned to look briefly at the other girls to bathe in their wonder. That's when she caught Mimi's smiling eyes. In that single moment, Mimi knew that she wanted to pledge her allegiance to this green-eyed angel from hell and would follow her anywhere and everywhere. Mimi stepped forward to show her support and solidarity with the girl, a grin on her face in defiance of the Captain, proud to become part of the rebellion, without a care when it came to the consequences that lay ahead.

The head counselor seemed to become more furious, as she pulled both girls by their arms to her side, twisting them around to face the whole squad of girls. Then she ordered them both to mop the restroom floors and scrub the toilets twice a day every day for the next four weeks as punishment. Shit, what did I do? Mimi thought. But when she looked over at the girl to find her grinning from ear to ear, she felt at once relaxed and happy. The girl edged closer to Mimi and took her hand, whispering, "Call me Cassie. I'm your new friend."

The two girls bonded like sisters that summer, despite having to deal with the stench and ugly mess of toilets soiled by preteen girls who scummed up the restroom stalls with their blood, many experiencing their first monthly period, not knowing the appropriate and hygienic protocol for used sanitary napkin disposal. It was a gross assignment, but it only fueled the fire for Mimi and Cassie in seeking revenge on the head counselor.

At least once a day, the two girls pulled a prank on Captain Libby, the four-eyed Gestapo leader. They put mustard in her shampoo bottle, thumbtacks between her sheets, used sanitary napkins in her dresser drawers, soap in her morning cereal. After a few days, they reeled in other girls to help them increase the number of pranks they pulled on Libby, who seemed to fume, but failed to catch anyone actually committing the offense.

Libby left camp within eight days and a gentler Sylvie took her place, having been duly warned about the two fearless girls. Sylvie took a different approach. Recognizing the duo's talent, she placed them in more formal leadership roles, where they assigned the other thirteen girls tasks to complete, including toilet-cleaning responsibilities. But they used the art of job rotation and awarded lighter duties to the girls who gave them gifts in return, such as flavored straws, chocolate Mars bars, or fancy underwear they'd finesse from the guilty parents who visited weekly for two hours.

Cassie and Mimi were inseparable partners, becoming the best of friends beyond the confines of the summer camp. They constantly created trouble, either as a solo act or with others, meeting up in Dublin for their shenanigans. This made it possible for the two to attend this delinquent summer camp for four consecutive summers, where they honed their leadership skills. They also met on the outskirts of Dublin at a gun range to practice shooting. And they enrolled in martial arts programs together, Cassie paying for Mimi when she couldn't get the money together.

Both girls grew into attractive women, Cassie, with her long flaming-red hair and green eyes, and Mimi, with her caramel eyes and flawless coffee-colored skin. When Cassie met Wendall, she fell for him hard, and the two wed seven months before she turned nineteen. Wendall's half-brother, a brooding gypsy boy, had an eye for Mimi, but Mimi initially had little interest in him.

He showed up on her doorstep one night, and her drunken father went into a screaming tirade, until he played "Danny Boy" on his black-lacquered guitar, dropping a twenty-pound note at the old man's feet. The old man smiled and grabbed a beer from the fridge. He then picked up the twenty-pound note and sat down in his threadbare easy chair to listen to the young bearded gypsy sing Irish ballads into the early morning. Mimi fell in love with Antonio that night, watching him cajole and seduce her pathetic father, turning him into a sobbing mush ball.

The two became lovers and Mimi soon moved into the flat Antonio shared with the newlyweds. Wendall and Antonio were already deep into arms trading, making decent money, hooking up with Middle Eastern, Russian, and Turkish buyers and sellers. The two women started getting involved in the gunrunning end of the business, moving guns from one town to the next, using their feminine wiles as defense whenever things got tense and they might be discovered. Cassie coached Mimi, looked out for her safety, and was her protection in edge-of-seat scenarios.

When the two brothers proposed that they move the business to America, with the potential of a much greater financial return on each deal, Mimi and Cassie enthusiastically agreed.

The night that Cassie was shot and killed by the CIA agent, Mimi's heart was crushed, her best friend dead. The idea of seeking revenge on the murderous agent, and his family members, drove her to work with Wendall, who started calling himself Zachery in California. When Wendall learned Stonemeyer's name and researched his family ties, he hatched a plan to torture the agent's family members, one-by-one, then kill them all before he personally finished off Stonemeyer for killing his wife. Mimi agreed to be part of the whole operation, gaining the trust of Sandy Stonemeyer, the agent's ex-wife.

Getting a resume and false credentials together for Mimi to prove her experience as a preschool teacher proved easier than expected, as Wendall and Antonio made use of their underworld connections. What surprised Mimi though was the subtle racism she experienced as a black woman in America, a racism that was hardly present back in Ireland. Now hiding behind the false facade as Luke's preschool teacher and Sandy's close friend, Mimi couldn't wait to be part of the plot to avenge Cassie's murder.

◆ ◆ ◆

The classroom noise level jolted Mimi from her thoughts, as Luke and Tricia came running up to her, wanting to explain their drawings.

After describing his picture that showed going to Disneyland with his mom and sister and Mr. Zachery, Luke looked up at his teacher and asked, "Aren't you going to have story time today?"

"Yes," Tricia chimed in. "Please read us a story! Please!"

Mimi produced a plastic smile and nodded in response, nudging the two pleading children over to the rug in the reading corner, but inside she was dreading to have to read another inane children's book aloud. She was annoyed at Wendall, who hadn't yet succeeded at harming Sandy Stonemeyer or her two children, as he had promised. Yes, he and Antonio still had important arms trading to do in Northern California, but she was getting impatient.

Chapter Twenty

Requesting Your Permission

In his car, Albie sat ruminating about the preschool teacher's hard edges. She was insulting in her words and manner of speaking. Trying to put these thoughts out of his mind, he picked up his cell phone and wondered if he should punch in Sandy's number. Having second thoughts, he put the phone down and plugged it into the charger. Forget it, he thought, Sandy's done with me and I should let her make her own decisions about the company she keeps. She's single now. She's got a new guy and this Mimi, this ice queen, is her good friend. Pack it up Stonemeyer, he told himself as he looked at himself in the rearview mirror. His hair was matted down from the rain and his eyes appeared vacant.

Reaching to pick up his sunglasses from the passenger seat before starting the engine, he saw Manny appear, in his mind's eye, as clear as day, sitting in the passenger seat, donning his very loud flowered Hawaiian shirt, the one he wore to the bars on their nights out.

A familiar grin on his face, Manny nodded his head. "Yes, do it *amigo*," his partner said, encouraging him. "Your family needs you. Don't run away. It would be a crime. A crime," he repeated, shaking his head. "Not wise, *amigo*." Manny's image then instantly faded at his side. Only the dark Air Force sunglasses sat on the seat beside him. "God, I have to stop drinking bad whiskey or I'll be joining Manny before my time. Freaking hallucinations..."

He grabbed his cell phone.

"Sandy Stonemeyer, speaking," she answered.

"It's me, Albie."

"Oh good. I tried to call you last night. Listen, did Mimi tell you that she'd have the kids this afternoon? I've got a big story to cover. I wanted you to know."

"Yep, she gave me the message..."

"Hmm? Sorry Albie, but I...I'm in the middle of preparing for this shoot and the producer is due here in a minute to brief me. Gotta go. Anything I should know? Kids all right?"

"Yeah, yeah. They're fine. I dropped off Jenny, then Luke at school. That...that Miss Webster would have curled my mustache if I had one. Are you sure she's your ally?"

"Albie, what did you say to her? Did you insult her? She's a gem and one of my best friends."

"Hmm. Yeah, that's what you said, but I think you can do better, Sandy. Chill, I didn't insult her. It was the other way around by my book. Look, that's not why I'm calling. I have an idea—there's something I've been meaning to talk to you about."

"God Albie, can't it wait until later? I'm in the middle of this TV gig and—"

"Well, it's kind of important." His words tumbled out quickly before he changed his mind. "I'd like to build Luke a tree house in your backyard. I noticed the perfect tree out next to your back fence. It would be a haven for Luke, his own get-away. Remember, that was my plan before, well before all this happened. You know I've got the skills—remember that deck I built for our last house?" Following an awkward silence, he cleared his throat and continued, "I...I have several days off with my partner having died and well I thought I could begin the tree house construction today. I'm already here in Felton. How about it?"

"Um-um, a tree house? It's not a great time, Albie. I have a big party planned in the backyard for Saturday, four days from now. It would be awkward..."

"Wait, no worries on that. I'll be mostly done by Friday and then I can come back on Monday to finish up before I'm due to be back at work on Tuesday."

"Albie, I'm just not sure it's—"

"Come on Sandy, Luke will love it and honestly, not that it's your concern, but it will help me put my mind on something positive. I...I'm..." He could hear other voices on her end in the background. Her producer must have arrived.

"Um, well, okay. Okay. You can do it. But don't be near the house on Saturday. Okay?"

"Okay. Thanks, Jelly Bean." He paused, realizing he had used his pet name for her. "Listen, I need to somehow make it up to Luke. With my being gone so much lately, he's feeling rejected I think more than Jenny. I can see it in his eyes. Like I cheated, or...um, I...I mean like he doesn't trust me. Look, I'm not making much sense now. I'll let you go."

Just as he clicked off, he felt his phone vibrate, another incoming call, this one from Emily Kota.

"Albie..." She was crying.

"What's wrong, Emily? Are you upset about Manny?"

"Yes, Albie, but there's something else you should know. My mother found some papers about the CIA tucked away in my garage and she heard us on the phone that night and..." She stopped, her sobs increasing. Albie felt sad for this young woman. "And Albie, I...I saw your wife in a restaurant in San Jose a couple of days ago."

"My wife? Sandy?"

"Yes, she was there with another woman having lunch. I was with my mother and my daughter. My mother figured out it was your ex-wife. How, I'm not quite sure. It just happened, Albie. I'm sorry. I never would have gone to that restaurant if..."

"It's okay, Emily. Try not to stress about this." All he could think about was that Emily Kota did not make a good CIA agent. There was no question in his mind about that. Too sensitive.

"I'm afraid that my mother, who is here from Japan, will seek out your wife and tell her...tell her about the faked infidelity. She's a headstrong Japanese woman with a strong sense of right and wrong. I asked her to be quiet, begged her to stay out of my business. She has agreed, but honestly I don't know. Please help me. I can't be fired from my job, not after all this, but my mother feels that I've wronged your wife, and dishonesty is in conflict with our culture, our way of life. What can I—"

"I'm the one who needs to apologize to you, Emily. I should have stood up for you when Ashcroft introduced his plan to deceive my wife and separate me from Sandy and the kids. It must have been traumatic for you to agree and then to actually have to go through with the charade. I'm the one who's clearly responsible for your unhappiness."

"Albie, your wife...she is very beautiful. You are a fortunate man."

"Yes I *was*. But that's behind me. That's over. Listen, are you in the office today?"

"Yes, I am here now."

"Good. Just keep your head down on your assignments. Don't show Ashcroft any weakness. I won't be in until next Tuesday. I'm taking some time off, you know...with Manny and everything. I'm doing some positive things for my family. Stay calm, Emily."

"Okay, Albie. It's good to hear that you're with your family. Does that mean that you and Sandy might...?"

He grew silent, then responded, "No, nothing like that. I'm building something for my son. A tree house. Look, gotta go, I'll see you next week. Keep your eye on your mother. I'd rather not give Sandy additional stress, especially related to me."

Driving down Graham Hill Road, he checked his GPS, on the hunt for a local lumberyard. About to get out of the car at San Lorenzo Lumber on River Street, he tried to put his rage at the Irishman for killing Manny on the back burner. If he succumbed to his anger, he would become like one of them, just like the men who brutally torture and kill the relatives of their enemies, be they women, children, grandmothers, in-laws, whoever. The Brethren had no limits—that was their signature reputation. He needed to rise above that and instead focus on building a dream tree house for his son, an antidote to the devil inside him who longed to kill for revenge.

After entering the Home Depot, he picked out the finest slabs of rich redwood he could find in their lumberyard and purchased an electric saw, several bags of nails of various sizes, four metal latches, a gallon of wood stain, a few paintbrushes, a can of black paint, and six feet of wood molding. He then loaded the goods into his SUV, one of the shop assistants helping to tie it all down and offering to mount a small red flag on the end of the stack, which he accepted. Next door to Home Depot was a Togo's Deli. He grabbed a sandwich and a drink, took it back to his motel room on Ocean Street, and then headed up to Sandy's house to launch the project. He knew his ex-wife had some reluctance, having shared her childhood tree house accident story with him just a week after they met. She said she had smashed her nose, probably broke it, but to him Sandy had the most perfect nose he'd ever seen.

A phone call from Ashcroft interrupted him as he was sketching out a tree house design on the brown paper he had laid out on Sandy's back lawn.

"Yeah, Stonemeyer here," he answered.

"Albie, I'm just checking in, to see how you're holding up, man."

"Yeah, fucking great now that I hear your voice," he said, faking a laugh. Then he grimly added, "I'm surviving, getting better control over my anger."

Ashcroft chuckled. "Yeah, good. I see you're getting your verbal mojo back. Look, on a serious note, when you return on Tuesday, let's meet so I can brief you on the Irish. There are some updates; it might be another opportunity for a bust end of next week. Another big trade going down. At least that's the information we're getting from a covert call just received today. But it could be a setup solely for our benefit. We're looking into it. Where are you anyway? Home?"

"I'm in Santa Cruz." He paused. "Shit, I guess I shouldn't be telling you this."

"What? You're not there to...? Did any of your colleagues leak any new information to you?"

Albie knew Ashcroft would be livid hearing that he was anywhere near Sandy and the kids, but what was he talking about...new information? His curiosity piqued, he wondered how he could finesse his boss into telling him more about what he was talking about. He decided to play it cool. "Yeah, well... he didn't mean to let it out," he said, "but..."

"So, you know the Irish have moved to the Santa Cruz Mountains? Look, don't do anything stupid, Stonemeyer. We'll track down the heart of the Brethren, but we'll do it right so it sticks...catch them in their crimes, not kill them prematurely for sport or revenge."

"What the hell are you talking about, Ashcroft? The Brethren are somewhere around here? That means that Sandy and the kids are being targeted. The Irish are still out to kill my family, avenge the death of that fucking Cassandra. Didn't you think I needed to be informed about that? It's a no brainer, man. Why would the Irish change their base location to this area? Why? Damn you and the whole CIA. I'm with my family, that's why I'm here. Okay, I'm copping to it...against your advice, I know. But you assholes are keeping important details from me."

"Albie, pull yourself together. We have information that they're doing a couple of big arms deals in that mountain area, the first of these deals going down the end of next week. We won't know anything until late Monday when our source is expected to get back to us. Nothing for you to do until Tuesday morning when you show up in my office. Got it, Stonemeyer? Nothing! I don't want to have to repeat this command again. Understood?"

"Yeah, sure."

Ashcroft softened, "Look, Albie, we don't think their motivation for a move to those mountains has anything to do with your family. We're ninety-nine percent sure of that. It's clearly their business plan that's driven their location change."

"Okay, I hear what you're saying," Albie said and hung up.

Chapter Twenty-One

St. Patty's Day in Northern California

When I explained Albie's tree house project to Zack, I could sense his dismay at having my ex-husband hanging around. Zack wanted to see me at night once Albie was gone. I agreed but insisted that he arrive sometime after 10 p.m. The kids would be asleep, unaware that I was waiting in bed for the man they now referred to as their "Uncle Zack," something Felicia had suggested a couple of weeks ago.

Having left the key under the doormat, I waited, curled up, listening for the turn of the front door lock and then for his footsteps coming up the stairs. His long hair brushed my forehead as he bent down to kiss me hello. "Are you awake?" he whispered.

I didn't respond with words, but stroked his face and nuzzled his neck. He left the house well past midnight. I still had concerns about him staying till morning. We did this three nights in a row that week.

It was an emotional roller coaster for me, arriving home in the late afternoons after an array of local TV shoots, to find Albie still working furiously on the tree house with Luke in tow, having picked up the kids from school and usually having prepared something for a light dinner.

Keeping his physical distance from me, Albie showed respect, a silent acknowledgement that he sensed that I was involved with someone else, but never asking me about it. If Albie had a grudge or a jealous bone, he kept it under wraps, faithfully excusing himself right after dinner. The kids seemed to be in heaven, their faces aglow, enjoying the family time, although Luke had asked me about Zack when we were in the kitchen alone one night, somehow knowing that mentioning another man, even Uncle Zack, in front of his father would be awkward. That's when I realized that my little boy was growing up, becoming more sophisticated, more knowledgeable about life.

I observed Albie's behavior during the few hours I saw him each day, searching for hints that he might still be involved with the Japanese woman, or perhaps someone new, but he didn't seem to phone anyone or appear detached or distracted by some romantic relationship. He was clearly 100 percent focused on his kids. On Wednesday night, while we all enjoyed a pepperoni pizza and some salad I made, I decided to ask Albie if he'd stay a bit later the next day until maybe 7:30 or 8:00 because I needed to shop for decorations for Saturday's St. Patty's Day party. Luke and Jenny had finished their pizza and were fiercely engaged in a Nintendo game in the living room.

"Oh yeah," Albie smirked, "a big holiday in these parts, huh? St. Patrick's Day, honoring the Irish, both the good and the bad."

"The good and the bad? What do you mean? Are there a bunch of bad ones, Albie?" I asked, thinking his comment slightly comical.

"Look, I know some Irish that would leave you breathless, and I don't mean in a positive way." He slugged down his last sip of Corona. "No, not in a good way at all. The Irish I know would happily rip your heart out if you crossed them. Ruthless gangsters." I hadn't seen his anger surface like this since the day he told me that his close colleague at work had been killed.

Saturday morning was hectic. Jenny had a rehearsal for a new children's show, this time playing Mrs. Hannigan in a production of *Annie*— not exactly against type, I thought. I dropped her off, rushed back home to start decorating the patio area, and sent Luke out to play in the yard, reminding him not to climb up to the tree house until his dad came by to finish it tomorrow or Monday.

Albie eased the car near Sandy's house. He had promised to stay away all day today, but he realized that he left his cell phone in the tree house last night when he was cleaning up and he needed his phone, especially to call Manny's wife today to express his sympathies. Sandy's party wasn't starting until sometime this afternoon, and it was only 11 a.m., probably nobody arriving for at least a couple of hours. He could see the backyard from the side of the house decorated with bright green shamrocks strewn on crepe paper over the patio and then winding across the yard between the two lemon trees. The large oak containing the almost completed tree house sat several yards behind the long picnic table, which had been meticulously set for a St. Patrick's Day celebration.

Sandy had crafted a centerpiece of gold, glittery shamrocks surrounding a green elf, giving the table a festive, party feel. Not only was she an intelligent journalist, but very creative as well. Great for the kids, Albie thought, smiling. He took in the tableau, wishing he were part of the festivities, enjoying the day with his family.

Sitting on the wooden bench was a black beret with some type of large metal pin attached to it—at least that's what it looked like to him. It seemed an oddity to Albie since he knew that Sandy would never wear a beret, preferring a broad-brimmed winter or summer hat. But it looked like it belonged to an adult.

I'll just sneak into the yard, climb the ladder, and grab my phone. No need to upset Sandy with my presence. Surmising he had parked too close for comfort, he backed up the car another half block and briskly walked to the side of the house, opening the iron side gate to the backyard. After climbing the wooden ladder, he spotted the cell phone by his toolbox at the back of the tree house.

Starting his descent, he heard the glass door to the patio slide open. Then Jenny came running out, a skinny red-haired girl right behind her.

"Come on Felicia, let's get the hula hoops and see who can do the most turns," Jenny said. "I bet I can do at least fifty more than you."

"Okay but I want to rehearse our lines first before we do that. I'll get them from my backpack, okay?"

"I'll get the hula hoops out of the shed," Jenny replied.

Luke came running out, flying past Felicia. "What are you guys doing? Can I play too?" he shouted, as he watched Jenny grab the hula hoops from the small metal shed, which was painted brick red like a miniature barn.

"Luke, find something else to do. Go play with your Legos or something," Jenny said. "Felicia and I are going to study our lines first anyway."

"Lines. What lines?"

"Lines from our play, stupid-head."

Luke shrugged and ran back inside the house. "Mommy, can I have my Legos down from the shelf?"

Damn, I'm stuck now, Albie thought. I don't want to engage the kids. Sandy will be livid. I should have just left the damn phone here until tomorrow, but what if Ashcroft called, or Emily? He squatted in the tree house, out of sight, tucked in a corner by the door that opened down to the ladder.

Aunt Sylvie appeared on the patio, using her cane to step over to the picnic table. Albie noted her having aged quite a bit since the last time he saw her one afternoon in San Francisco. That was over a year ago before the split, he recalled. Funny old woman—never said much to me. She was quite the intellectual, probably thinking I was just a bad penny who craftily lured her niece into a no-win marriage. The truth is, that woman never warmed up to me, he thought, but who can blame her. I wasn't exactly focused on building bridges with her either. Aunt Sylvie settled into a patio chair and opened a magazine and started reading.

"Come on out here, you guys," Sandy called back inside the door. "I've got the salad and appetizers ready. Let's start!"

Sandy emerged on the patio, dressed in a bright green sundress, her hair pulled back, half up, half down. Seeing his ex-wife, he sighed. He'd been known to whistle, but now resisted showing the reaction he used to have when she'd come down the staircase dressed and ready for an event. She had that knack of going from ratty jeans and mussed hair to looking like a model dressed for a fashion show, all in a matter of fifteen minutes. It had always dazzled him.

"Aunt Sylvie, you okay?" Sandy asked. "How about some St. Patty's Day punch? I don't think it will be too sweet. The men are busy concocting it in the kitchen. I'm sure it will be delicious."

"No thanks, maybe just a glass of water with lunch. Have you read this article in *Time* on the impact of the press in local politics? It's got some alarming examples of local media's manipulation and interference. You should read this. It's relevant to your work."

That's Aunt Sylvie, Albie thought, frowning to himself, faithfully offering Sandy her opinionated unsolicited advice.

"Sounds like it. Thanks Aunt Sylvie, I'll be sure to take a look at it later."

A tall, slender black woman dressed in khaki Bermudas and a white cotton shirt stepped out, holding a serving plate loaded with green snacks. Luke's witchy teacher, I guess she's here too, Albie acknowledged.

What a crowd, all my favorites so far. It'll be ages until they vacate the back patio. Jesus, I can't just appear before their eyes now. He sat down and crossed his legs, trying to find a comfortable position in the cramped space.

A man's voice came from inside the house, and Albie tried to make out what was being said.

"You leprechauns get..." That was followed by several inaudible words. Then as the voice came closer to the patio door, Albie heard, "The famous punch is about ready. Get yer cups. We got two versions, one for kids and one for grownups."

Another man's voice broke in, this voice gruffer and louder. "It's me brother's gift to you—come sample it."

Everyone except Mimi and Aunt Sylvie rushed inside.

"How about if I get you some punch, Aunt Sylvie?" Mimi asked.

"Well, I just got comfortable and this is such an interesting article. But okay, I'll try a sip of that Irish drink."

Sandy came rushing out to gather the plastic cups from the picnic table, smiling over at the two women.

The patio emptied, giving Albie an opportunity to make his get-away. Just as he stepped off the last rung of the ladder, he heard something behind him. It was Luke.

"Come and see my rabbit. It's in the cage out here. His name is Mr. Nibbles. You didn't meet him yet. Come and see!" Luke said, running back inside.

As Albie made a run for it, leaping over the iron gate, set to sprint down the road, Luke emerged, witnessing his father's escape. He realized that his father was somehow stuck in the gate, vigorously tugging at his left pant leg, trying to unhitch himself. Excited at unexpectedly seeing his dad, he rushed over and said, "Daddy, you're here. Come inside and see the party. Come on."

Albie yanked his pant leg again, this time tearing the fabric, getting himself freed. A small patch of cotton was left hanging from the black metal gate. Noticing that he had nicked his thigh and was bleeding, Albie whispered, "Luke, listen, don't say a word about seeing me. I promised your mom that I wouldn't be here today. But I left my phone in the tree house. Okay, son? Promise?"

"Okay Daddy," Luke said, disappointed. "But why can't you just come in?"

"It's complicated," Albie said, kissing the child's head. "I'll explain tomorrow when I come by and we have more time. Okay?"

"Luke, Luke, come into the kitchen and join us," Sandy called out, standing by the sliding glass door. "There's a cup of green punch calling your name. Luke, where are you?"

Albie quickly pecked his boy's head and sprinted away.

Luke shrugged his shoulders, went to check on Mr. Nibbles, picking up a carrot to feed him, and then ran back into the house. "I'm coming," he called, racing inside.

Everyone sipped on the green punch, praising its sweet flavor.

Mimi stood next to Antonio, her eyes locked with Zack's as she sipped on her punch. "I love this stuff, always have," she said, beaming.

"You've had this punch before?" I asked Mimi, taken aback.

Mimi chuckled, taking another long sip. "No, not exactly," she replied, "but I've been to St. Patrick's Day celebrations many times in the past and they always have this same delicious green punch." She looked over at Antonio and Zack. "So, what's in this adult version? I never asked anyone before. I just love it."

"Indeed, love, well it's an old Irish recipe," Zack responded. "There are lots of tasty ingredients, including balls of lime-flavored sherbet, pineapple juice, ginger ale, and generous amounts of vodka, of course. It's our appetizer to our Guinness, which is coming up next. Can you feel this drink already grabbing at ya?"

Antonio moved closer to Mimi, brushing her body with his hip, pressing his shoulder into hers. Noticing this, I thought, Wow, maybe there's a match here. Not quite what I expected. And they sure do move fast, having just met.

Enjoying my second cup of spiked punch, I realized I'd better slow down my intake—I was already feeling a buzz. My kids are here for God's sake, and I needed to deliver on a decent corned beef and cabbage meal. No more punch, I told myself.

Taking out my cell phone to snap a photo of this happy gathering, I pointed my lens at Zack, Antonio, and Mimi. "Get closer together you three," I said, starting to slur my words.

Mimi rushed over to me and snatched the phone from my hand. "Uh uh. I hate having my picture taken," she said. "I always look anorexic and my hair is a wreck. No photos, please."

"I'm the same, love," Zack said. "Hate to see myself in a photo. Gypsy superstition."

Antonio nodded in agreement. "The honest truth."

Mimi filled the awkward moment. "Let me take one of you, Sandy, with Jenny."

I posed with Jenny. Then I put my cell phone back on the coffee table in the family room, noticing Aunt Sylvie slumped down in the easy chair, the magazine open on her lap. She had fallen asleep, her head back on the cushion, her mouth open. I could hear the sound of her gentle breath-ing. Picking up my phone, I snapped a picture of her, aware that I was already more than a little tipsy.

"Mommy, Mommy, can I show Mr. Zachery my tree house? Can I?" Luke pleaded.

"Um, well, it's not quite finished yet and I don't want you hurting your-self on any debris up there." My brain shot back to my own tree house experience when I was nine, which I never told Jenny or Luke about. "Your Daddy needs to finish it before you play in it. Remember, that was our deal. There's a sign at the bottom of the ladder that says, 'UNDER CONSTRUCTION.' You've seen it, Luke, right?"

"Oh come on, love," Zack said, turning to me, taking my hand, and pulling me close. "Let me go out there with the lad so he can show it to me."

"Well, maybe that'll be all right," I replied, walking over to the sliding glass door and looking out at the tree house, reconsidering. "Oh my God, it looks like it's going to rain! Do it quickly then."

"Come on Luke," Zack said. "We'll be right back, love. We'll just have a quick look."

"Okay, maybe I'd better move the party inside, gather up our stuff," I said. "What a shame!"

"No, wait for that," Zack said, putting his arm around my waist. "It may not turn into a full-fledged storm. We're supposed to be in a drought," he laughed. "Anyway, would be nice fer us to be outside. I can see the sun peeking through the clouds."

His Irish lilt was more pronounced after a few cups of that adult punch. He took Luke's hand and started out to the tree house, as I retreated into the kitchen to prepare the meal.

When they approached the tree house, Zack removed the "UNDER CONSTRUCTION" sign and, chuckling, said, "We don't need that now, do we?"

Luke smiled back and said, "I'm glad you wanted to see the tree house, Mr. Zachery. I can't wait to show you."

"Sure thing, lad. I knew yer dear mum would cave in. Let's get up there, shall we? I'm anxious to see it."

He followed the boy, helping him navigate, as the tyke climbed up the steep ladder. When they got up to the tree house, they both sat down, legs crossed, facing each other. "Pretty darn cozy up here," Zack remarked, his body scrunched down to avoid hitting the ceiling. "Good construction. Yer dad's got some talent."

"Yeah, he promised a long time ago he'd build it for me but then they got divorced."

"I see. Listen, I've got a surprise for you, Luke," Zack said as he reached into his pocket. "It's bubbles. I thought we could blow some cool bubbles up here. Blow them out of the tree house door. I've got some for me and for you." He placed the two small plastic bottles of bubbles on the tree house floor.

"Wow, great idea, Mr. Zachery."

They both sat quietly blowing bubbles, dozens and dozens escaping down into the yard, across the green lawn, some of them floating out to the patio area, landing on the St. Patty's decorations. Then the rain started to come down, at first sprinkles, then turning into a heavy rain. They could see Sandy and Mimi out at the table, gathering up the place settings and table decorations, and then disappearing back into the house.

"We'd better go down now, lad," Zack said. "This was fun but we don't want to miss our meal. Give me yer bubbles and I'll lead the way down. Okay?"

"Okay, wow, it's really raining hard," Luke said, sounding apprehensive. "I...I don't..."

"You'll be fine, lad. I'll yell up when you should climb down. Just don't come down until I say so. Got it?"

Luke nodded. "Okay."

"Now turn around to face the wall so you don't get nervous watching me go down."

"Um, okay." Luke shifted his little body around and faced the back wall as instructed.

As Wendall stepped down, he removed the two bottles of bubbles from his pocket, tossing off the bottle caps onto the ground below and spilling the liquid over each rung of the ladder as he descended, generously drenching the one above him at every step. When he got to the bottom, he looked up to see each rung dripping with the liquid bubbles. He also added oil to each bottle before he left his house.

"Okay, lad," he called up to Luke, "it's fine for you to come down now. Do it like you're sliding down a firehouse pole. Do it quick, Luke. The rain's started to come down really hard, so hurry!"

Luke began his descent, following Zack's instructions. He stepped down quickly on the first rung, then onto the next, losing his step on the third rung. He was caught by surprise at how slippery it was. He slid down the remaining steps, his face bumping each rung. When his body hit the ground, his leg twisted up beside him. Splayed out on the hard earth, the rain coming down, he screamed, "Oww, owww!"

Chapter Twenty-Two

Manipulated

From the kitchen, I heard Luke's wail. Panicked, I looked over at Mimi, whose eyes were like saucers, Antonio close by at her side. I took the snapshot in my head, Antonio's hand on her back, down at her waist, then gradually sliding down her Bermuda shorts, massaging her lower back as he stood there, sipping his punch. My son was screaming out from the backyard. I turned and ran, my peripheral vision noting that Aunt Sylvie was awakened by Luke's howls. The girls came running out of Jenny's room to see what happened. Sliding open the patio glass door, I could see Zack bent down on the grass at Luke's side, my boy's leg looking very twisted, the raining coming down heavier now.

"Call 911, hurry," I yelled back to Mimi.

I looked over at Zack. "What happened?" I asked, hugging Luke.

"I don't know, love," he replied. "I was already down here and he said he was coming down in a minute. He was afraid of the rain, so I let him stay up there for a few more minutes, until he got up his courage. I was turned around when I heard the thud. We need an ambulance."

Luke seemed barely conscious, his eyes appearing to be moving in and out of focus. "Mommy, I hurt," he said weakly.

It was a day that frightened me to my core. At first, I was angry at Albie for constructing that nightmare. Luke's leg was broken in two places and required surgery, setting, and a full-leg cast likely for at least a couple of months. His left wrist was also fractured, fortunately not broken, and he had a concussion, which the doctors were afraid could cause some long-term problems.

But two weeks later, he was sitting up in his bed, his leg in a raised lift sling, his cast full of colored marker cartoons and captions, compliments of his sister. Aunt Sylvie sat in a metal chair at his side, reading *Time Magazine,* her wooden cane propped against her leg.

Albie had become quiet again, only calling twice after his one visit to Luke in the hospital. His job seemed to overtake his life, which wasn't surprising. I felt guilty that I had agreed for Luke to climb up to the tree house with Zack that day, knowing it was about to rain, but more than that, it was against my better judgment. I couldn't blame what happened to Luke on Zack. He was overly apologetic, but didn't see how he could have prevented such an accident. He slept cramped on a rickety chair in Luke's hospital room at least three nights during his first week of recovery, sending me home to get some decent rest and see to Jenny. I made sure that Albie and Zack didn't cross paths at the hospital, but that was indeed made easy since Albie had retreated from his family yet again.

Chapter Twenty-Three

Stairway to Justice

Mimi proved to be my savior, keeping tabs on my sanity and supporting me on the numerous Channel 6 stories that fell into my lap after Junipero Serra. Single parenting was almost fully on my plate again, with one child crippled at least for the short-term, a resentful daughter, and a romantic relationship I seemed to covet one day and question the next. Therefore, when I got the call from Jon Novak about being selected to cover a high-profile murder case in Monterey, I almost turned it down. Unaware that I was nursing an injured child back to health, Jon threw me a bone and expected me to explode with appreciation.

"So, we're doing a briefing tomorrow in my office at eleven o'clock," he said. "It'll be you, me, and Dan Spears, who has covered many of these murder trials in the past, including O.J. This Bob Giffendorf child-killing story is monumental for this station. You'll need to be at the courthouse starting at 1 p.m. tomorrow, then each day at the start and end of the court session, grabbing the attention of the prosecuting DA and the defense attorney, collecting their fresh impressions of the proceedings. That'll mean about six to seven hours a day for the next two weeks, maybe three weeks. The proceedings are open to the press and you'll be on camera twice each day, Monday through Friday."

"Wow, that's very flattering, Jon," I said. "I appreciate you selecting me for this. I...I..."

He sensed my hesitation and broke in. "This is your path to much bigger assignments, Sandy. You know that, right? Not something you want to pass up. You're at a crossroads here. You're good but I don't want to be walking on eggshells and I'm feeling those shells beneath my feet right now. Get me?"

"Yes, yes, I'll be there tomorrow. Forgive me, Jon, but I recently had a personal issue come up with my son. I think I can work out the logistics, not a problem. I want this assignment," I told him emphatically.

"Good. It's perfect for you at this juncture, especially since you're also the mother of two young children. It will be easy for you to relate to what it means to the mother in such circumstances. You'll be able to identify all the right angles. See you at 9 a.m. tomorrow in my office, plenty of time before you're at the courthouse at one o'clock all set up to roll. Jury selection begins at 2 p.m."

Oh God, the Bob Giffendorf murder trial. Immediately searching Google, I found a foundry of details. The story centered on the killing of two young children, three-year-old Tammy and six-year-old Ricardo. The mother, Rosa Torres Giffendorf, was the only family survivor, her ex-husband Bob having taken the children hostage, accused of locking them up in an abandoned storage locker for sixteen days. The Grady's Storage Lockers facility located on the outskirts of Salinas was set to be demolished within the next two weeks. Bob Giffendorf allegedly made the decision to suffocate the two children and then stuff them into two oversized suitcases that he stored in the locker. The coroner contended that the kids had been killed at least twenty-four hours before being placed in each of the suitcases and were discovered just five days ago.

The facts were grotesque, making me almost heave on my keyboard. Rosa Torres Giffendorf was a mother in great distress—there was no doubt about that. I watched a short clip on YouTube, a bystander having caught her exiting the police station just minutes after being informed of the tragedy. Her face was streaked with black lines of makeup, her shoulders were hunched, her eyes vacant. Rumors were that she had informed her ex-husband, a seemingly caring father, that she was engaged to be married and that her two young children would have a new stepdad. The mystery was, at this stage, what made a father of two beautiful children snap without any apparent violent history or trouble with the law in his background? What was it? Jealousy...? What?

Mimi was due to arrive at my house at 6:30. Jenny and Luke were arguing over some scenario centered on the Hungry Hippo board game. I had already changed into my black velvet skirt and frilly white blouse for a planned dinner out with Zack. My hair was half up, still quite a mess from my hurried errands earlier that day. It was difficult for me to leave the computer. I needed another half hour to complete my research to find out if there was anything else out there about Giffendorf or his wife.

It would be a treat going out for dinner on a Thursday evening, after being so focused on Luke's accident, catering to his whims, giving him as much motherly love as possible, while his dad was once again MIA, supposedly totally absorbed in his precious investigations. I was meeting Zack at the Cuba Café. Then he was planning to spend the night once the children were in bed and asleep, something Mimi would undoubtedly make sure of while Zack and I were out to dinner.

When I entered the restaurant, Zack was standing by a table, the host seating him. Sporting a heather gray turtleneck, a black beret still cocked perfectly on his head, and a black-and-white herringbone wool scarf around his neck, he looked very European, a bit out of synch with his surroundings in Santa Cruz. When he saw me walk in, his face seemed to light up. I was intentionally wearing Zack's favorite outfit, the same one I was wearing on the first night he kissed me. As I approached the table, he removed his beret and placed it on the corner of his chair. His hair was so long now that he pulled it back in a little blond ponytail. I found this look sexy but had never mentioned it to him. He waited for me to be seated by the host, then reached over and tenderly kissed me.

"You have it on," he said, glancing at my clothes. "I think I'm crushing on you. Isn't that how you Americans say it?"

"Hmm, is that a cross-cultural jab or just a compliment?" I replied.

Sitting down, he closed the open menu left by the host and reached over to touch my hand, my fingers already busy tracing the offerings on the menu. "Both," he said, rolling his eyes. "Now, let's see, what are the entrées?" He didn't open his menu but instead was fully focused on me to give him an overview. "I'm starved."

I looked up into his eyes, a kaleidoscope of watercolor greens and blues gazing back at me. "By the way, forgive me for being nosy," I said, looking back at his beret, "but that metal brooch on your beret, I never asked you before, does it mean something special or is it from some Irish rugby team perhaps?"

His eyes went cold for a moment as his hand slipped away from mine. He cleared his throat. "Yes. That brooch belonged to my brother's wife, Felicia's dear mother. I don it to honor her spirit. Antonio is too angry to wear it. I see it warms little Felicia's heart to see me always wear it." He reached back to clutch the beret, and then held it up in front of me. "The brooch has two open hands, the wrists shackled by chains. It's an ancient Celtic symbol," he explained as he outlined each part of the design with his index finger. "In the artist's actual painting, which hangs in a Dublin art museum, the hands reach up to almost touch a beautiful green and orange butterfly. This pin depicts only the shackled hands. Antonio's dear wife wore this brooch every day. The woman was not only stunning but a passionate intellect and a great supporter of freedom," he added, his eyes moist with tears.

"It's a lovely pin," I said as he handed me the beret. "What's it made of? It looks special, not made of ordinary silver."

"You *are* observant. It *is* special... The slender hands are made of pewter and the shackles of solid gold." He became quiet for a moment, almost hypnotized by the brooch.

Returning to the here and now, he continued, "So, love, let's focus on you. I see you're a bit flushed tonight. I hope it's a reaction to the sight of me."

"You noticed," I replied, beaming. "May I tell you about what happened to me today, my amazing news?"

Arms folded on his chest, offering his undivided attention, he leaned back. "Okay love, me ears and eyes are all yours."

"Good. I'm honored. Well, it's an assignment, a hefty one from Channel 6. Zack, this is the break I've been waiting for, a high-profile murder case, a heartbreaking story. Bob Giffendorf, a divorced father of two young children, allegedly kidnapped and then tragically murdered his three-year-old and six-year-old, leaving them dead in suitcases just outside of Salinas, in some abandoned storage facility. The ex-wife, the poor children's mother, is the family's sole survivor." As I described the gruesome circumstances, shivers went through my body, yet I felt pride in having been awarded the assignment.

I continued, Zack sitting silently, listening to every word. "After a meeting in the morning with the producer, I'll be outside the courthouse beginning tomorrow afternoon at one o'clock to interview the prosecuting DA and hopefully the defense attorney before they begin proceedings each day, probably going on for at least two weeks, maybe longer."

His eyes closed. The next thing I saw scared me. He picked up the steak knife from his place setting and threw it down at the floor, as if wanting to stab something. Simmering, he yelled out, "Bastard! Killing someone in his own family!" His voice was suddenly strained, raw. "I'd like to fucking wring the shit's neck."

I couldn't comprehend where Zack was coming from, feeling stripped of my elation. There I go again, I chided myself, alienating those closest to me, same old story. "Yes, it is the most tragic story I've heard in a long time. Look, Zack, I...I'm sorry I mentioned it. I didn't mean to spoil our dinner."

Still heated, he interrupted me. "Do you, Sandy Stonemeyer, star reporter, understand what it's like to lose a family member to cold-blooded murder? *Do you?*" he said, his voice raised, his hands clenched into closed fists.

"Zack, I...I'm so sorry, let's talk about something else. I wasn't thinking about how this topic might affect you." His cold eyes penetrated mine, his skin pale. I noticed the couple sitting across from us turn their heads and stare. Then it hit me. "Oh my God, Antonio's wife! Oh God, I remember now that you lost her because of a violent, senseless crime.

That's why this is..." I stopped myself and reached across the table to place my hand on his, to sooth his pain, regretting having opened up this wound.

Color gradually returned to his face, his eyes back to how I knew them. "No, I'm the one who should apologize," he said, shaking his head. "Please love, I must excuse myself and visit the loo, get myself together. It was foolish of me to respond in such a way, a senseless outburst to be sure. You're excited about your work. Why shouldn't you be? Please, I need a moment. I'll be right back," he said as he got up and left.

All I could think about from the moment he left was how unsympathetic I had been. Those I love I hurt, and my God, I love this man.

The waiter approached. "Can I offer you a rundown of our specials tonight while waiting for your husband to return?" he asked.

My husband, I thought, my head reeling. Could that ever be in our future? I refocused on the present. "Yes please," I replied. "I'd love to hear about your specials."

"With pleasure," the young waiter said. "Everything Cuban, let me say first. Our Pork Fiesta, served with plantains and cilantro rice, is our renowned specialty. The sauce is to die for," he said, wriggling his body. "We also have a divine Chicken Mole, Cuban style, a collection of spices to make your mouth water, served again with plantains and a special lime and coconut fried rice. Our special appetizer tonight is a mini paella dish also boasting an assortment of Caribbean spices, including caramelized chunks of juicy pineapple and lots of seafood."

As the waiter described the dishes, I kept my eyes on the alcove where the restrooms were located. Happy to see Zack emerge, I was looking forward to telling him about the specials that I tried to carefully memorize. But instead of heading back to the table, he was taking a call on his cell phone by the ATM machine. His face intense, he seemed to be upset with the person on the other end, until I realized that it was more like he was giving the other person instructions or orders. I was curious about the call but didn't want to be intrusive, so I didn't plan on asking him about it. He came back to the table seemingly in a better mood.

"Do you want to hear about the specials?" I asked, not wanting to forget them, my brain flooded with all the fabulous choices.

"No worry, love, how about if you order for me? You know what I like." He took my hand. "Ya do, my love."

"Really? You want me to decide your fate tonight," I teased, hoping to get the evening off on a better note.

He nodded. "Probably more preferable than me deciding my fate, or yours for that matter," he said, a hint of his angry mood returning. Then he grinned, saying, "Yes, please you decide for us."

I liked the sound of that. I ordered the mini paella for us to share, then chicken for me and the barbecued pork special for him, knowing he was a dedicated carnivore. We ate peacefully, him talking about his niece Felicia learning new vocabulary words on a daily basis, and me describing Jenny's fixation with learning every speaking line of the new play, even the parts of the other actors, including Felicia's lines. He laughed and asked several extending questions, the perfect interviewer, and the perfect lover, I thought.

We ate dessert in silence, him ordering the Guava Cheese Flan and me the Bacardi Rum Cake, sharing our two dishes. He occasionally reached over and touched my cheek, apologizing for his earlier behavior with his eyes and his grin. Men have a way of saying "I'm sorry" nonverbally, I thought, a trait that women in general could benefit from utilizing more often themselves.

After two cups of coffee, Zack pulled my hand to his lips to kiss it. "Look love," he began, "I need to make a confession. It's about what's causing me to be so emotional tonight."

I smiled, resisting the urge to talk.

"Last night, as I drifted off to sleep, I had an epiphany." He paused. "About us."

Dammit, here it comes, I thought, cringing, my hands trembling, my coffee cup teetering on its saucer. His face seemed to blur, then morphed back to clarity, then blurred again.

"Sandy, I'm falling for you. No, correction, I have already fallen hard for you. I believe it's a love that will grow even further. I've been fighting it ever since the night I picked you up in my arms and carried you to my car. To me, you were a sleeping angel." He laughed at himself, seeming to realize how cliché his words probably sounded. Sitting back in his chair, he scratched his head and said, "Who am I fooling? I'm bewitched and insanely in love with you, besides wanting to remove your clothes every thirty minutes or so. Can you stand it, love?"

"Does the sun come up every day? Yes, of course, I can stand it. I can more than stand it," I replied.

Giddy, I broke into giggles. He walked me to my car, and without warning pressed me up against the passenger door, giving me a long kiss. Then he stood back, his arms still around my waist, but his head down. I watched his confident Irish charm shift to the demeanor of a shy boy.

"I'm emotionally wiped out, love," he said. "It's not so easy for a lug like me to express his deep feelings. Do you mind if I go home tonight? It's been a tough day in the import/export business as well and tomorrow's Friday, so that means early-morning meetings with the French and Germans."

After the extreme swings of the evening, I thought I would be content to be alone in my bed, to process Zack's confessions of love.

"I feel lucky to have you, Sandy Stonemeyer, star reporter, in my life," he said, looking down at me. "I used to think if you're lucky enough to be Irish, you're lucky enough." We both chuckled. "But now that I've fallen for you, being Irish is nothing compared to being in love. First time in my life, really."

I grinned, still not quite believing my own luck, just when I thought my love life had ended for good after finding Albie with the Japanese girl.

"I'll see you tomorrow night then, love," Zack said, smiling. "Shall I bring Felicia if Antonio doesn't have plans, though I doubt that will be the case. The man's still in the doldrums—the lows never seem to leave him."

"Sure, you bring the pizza for us and I'll have the beer and lemonade. How does that sound?"

The next morning, I was up and out, Mimi graciously picking up the kids for school, Luke hobbling along now with a soft leg boot, getting around better than in the earlier days. The meeting with my producer, where I talked about approach, demeanor, and direction for questioning both sides of the legal team, couldn't have gone better.

At the courthouse, standing on the top steps by the entrance, a little before one o'clock, my cameraman was ready to roll and I was positioned, wearing a pale-pink suit, my hair neatly swept up in a French twist.

A crowd of observers stood below, some holding signs. One read "Convict Giffendorf!" and another "Show No Mercy to Child Killers!" Gus, my cameraman, panned the people holding signs, zeroing in on a Hispanic woman, her baby in one arm and a protest sign in the other. Panning back to me, he focused his camera on me, as I made some introductory remarks, and then waited for the first interviewee to arrive.

Arnie Zaragoza, Giffendorf's defense attorney, was the first to climb the concrete courthouse stairs, flanked by his legal team, and out of the three reporters on site, was headed toward me. Another reporter approached, trying to get Zaragoza's attention, but he waved them off and waited for me to reach him.

"Ms. Stonemeyer," the defense attorney began, "I recognize you from the Junipero Serra story. I'd like to talk to only you today."

I smiled and then nodded over to Gus, who had closed in on just the two of us. I shot right into it. "Mr. Zaragoza, as Bob Giffendorf's attorney, what are your first thoughts on defending him when the story that's out there right now leads the public to, as you can see, already have him convicted as a child killer?" I was being provocative but felt it appropriate. He nodded back, acknowledging the plausibility of my question.

"Bob Giffendorf deserves a fair trial, just like everyone in this country," he said. "I'm here to ensure that happens. It's my intention to present the facts, including any and all evidence that would show reasonable doubt."

Good answer, I thought. "Thank you for sharing your approach to his trial. Do you see a chance that he's not guilty?" I held the microphone out to him, wondering how he'd reply.

I heard his first two words, "Justice is...," and then felt the jolt, the piercing pain shooting into my shoulder. The microphone fell to the ground, as I collapsed on top of it. My vision faded in and out, as people were screaming around me, many running, dispersing from the area. Lying on the ground, I spotted the woman I had seen earlier with the baby, who had dropped her sign and ran, shielding the girl in her arms.

Gus moved in, swooping me up in his arms, headed into the courthouse entrance, out of harm's way, while leaving his camera somewhere outside. He put me down on the cold floor in a corner to examine my injury. "Oh God, Sandy, it's your shoulder. I know it's bad, but it could have been a lot worse. Do you hurt anywhere else?" The left sleeve on my pink suit jacket had turned red.

"I...I think I'm okay, Gus. A bullet, wasn't it?"

"Sure was, here's the EMT," he said, looking up, relieved. "I'll get out of the way, but I'll be close by."

A young man, with the face of a teenager, bent down and introduced himself. "I'm Alan here to take a look at you. Let me get that jacket off. Can you sit up a little?"

I sat up against the wall. He carefully removed my jacket and examined the wound. "You're a lucky lady. Looks like a bullet grazed you but didn't hit the bone." I didn't see Gus anywhere. The EMT was more upbeat now. "This should be cleaned and bandaged up, but first let me take your vitals. Then we'll get you to the hospital so they can do a thorough check."

"But why...who would do this?" I said.

He shook his head, not knowing what to say to me.

Realizing I was thirsty, I asked, "Can I have some water?"

Alan glanced over at his partner and gestured. A bottle of water, cap off, was in my hand in a few seconds. I gulped down half of it, staring at my shoulder, which Alan was cleaning after having cut open the sleeve of my white blouse.

"No bullet. I was right—it just grazed you."

I should have been thankful, but I couldn't help but wonder if the shooter wanted me dead. I looked up at the hordes of people who had gathered around us, and through the myriad of legs, I could see a court official I recognized emerge from the courtroom to the right. He seemed determined to make some sort of announcement.

Looking up, I saw that Gus had returned inside the building and was holding his camera and his bag, my microphone sticking out from his side pocket. I wanted to signal him to get over to the official and start rolling, but he was way ahead of me, already in front of the suited man before I could hold up my hand. He held up my microphone with one hand, the camera on his opposite shoulder. I noticed several police officers standing around the perimeter of the lobby area, hands on their weapons, ready to react if needed.

A thin man in a navy blue suit with black-framed glasses read a statement from a notepad: "This is an official announcement from the Monterey County Courthouse. Judge Sanjit Singh has cancelled to-day's proceedings in light of a shooter in the area. Regretfully, Judge Singh has decided to instead begin proceedings tomorrow morn-ing at 9 a.m." Murmurs came from the crowd. The man continued, "Please don't leave the courthouse until the police give you clearance instructions."

Audible reactions came from the crowd. "Oh God, is the sniper in-side?" somebody yelled. A few people screamed in fear.

A policeman grabbed the Channel 6 microphone from Gus's hand and said, "We've checked the interior of the courthouse. You can see the police standing around you. There is no evidence of a shooter inside. The bullet and the gun were located outside. The victim, a Channel 6 news reporter, is okay, as you may have noticed." He pointed over to me, sitting on the marble floor against the paneled wall.

"We all thank God that she was barely hurt, but of course, this is serious. Because the gun was found, we think the shooter has escaped and is no longer a threat, but we can't be sure."

"You mean *sniper,* don't you?" a man yelled out.

"God, man, yes, you can call the person a shooter or a sniper, whatever you want." The policeman, holding himself like a seasoned professional, shook his head. "Always one in the crowd," he said. "In any case, ladies and gentlemen, a member of our police squad here today will be taking you all out through an alternative exit door, releasing you onto King Street and escorting you, one-by-one, out to your vehicle or if preferred to your desired mode of public transportation. Please follow me and line up single-file at the alternative exit door. Thank you and God bless."

More murmurs, but this time more subdued. Gus came through the crowd. I felt weak, but gestured for him to hand me the microphone.

"I need to make some ending statements here Gus, and show the viewers I'm all right."

"Are you up to it?" he asked.

I nodded. Then I propped myself up so I could sit up straight against the wall, straightened out what was left of my white blouse, smoothed my hair back, made sure my legs were closed, my feet tucked under me. "Gus, please roll the camera," I said. I didn't smile but spoke with a mixture of physical fatigue and informed reason. "As you witnessed on camera just minutes ago, I was shot in the shoulder by an unknown sniper. Fortunately, very fortunately"—I spoke slowly and clearly—"I'm not badly injured. I was only grazed by the bullet."

I could see the man who had just spoken on the microphone looking down at me, a grimace on his face. The young emergency responder touched his watch, a signal that I should cut this short so he could get me to the hospital. I focused my attention back to the camera.

"We here at Channel 6 pledge to keep our viewers informed of any new developments," I said. "I'm sure the police are out combing the vicinity searching for the shooter. Further good news, the weapon used was found not far away. Court proceedings on the Bob Giffendorf child murder case have been delayed until tomorrow morning at 9 a.m. We will be back here following every minute of this case. And finally, for those of you with loved ones at the courthouse today, we want you to know that the police are personally escorting each individual out to their vehicle or preferred mode of public transportation keeping them safe. That's all the information we have at this point. For Channel 6 News, this is Sandy Stonemeyer, *live* at the Monterey County Courthouse."

Gus kept the camera on me as the EMT helped me up from the floor and onto a waiting wheelchair. Although a harrowing experience, I took pride in what I just delivered, a quality piece of work in a stressful situation, and was grateful to be alive.

Chapter Twenty-Four

On the Bluff, in the Rough

My nerves were in shambles for days, as my life had been threatened, and I wondered who the shooter was gunning for me, or the defense attorney, or was it someone else? The police were investigating the scene, but without any solid leads, and it was difficult for me to accept or comprehend that it remained an unsolved mystery. The court case ensued the next day at 9 a.m., as announced, and I covered the story. Life gradually went back to normal. I counted on Zack and Mimi for emotional support as well as raw luck when it came to my well-being.

The police had shifted their attention away from an initial concern for my safety and instead became convinced that because of the heinous crime committed against two helpless children, there was at least one angered citizen, who had evidently taken the law into his own hands, and I had been the unlucky recipient of the bullet grazing. Every day, every minute of the disturbing two-week trial, badges and uniforms flanked both attorneys and defendants.

Overnight, I became the station's "It Girl," covering the Giffendorf story in addition to other news events, including real-time on-camera studio time versus only being exclusively on location. Fatigued from the volume of work, and stressed by the threat to my life, I ploughed through the next several days, becoming more accustomed to the grueling work schedule. Jenny and Luke were concerned about their dad disappearing yet again out of their lives, realizing just how close they had come to losing their mom.

Zack was by my side as soon as he heard about me being hit by the bullet, although he seemed somewhat distracted, emotionally distant, not unlike that night at the restaurant.

I was on the steps of the courthouse, my right arm in a soft sling, my microphone in the other, faithfully interviewing both attorneys before court proceedings. On the last morning of jury selection, court was scheduled for 11:00 a.m., with jury prep from the judge scheduled for the afternoon. Both attorneys were in a rush to get inside the building, but were generous with answering my few quick questions, knowing that I had been the recipient of a bullet probably meant for one of them, which had resulted in a journalistic edge for me over the other three reporters.

I was meeting Zack in an hour at his place, so I rushed to my car. Walking through the alleyway, I heard his voice coming up behind me.

"Going in my direction?" he said, kissing my neck, beaming as if bursting with anticipation. "Ready for our picnic? Wait, you don't look ready to me."

I smiled. "I was going to meet you at your place, remember? My clothes are in the car. You know, I have to pick Luke up at noon and take him to Aunt Sylvie's first."

"It's already done, love," he replied. "I spoke to your Aunt Sylvie and to your friend, Mimi, and she's bringing Luke over to your aunt's house, so no problem."

"Mimi? But she's not at school today. I tried to call her this morning, and last night my message went straight to voicemail twice. Is she okay?"

"Yes, she sounded fine when I talked to her just before school started this morning."

"Well, you do have special powers. Must be the Irish in you, only I'm the lucky one," I said, wondering why Mimi hadn't left a message for me in return.

"Listen love," he continued, "I need to make a call in my car. How about I drive into this side street and you change in the courthouse restroom and meet me right here. We can leave your car here. You can pick it up later after our picnic. Okay?"

"Sounds fine by me," I said, feeling free.

The sun was shining brightly, and a relaxing afternoon with Zachery was in front of me, and as agreed, I didn't spill our plans this afternoon to Luke and Jenny for fear they'd nag me into bringing them along, wanting every moment they could get with Zack, especially now that their father had melted into the ozone yet again. Aunt Sylvie did not get informed either, as I thought she'd probably spill it to the kids although unintentionally. She thought I was on a TV assignment and would be back to pick up the kids later in the evening.

Zack had prepared a special picnic lunch and laid it out on a red-and-white checked gingham tablecloth: two turkey and cranberry sandwiches stacked high on San Francisco sourdough with a touch of lettuce and mayo. Sometime ago, I remembered confessing to him a wish to fast-forward to the winter season, when I could once again savor my favorite holiday lunch, the turkey-cranberry sandwich, which would be available in just about every lunchtime restaurant I frequented. Zack must have filed away this wish, stashed it in his Sandy Stonemeyer cabinet, hoping to take my attention away from my manic life, having been a target for violence and now totally consumed with the murder trial coverage. Jenny had the day off from school because of teacher in-service training so she was already with Aunt Sylvie.

He handed me his sandwich surprise, and I squealed in appreciation, reached over, kissed him, and took my first bite. From the picnic basket, he pulled out a bottle of champagne. Although the sun was retreating behind the clouds, the temperature was still warm, almost sultry, the humidity higher than a typical early-spring day in Santa Cruz.

I was impressed with Zack's plan to get me away from the children, away from my now hectic work life. I had almost forgotten the concern I had the night before I invited him to stay the whole night in my bed, my children in the next room. This was the one thing I had promised myself never to do, but it had unfolded so naturally, without any drama or attention being paid to it. The time with Zack had passed so quickly, as we saw each other regularly but usually with kids all around us.

◆ ◆ ◆

Last night had been different though, more intense, our passion erupting minutes after Jenny and Luke had gone off to bed. Then, at about 4:30 in the morning, I awoke with misgivings swimming around in my head. Feeling the heat of the rugged Irishman who lay there beside me, I pushed those thoughts away and smiled before I whispered in his ear, "Zack, you must go. You know the drill. Jenny and Luke will be up in no time. I still don't want them to see you here in the morning."

He turned into me and said, "You don't really want me to leave just yet, do you, love?"

"Zack, I...I'm not sure what I want," I replied, "but I know I want to be cautious when it comes to my kids. I...I'm just confused right now. I can't make any rash decisions."

He said that he understood and he would leave in a few minutes as he sprinkled tender kisses all over my face and neck. Closing my eyes, I unexpectedly imagined Albie back in my bed, just for a hair of a second, with that saucy grin of his. Why was I thinking of Albie, I wondered, when lying there so content with Zack?

Falling, I knew that I was falling for this Irishman, only the second man in my life who had successfully lassoed my restless heart. I watched him dress, his strong body slipping into his tan slacks and dark-green shirt. I nervously bit my lip when he said his goodbye, promising to come back later to take me on the picnic he had planned.

"Dress appropriately, love," he said, "it's supposed to be warm today, but as we know that can quickly change. So...layers, yes?" He then left, closing the door behind him.

◆ ◆ ◆

Sitting on the bluff, drinking champagne from a slim glass flute, I felt special. Zack took my glass and set it in the picnic basket, then lay down on the gingham fabric next to me.

"Close your eyes, love," he said. "I have one more surprise for you."

His magical Irish lilt warmed my heart. "I don't think I can accept yet another surprise after that delicious sandwich," I said, grinning up at him. "Some kind of dessert, maybe?"

"Maybe," he said, winking.

"Okay then," I conceded, closing my eyes, the image of Albie's face unexpectedly leaping across my consciousness for the second time.

Feeling a streak of guilt, I waited for Zack to present me with his next surprise. I tried to recall if I had previously divulged any of my "sweet tooth" preferences to him, thinking if he had chocolate-covered strawberries in that basket, I'd plant a very long "thank-you" kiss on his soft Irish lips.

He paid attention to me, picking up on the subtle, yet important things, and I was becoming used to it. He brought his enchanting niece Felicia into my daughter's life, had been a catalyst for improving my relationship with Jenny, and had captured Luke's heart with his storytelling, especially attentive to him after the tree house accident. Zack had proven to be my lucky charm, easing my transition into single parenting, filling the dark corners of my loneliness with his easy loving.

◆ ◆ ◆

My eyes were still closed, ready for his next surprise, when I was suddenly gagged. My eyes popped open. The black cotton headband from my straw hat was now being tied around my mouth. He must have yanked it from the brim. What the hell? I could feel him quickly knotting the two ends of the cloth, and then he gave it a tug to ensure a tight fit. I was overcome with shock. He pulled my wrists together and springing a zip tie from his pocket, snapped it together. I kicked him, but he gripped me harder, then he sat on me, straddling his legs on either side of my body. His face had transformed, as though the devil had taken over.

He shook his forefinger in my eyes and bent down, whispering in my left ear. "You kick me again and I'll kill you right here. Your ex-husband, Albie Stonemeyer, will be very upset with me. But then I don't give a shit."

He sat up again as if looking forward to my reaction. My body stiffened, the zip tie cutting into my wrists. I struggled to breathe, thinking that I was headed for hyperventilation if I didn't get control of myself.

Zack knows Albie. Images of the time spent with Zack flashed like a movie across the screen of my mind: in bed with Zack, Zack and Jenny laughing, Zack caressing his niece Felicia, Zack pushing Jenny high on the swing in the local park, Jenny enjoying the company of the man who was filling the void left by her estranged father. My unanswered calls to Mimi...did that have anything to do with this man who had suddenly become a monster? My mind filled with fear and a host of terrifying possibilities. I felt so betrayed.

I looked up at the sky, thunderstruck by what was happening. The clouds seemed to thicken. A curtain of fog now hung over us. The sound of the waves had intensified on the deserted beach below. He wants to kill me, I thought.

He pulled the iPhone from his back pocket and snapped a photo of my twisted face, my eyes undoubtedly screaming panic. "Say cheese," he said, zooming in and snapping another. Like a tornado, he pulled me up and dragged me to the Range Rover, releasing the hatch and throwing me into the back. Hanging over me, he pulled out another zip tie, grabbed my ankles, and bound them together. He rushed away, returning within a few seconds, throwing the wicker picnic basket inside the SUV, hitting my bare legs, the thorny edges of wicker scraping my leg. The gingham tablecloth was then tossed inside, landing on my upper body, covering my right eye. The champagne glasses were next, flying in, one of them hitting me sharply in the knee, the other slamming against the backseat and smashing in pieces. Pulling the gingham tablecloth away from my face, he snapped a third close-up. I tried to move my legs, but couldn't budge them.

"Your Albie is going to be upset when he sees a shot of his lovely Sandy girl in distress, tortured just before her tragic death." I narrowed my eyes in horror. "Why am I doing this? That's what you're asking with those eyes, isn't it?" He pulled my hair hard until my eyes welled up with tears. "Your arse-hole of a husband murdered my wife, that's why, Miss Muffet. Cassandra's dead because of him! And now you're going to die, too. Quid pro quo, as they say. Then I'll focus on your two dear little children. Dead, m'dear! They'll be dead, just like you!" He slammed the hatchback shut. I could hear him slide into the front seat, close the door, and start the engine.

I'm going to die, then my children, because Albie killed his wife? Oh God, how did he kill her? Why would he do such a thing? It doesn't add up. Nothing made sense. Where was Zack taking me? Somehow I must get free. The ride felt like an hour. I couldn't make out the time on my watch in the dark SUV. But I did see something glistening in the corner. It was a long sharp chunk of glass from the broken champagne flute now wedged in the crevice between the backseat and the carpeted floor of the cab. I moved my bound legs closer, desperately moving the plastic zip tie up and down against the jagged edge of the shard.

The SUV rocked, bouncing me around, but I persisted, thrusting my ankles back to the glass. Another big bump. The glass cut into my ankle. I had to ignore it, though it stung like hell. I went back for another round of grinding the plastic on the glass tip. Finally the plastic band snapped open, springing my ankles free. Thank God. Flipping my body around to the opposite side of the vehicle, I prayed that I could repeat my feat, cutting the zip tie binding my wrists. Dammit, it's too late, I thought, as the SUV came to a jolting halt. Where were we? I wondered as the hatch popped open. I kept my ankles close together as if still bound so he wouldn't suspect anything.

His face lowered close to mine. "Before you die," he said, "I'm going to film the whole gruesome thing for your ex-husband."

He started to lift me from the enclosure, like a bag of dirt. Mustering all the strength I could, I turned onto my back as I was being pulled out and kicked him with full force in the groin, then shoved my foot upward, catching his chin. His legs buckled, causing him to almost fall, but he managed to rebalance himself, shooting up again, now enraged. I kicked hard until he fell down onto the ground.

Although my wrists were still zip-tied and my mouth gagged and dry, neither stopped me from jumping out of the SUV and bolting away like a freed animal. Zack reached out, clutched my bleeding ankle, and yanked hard. I didn't surrender, but instead pivoted around, smashing him with my other foot right in his mouth, forcing him to release my ankle. "Agh," he moaned. "Bitch!"

Run. Run, I screamed inside my head, my heart jumping in my chest. He grabbed me by the neck from behind and pushed me to the ground, holding my face down in the dirt. I had managed to pull the stick of glass from the Range Rover, and it was cutting into me, as I lay there pressed on the ground, feeling the dirt and leaves on my tongue and in my teeth, despite the gag. I held the glass shard firmly in my bound hands, desperate to keep it camouflaged between my thighs. Zack flipped me back over to face him and laughed, his spit hitting me in the face.

"You tried to get the better of me, love," he said. "I don't appreciate that." His iPhone was out again, positioned to film this abhorrent deed. "Me mum always told me to never leave a pretty lady waiting." He put down his phone and started to unzip his jeans. "I've been hungry for this, to take you for a change when you least desired me." He was on fire with hatred. "I guess you don't have affection for me anymore, do ya now?" Leaning closer, he spat in my face again, saying, "Revenge...so fucking delicious."

I wanted to kill him.

He sneered, "Your husband, a CIA loser..."

I didn't wait for him to finish his sentence. Turning into him, shifting the sharp tip of the glass away from myself, I thrust it upwards, with no idea what part of his body, if any, it would hopefully pierce. His neck ripped open, blood pouring out. Good.

Rolling onto the dirt, he held his neck with both hands, screaming, "Bitch. You'll pay, you bitch."

I scrambled to get up, and then glancing down, I noticed that my left ankle was covered in blood, my white sock and pale-blue Nike sneaker darkened with crimson stains. Running for my life, I headed deeper into the woods. The ground was covered with crisp leaves, jagged branches, and pine cones. It had been mostly a dry winter and a warm balmy spring in the Santa Cruz Mountains, but I knew that the temperature could change from cold to warm to hot and back to bitter cold within a matter of minutes. Just run and hide, I told myself over and over. I didn't hear him following me...a good sign. Maybe I killed him, maybe I stopped him. Maybe he's dead. I feared his arm reaching out from behind me to take me down. Did he say CIA right before I cut him? CIA? Albie, was he somehow connected to the CIA? It didn't make sense.

I kept moving. Every twenty yards or so, I'd pick a tree and hide behind it for a few minutes, look around, listen carefully, checking to see if Zack was tracking me. Still there was no sign of him. After about thirty minutes of running and hiding, I stopped a little longer to catch my breath. My bound wrists were slowing me down, the zip tie cutting deeper into my skin, with each jerky movement. I recalled watching an episode of *60 Minutes* a few months ago where a renowned survival expert advised viewers how to defend themselves if they found themselves zip-tied in a home robbery. A young woman stood next to the expert, demonstrating the right moves, as he gave his instructions. Maybe I could try this method, I thought. It's worth a shot. Holding my arms straight down, my elbows locked, I attempted to imitate what I had seen the woman do on the TV screen. I raised my knee up high and slammed my wrists down hard, hoping to break the plastic tie. It didn't work. How the hell did that woman do it? I wondered. I straightened my leg back down and concentrated, thrusting my arms straight down again, but this time with a sharp single movement, slamming my wrists down hard on my thighs. Snap, the zip tie sprung open, flew off, and landed in the dirt.

Thank God. I rubbed my stinging wrists, wriggling them about, looking for any sign of injury bar the deep bloodied creases in my wrists. No time for self-pity, I thought. Reaching up behind my head, I worked the cloth gagging me, furiously untying the double knot and flinging the fabric onto the ground. I moved my jaw, opening and closing my mouth several times, an audible snapping sound each time. God, that gag was uncomfortable. It felt like my jaw was injured. Then I retrieved the black fabric from the ground, wrapped it around my bleeding hand, and buried the zip tie under a pile of dry leaves. Leave no sign. Leave no sign, I told myself.

I need to get out of these woods, find my kids before he finds them. They're with Aunt Sylvie. Oh God, she'll be in danger, too. The light of day was fading. I still had on my watch, the Movado, which Albie had given to me two years ago on my birthday. It was 6:32. Suddenly I heard some rustling in the bushes to my right. Damn, it's him. Oh God. No...just a squirrel hurrying up a tree. Keep your senses, Sandy. Keep your senses! If Jenny were here, she'd chide me: "It's just a squirrel, Mom, chill. Don't panic over a squirrel." I longed for the sound of her voice, and wished that I had apologized for my many failures as a mother, especially how I had so poorly communicated the separation.

The underbrush crunched beneath my feet. The cut on my ankle was bad. I reached down to assess the damage. It was getting worse—it was much deeper than I had thought. I'm lost and I have nothing to help me: no wallet, no money, no phone, no protection. If I could just find the road, just find the road. God willing, I had gotten further away from the Irishman. Nothing, I knew nothing about camping, zippo about wilderness survival, didn't even know how to conjure up a campfire. I glanced at my watch, the tiny silver hands now barely visible under the thick canopy of tall trees. It was 7:06 and the sun was going down. Then I heard something new, the trickling of water, and was that singing?

Hurtling through the trees, I followed the sounds. Finding myself at the edge of a bluff, I looked down. A river...that must be the San Lorenzo,

I thought. The voices...they were coming from below. Spotting some ca-noes just a short distance away, over a dozen of them, I saw more than twenty people, maybe even thirty, all wearing Santa Claus costumes, red hats and suits, white beards, singing a Christmas carol, belting out the song at the top of their lungs. "We wish you a merry Christmas, we wish you a merry Christmas. We wish you a merry Christmas and a happy New Year!" Christmas songs and Santa costumes in the Spring? I didn't understand but didn't care.

People to help me, was all I could think about. Thank God. I cupped my hands around my mouth as if holding a megaphone and yelled out, "Help. Help. Up here, up here."

They kept singing, booming their lyrics as they moved their paddles through the water.

I tried again. "Hey, help me. Up here. Help. Please."

My throat was raw, weak. If only I had a whistle. I flashed on the red whistle that Albie had given to Jenny the day she turned five. He wanted her to have something with her at all times enabling her to call for help if she got into any kind of trouble. She wore it every day, and when she forgot to have it on her, either around her neck or in her backpack, she'd want to go back home to get it right away. I noticed that she hadn't worn it since the night I told her that Albie and I were separating. Dammit. I wish I had that whistle now.

I started to cry. Then in the loudest voice I could possible summon, I yelled again, "Help me! Help me!"

"Good tidings we bring to you and your king," they sang out.

I waved my arms high in the air. They were passing me by, taking no notice of the mad woman jumping up and down high above them. Gone, they were gone and I was alone again.

Slivers of yellow and amber sunlight threaded through the trees and then started to fade. A light rain began to fall, raindrops hitting the red-woods around me, everything glistening. Now I was limping, the cut above my ankle having caught up with me. Kneeling on the ground and then sliding down onto my side, I found myself giving up, surrendering to my circumstances, my tears flowing. The forest started to get cold as the rain got heavier. I noticed what looked like a long brown worm creep through a thicket just an inch or two from my face, wriggling across my line of sight. A crowd of black ants marched in perfect formation just behind the worm. Rolling onto my back, I gazed up at the towering redwoods, my face wet, my ankle stinging, yet I suddenly felt at ease, taking in the striking natural beauty that enveloped me, the arms of Mother Nature wrapped around me like a blanket. Will she prove protective? I was hoping against hope.

My thoughts shifted to Albie. He knew Zack and his wife Cassandra. Now the Irishman was out to kill me, my kids, and probably finish it off with killing him, all to avenge his wife's death. Had his wife been a criminal like him? Or was she merely an innocent casualty? Was Albie really in the freaking CIA? I tried to imagine it, thinking back to his extended business trips, his military expertise acquired from his stint in the Army, his passion to bust the bad guys. He was a good private investigator, but a CIA agent?

A beam of light from a flashlight hit the ground about six inches from my bleeding ankle. I got up as quietly as I could and stepped behind the nearest redwood, keeping myself from making the tiniest of sounds. I heard only the rain trickling down into the dark woods and the birds chattering their *adieu,* introducing the night, then the crunching of leaves under his shoes. The light moved to a tree adjacent to where I stood. Damn, Zack, I thought, shivering and wet, standing there like a stone. He's alive. Dammit, he'll see my tracks. The wind came up, leaves falling around me. My enemy was closing in, his flashlight now aimed at the tree I stood behind. Then it shifted away, hitting another tree and then another. He was searching.

My acute peripheral vision kicked in. I could make out Zachery darting around, the light showing his silhouette, as he moved clumsily until resting at the tree just on my left. Carefully slipping to the opposite side of the tree with a degree of agility, I managed to remain out of sight as I held my breath to keep silent. I was in a war battling a monster and my senses were on high alert. No room for mistakes, I warned myself. Take chances to survive but be careful.

Something suddenly moved close to my feet. It shot out of the dark underbrush, the beam of light instantly responding in my direction. "Gotcha," he yelled out victoriously when some kind of animal ran straight toward him. A rabbit, I thought. No, a skunk, I realized. The white-striped mammal took notice of Zack, seemed to panic, then rushed toward him, making a loud hissing sound, whisking up its tail, and squirted out a liquid. I took a quick peek from behind the tree to see Zack twisting in his tracks to escape, but then tripping himself up, and dropping to the ground, his flashlight landing beside him, now pointed at the tree that camouflaged me.

"Skunk, bloody skunk," he screeched, scrunching his nose and rubbing his eyes.

Grasping for my next move, I anticipated Zack recovering quickly, imagining him pulling me to the ground, ripping off my clothes in anger before he killed me, the noxious skunk stench the last thing I would ever smell. But I could see his body rolling around in the dirt, the flashlight beam upon him. I made a run for it, but not before picking up the flashlight. With his hands, Zack was still trying to wipe the spray out of his eyes. Disabled. Thank God.

"Bitch! Bitch," he shouted.

He knew I was watching him, which almost made me happy. I stumbled at first, but then forced myself to attempt a run, the flashlight, my new protection, enabling my escape into the night, as I left the depraved devil in the dirt.

Chapter Twenty-Five

Beam of Light

Hobbling in the darkness, I realized that the flashlight I snatched from Zack was losing its luminosity. I imagined what it would be like to die by myself, in the forest, all alone. Sitting on the cold ground, I felt momentarily defeated.

An image of my parents pushed the fear of mortality out of my mind. We were back in our living room and they were dancing to a big hit from the 1960s, the catchy tune blearing from our antique jukebox, a treasure my mother picked up in San Francisco. "Come on baby, do the locomotion. Do the locomotion with me." Every once in a while, my mom would signal over to my brother and me to join them. We'd laugh and shake our heads, shouting, "No way. No way Mom." Then, in the end, we'd acquiesce, the four of us dipping and shimmying across our Egyptian carpet. My life-affirming parents, taken out by a faulty airplane engine. Life is a poker game, each one of us in daily jeopardy, the only differentiators between us being the timing and circumstance of our ultimate demise. Over and over, we prove that the process of living is merely a game of chance.

Gazing down at the weakening beam, I had one consoling thought, and that was that my mom and dad wouldn't have to hear about their only daughter's pathetic end in the Santa Cruz Mountains. My kids would be motherless, at least for awhile. Would Albie survive as a single parent, team up with his young lover, and form a refreshed family circle? Or would Zack catch up with him, curtailing Albie's life before he had an opportunity to react after my death? Was Albie actually in the CIA? Had he lied to me all these years? The image of the older Japanese woman standing outside the restaurant hijacked my thoughts. "What you see not real," she had said. "What you see not real. You understand?" Did those words somehow complete the CIA equation? And how was the old woman's daughter, Albie's lover, involved in this convoluted scenario? With these thoughts, I struggled to stand up. It was as if my anger and anxiety plus my will to survive were lifting me from the forest floor.

Dragging my injured leg, I forged on. Heading down the slope to the river is probably the only hope for me finding a path out, I surmised. I could sleep once I got down there. If I survived the night, maybe the morning would bring someone to rescue me. What if Zack found me first? I pushed the depressing thought out of my mind and stepped down carefully, the dwindling intermittent light assisting my descent. Halfway down, I lost my footing. As I slid down the steep grade, a tree branch scraped across my right leg, ripping into my flesh. Why did I wear these damn Bermuda shorts? I yelled out in pain, anticipating my fateful end, as I smacked into something solid, my right side feeling the sudden impact. Oh God, that hurt.

The object I hit was a boat, some type of canoe, set there on the riverbank. Remarkably, my right hand was still wrapped around the flashlight. The sound of the moving water ahead of me seemed to soothe me. The boat appeared to be abandoned. I grabbed onto it, pulling myself closer, and clumsily heaved my body into its shallow bed, where I then passed out.

◆ ◆ ◆

Two strange voices in the night awoke me.

"Marco, darn, I forgot to bring the bacon," a woman said with annoyance. "You know how Carl loves bacon with his eggs." Her tone was shrill, almost whining. "They were supposed to meet us here over an hour ago. Where the heck are they? Marco, Marco, are you even listening to me?" Her voice was urgent and intense. "I hope you're hungry. The franks and beans are hot. Baked potatoes are ready, too. Let's eat now. God Marco, I hope nothing happened to those two. My brother is always late. Where are they? Marco, I'm starting to worry. It's cold, and oh God, what if they—"

"Stacey, please be quiet," a male voice broke in, "some vestige of peace, please? There's no need to panic. They'll be here. They know the way. I can't eat anything until I get out of these wet clothes anyway. Geesh, this damn thing is soaking wet. I never should have agreed to this fiasco in the first place. Dressing up as Santas in early spring? Ridiculous! For what reason? Well, it wasn't much fun! Damn, before I take this soaking-wet outfit off, I better get some more wood for the fire."

Peeking over the ledge of the boat, I wondered exactly where the two voices were coming from. Then a bright beam of light flashed before me, just about blinding me. Feeling around for the flashlight, I managed to stand up and step out of the boat, almost falling over twice, and then pointed my weak light, to find a man wearing a Santa Claus suit with a bewildered look on his face.

"What the hell? Who are you?" he asked. "That's our boat you were in." He stopped talking and stared at me for a few moments. "Hey, are you okay? Look, I...I'm sorry, I thought... Man, you don't look so good."

I must be a sight, I thought.

"I mean, I didn't mean to say..." he hesitated. "Are you okay?" he repeated.

"Yes," I replied with a raspy voice, leaning against the canoe. "But I'm lost, and I'm hurt. I...I'm in trouble. Someone is trying to k..." I couldn't get out any more words. In tears, I sat there, the wet mud spreading across my bare thighs, while I thanked God that I likely wasn't going to die in the woods that night.

"Stacey, Stacey," the Santa Claus yelled out. "Come quickly. There's an injured woman here."

He walked down the hill closer to me and reached out, gently touching my shoulder, taking care not to frighten me. "You'll be okay now," he said. "Don't worry." He smiled as he asked, "Do you like hot dogs and baked beans?"

Chapter Twenty-Six

Mission of Mercy

Tamakichi left her daughter's house in the mid-morning once she finished a round of pruning in the garden. Emily was at her daughter's soccer game and then planned on escorting Miyoko and three of her teammates to a popular animated afternoon movie. Miyoko had been excited that morning about these events. She pecked her grandmother lightly on the cheek while urging her mother to hurry up because she promised her friends she'd be there early for practice before the game.

Embarking on the journey she had planned that day, Tamakichi walked to the Greyhound bus station in Santa Clara to catch a bus that went over the Santa Cruz Mountains to Felton, her target being to get within a dozen streets or so from the address she had for Sandy Stonemeyer. It would be better than phoning her, she thought. Her discovery about Emily and Albie working for the CIA and the faked infidelity, she believed, would both need a face-to-face explanation. Perhaps she should have at least phoned first to see if Sandy would be at home. In any case, Tamakichi had been careful to check the return bus schedule and there were options for her throughout the day into the early evening. Before leaving Emily's house in Santa Clara, she had left her daughter a note saying that she was going to the Japanese cultural fair being held in downtown San Jose and might be late getting back.

The bus made its first stop in downtown Santa Cruz before it climbed the hill up to Felton. As they left the downtown station, Tamakichi was thinking that sharing that information with the American woman will help clear the slate for a new beginning, both for me and for my daughter.

Stepping off the bus onto the dusty road, she felt the rush of fresh mountain air on her face and in her hair. It was as if she were already beginning the cleansing process. Thankful that she wore her comfortable walking shoes, she examined her map, which she had purchased during the brief stop at the bus station. She carefully circled the area where Sandy lived and made an "X" on her street. It would likely take about thirty minutes, she thought, to walk down the road from the bus stop to Sandy's house.

Chapter Twenty-Seven

Temporary Respite

I limped up the steps to my front door after retrieving the spare key I hid under the mat on the back patio. Grimy and covered with dirt and leaves, I felt like I should be sprayed with disinfectant before entering the house. Why am I even thinking about the dirt? I needed to phone Aunt Sylvie immediately but realized that I had the AT&T landline disconnected a few days ago, finally taking action after agonizing over it for a year. Confident that my cell phone would cover all circumstances, I thought there was no reason to waste money on an outdated landline. Unfortunately, my cell phone was now either sitting in my purse on the bluff at the beach where I picnicked with the devil or it was somewhere inside his Range Rover. Zack could have survived the night even though he was unable to catch up with me. Maybe he gave up on that.

I caught my image in the hallway mirror. Oh God, I can't have Luke and Jenny see me like this. It would scare them. I scurried around, nervously locking every door, then peeled off my bloody clothes and stepped into the shower, the warm water cascading over the stinging cuts and bruises on my body.

A noise from downstairs startled me. The doorbell chimed, then again, and a moment later, a third chime. He'd never ring the doorbell. He'd just break in, cut my throat in the shower. I quickly toweled off, blotted my wet hair, grabbed my terrycloth robe, and hobbled down the staircase, noticing that the gash on my ankle was still caked with creased lines of dried blood that I failed to effectively wash off. I needed a doctor, of course, but that would not be my first order of business. The doorbell quieted, tangling me up with heightened fear. Was Zack hiding in some corner of the house, ready to pounce, distracting me with the doorbell? Guardedly, I stepped into the kitchen, stooped down below the counter, level with the stools, feeling the aches shooting through my body. Moving from counter to counter, I tried to stay out of sight.

Thoughts of last night trickled into my mind. Damn, I should have called Aunt Sylvie then. I chose not to ask the couple or their friends in the woods to use their cell phone, not wanting them in any way involved in my troubles or for them to hear any related cell phone conversation. It would have rattled them, especially the woman, who seemed so wound up, and when her brother and sister-in-law arrived, she seemed to get even more hyper. Instead, the next morning, I simply asked the couple to drop me at the corner of my road, thanking them profusely before we parted, praying that Zack wouldn't be waiting for me. Now, sensing someone's presence either inside or outside my house, I shuddered.

As she stood at the front door, Tamakichi felt her mood fluctuate between hopefulness and despondency. Sandy didn't seem to be at home even though a vehicle was parked in her driveway.

Tamakichi noted that it was a lovely cottage from the outside. She had studied the Chinese art of feng shui, which she hoped would help her be more of a success in her seamstress business. Tamakichi specialized in creating unique curtains and wall hangings for her clients, over time evolving into an interior design expert of sorts. There were two basic principles in feng shui regarding the exterior of the house, both of which Tamakichi had fully embraced. The first was to blend harmoniously with the surrounding area and the second to have an entry door that made a strong statement, being powerful yet still inviting. She noted that this house had both. The exterior was painted a deep taupe color with an understated pale-green trim, and the front door was a much deeper green with a tasteful gold antique doorknocker set just below an arched leaded glass window.

When nobody answered the door after her three attempts at the doorbell, Tamakichi peeked into the living room through the bay window, discerning a loving, happy energy within, yet there was some sense of shadow, some type of cloud hanging over the living space. What surprised her was the pile of toys and children's books spread out on the sofa. Children lived here, young children. This realization caused her to reexamine her wisdom at showing up unannounced. "I'd better go," she mumbled to herself. But something made her ring the doorbell one more time. There was a calm but distinct energy coursing through her veins, like a hairbrush running through long hair, as she was reminded of her mission.

Chapter Twenty-Eight

Visitors

Crouching down behind the sofa, I inched closer to the window. Oh God, was it really the old Japanese woman from the restaurant, Emily Kota's mother? The woman's words came back to me: "What you see, not real. Not real, Sandy Stonemeyer. You understand?" I didn't want to answer the front door. I didn't want to speak to this woman. Dammit. She must have something important to say though. Maybe something's happened to Albie; maybe she had something to tell me about her daughter and my ex-husband. I had no freaking idea. Could Zachery have tracked him down already, and that's why he ditched searching for me last night?

I felt the hair tie in the pocket of the robe I was wearing. Pulling back my wet hair, I straightened myself and opened the door to face the tiny woman.

"You here. You here. Good," she said.

I was confused but took the opportunity to do a quick scan for any sign of Zachery. Pulling the woman inside and slamming the door shut, I stepped back, placed my hands on my hips, shooting her a questioning look.

"Why are you here?" I asked with a slight frown. "What do you want?"

Tamakichi bowed apologetically, and with her eyes and delicate hand gesture, requested to sit down on the sofa.

I nodded, waiting to hear from the older woman, who looked embarrassed.

"Do you want some water?" I found myself asking. "I...I'm sorry but I was just getting ready to rush out and pick up my kids. But, please, let me get you some water."

Moving unsteadily into the kitchen, I took a clean glass from the shelf and tapped the refrigerator spout for some filtered water.

The woman followed me.

"My name is Tamakichi. "I...I need to explain something to you. Very important information you need to hear."

I felt annoyed at her terrible timing, but my curiosity had been piqued. The woman's eyes moved to the gash on my ankle and then up to the bruises on my legs.

She didn't comment on my injuries, but I felt her sympathy when she said, "I know you think my daughter, Emily Kota, did a dishonorable thing with your husband. But not true. Not true!" She shook her head back and forth. "All fake but with clear purpose."

"What? What do you mean?" was all I could say.

"Yes, for your benefit only," she said slowly, "to quickly separate you from husband. I don't know why they do this thing." She shook her head again, staring into my eyes, seeming to ask for forgiveness.

Why was she telling me this? Was it really all staged to cause me to leave Albie? I wondered. I sat shakily atop the kitchen stool, dropping my clouded head in my hands, tears rolling uncontrollably down my face, recalling that miserable night in San Francisco, the shocking bedroom scene, with the beautiful young Japanese woman on top of Albie, her head turning in my direction, her dark eyes slicing through me... Was it faked, the whole thing?

◆　◆　◆

Just then the kitchen door sprung open, interrupting my thoughts. It was Zachery, disheveled, filthy, his eyes bloodshot, his clothes ripped, his neck caked with blood, holding a pistol in his hand.

A tall woman followed in behind him, slamming the door shut with a thud. I froze, my neck stiffened, and I felt a tingling up and down my spine, as I searched the eyes of my good friend, Mimi, who now stood next to Zack, a sardonic half-smile on her face. At first, I was struck by the thought that Zachery must have kidnapped Mimi. Or maybe she was just about to knock on my door and the asshole grabbed her from behind.

"Mimi? You're with *him*?" I said in disbelief.

They both smirked.

"Why...why, Mimi? What the hell are you doing with *him*? I thought you were my good friend."

"You wouldn't understand," she said. Then she glanced at the old woman. "So you two are friends now?" she remarked, shaking her head.

"Who the fuck is *this one*?" Zack asked, looking over at Tamakichi.

"Well, I forgot to tell you about her," Mimi replied.

Thoughts were racing through my head as Zack gestured with his gun for me to move off the stool and into the living room. Mimi was also holding a pistol. I hadn't registered seeing it in her hand when she first entered the kitchen.

"Both of you get on the settee in the living room," he ordered. *"Now! Move!"*

Tamakichi hadn't taken her eyes from me as if all she cared about was my safety. Although she stood several feet away, I felt the sensation of her arms around me, hugging me to her breast, protecting me. But I was fading, exhausted from all I'd been through. I wanted to give up, beg Zack to spare this innocent woman, allow her to leave.

I was trying to think of how I could convince them to let her go when he said, "Your kids are next." Then he laughed. "I will savor your Aunt Sylvie watching me kill the precious Jenny and Luke. I think I'll do it silently and very quickly, but no, no, no...maybe slowly instead."

He had a look of glee on his face, the skunk smell exuding from his clothes and body, as he moved toward me, gesturing that I should get into the living room. Then he took an object out of his pocket. He was latching a long, gray, metal cylinder to his gun, a silencer. I sat down on the sofa. Mimi moved swiftly over to Tamakichi and pushed her gun already equipped with a silencer into the older woman's lower back.

I cringed. "She barely speaks English; she's old. Don't hurt her, Mimi, please. Why...why are you doing this?" I cried.

Mimi rolled her eyes and shook her head in annoyance. "Doesn't really matter now, does it? But for the record, I'm Antonio's life partner, his wife to be. Cassie, the woman your fucking husband murdered, was almost my sister-in-law, a fine mother, and my closest friend. Now get over to the fucking sofa," she said, turning to Tamakichi and nudging the gun more forcefully into her back.

I could see Tamakichi physically resisting. Furious, Mimi pushed her with her elbow and then kicked her leg straight out, swinging it in the air, landing her foot down into the frail woman's chest, as if calling on some long-studied martial art. Tamakichi fell back onto the sofa, yelling out in pain.

"Stop! Please, no need to hurt her," I beseeched.

Mimi looked at me and grinned nonchalantly. Turning to Zack, an Irish accent evident, she said, "Wait, let's have Sandy call the aunt and say she'll be over in thirty minutes to pick up the kids." She moved closer to him, as she pointed her gun at both of us.

Zack motioned to the phone hanging on the kitchen wall and looked over at me. "Call your grumpy Aunt Sylvie then," he said.

I didn't move, wanting to stay close to Tamakichi. He rushed over to the sofa and sat perched on the upholstered arm, pointing his gun at Tamakichi's temple.

"If you say anything, anything, to your aunt, other than you'll be over there in half an hour to get yer kids, and sorry you didn't call her last night, having lost track of the time, accidentally falling asleep, then I will put a quick bullet clean into this old woman's head. Then I'll rush next door and murder your kids and your sweet aunt. It's your call Sandy fucking Stonemeyer, and you know, I don't really give a shit which way we do this."

"But the landline's been disconnected. It's dead. I just checked it when I got home. Remember, I called AT&T the other day."

He bolted back into the kitchen toward the wall phone, then suddenly stopped and said, "Yes, I fucking remember! Well then, use your bloody cell phone to make the call!"

"But you have it. I...I don't know where it is."

"Here." He reached into his pocket. "Oh shit. It's in the bloody Rover."

"No, don't go to the car," Mimi shouted. "Your Rover's down the fucking street. Let's just get rid of these two, then surprise the aunt and the kids. It makes little difference. She obviously can't use your phone or mine! Come to your senses. This is it, exactly what we've been waiting for—revenge!"

I had managed to live through hell in the dark woods and now I was going to die anyway, my children never to see me again. I was searching my aching head for what I could do as a defense when I suddenly heard a choking, hacking noise and saw something brown and slimy splash onto my white robe. From this tiny Japanese woman came a flood of vomit alarming all three of us.

"What...the hell?" Zack barked.

Mimi stood silent, unable to speak.

Tamakichi wasn't finished, as she threw up again, hitting my cherry wood coffee table, showering the orchid sitting in the center.

"Fuckin' disgusting," the Irishman said, brushing the gun to his forehead, seeming to question how to handle the situation.

"Disgusting, huh?" I said maliciously. "What's disgusting is your stench, like the skunk you are."

"She's right about the stink," Mimi quipped.

Ignoring Mimi for a moment, Zack bent down on the rug and placed his face close to mine. His odor was overwhelming. He grabbed my shoulders, pushing me onto the sofa's left armrest away from the splashes of vomit.

"I hated fucking you," he screamed. "You're such a plastic cliché of a middle-class American mother, whose daughter thinks nothing of her. No resemblance between the father-daughter bond I have with my little girl. She hates you because you're a bitch!" He laughed again. "You were a fraud as much as I was!" he added, pulling me up, shaking me, then shoving me back onto the sofa next to the frightened Japanese woman.

"You're Felicia's father then...not her uncle?" I said. "Why bother with the façade? Why?"

"Anything to throw you off from my real identity."

"You drugged me at the gas station, didn't you? That pinch in my lower back."

He rolled his eyes.

"You bastard! It was you!"

Then he came up behind the sofa, and pulled my hair back, my eyes tearing up, and said, "I wanted to fucking kill you right there in the rain with your kids watching me do it, but decided to do it more elegantly instead. Reel you in first, make you need me, want me, hurt your children, then cut you into little pieces in the redwoods. But you got lucky, that's all. It's time for justice now."

"Shut up, Wendall. Shut up!" Mimi said, throwing the package of bundled rope and a roll of masking tape onto the area rug, away from the dripping vomit. She stood there glaring at him. "Let's get on with it," she continued. "We'll tie them up and gag them, as if there was a robbery at their house or something."

"Wendall? Your name's not even Zachery?" I said.

Tamakichi sat by my side, looking pale, convulsing, seeming to be on the point of another round of heaving. Oh God, I thought, will she die before he finishes us off? Or was she somehow intentional with this act of desperation? I struggled to get my bearings, floundering on how I could contribute to stalling our two enemies.

"I'm not touching *that*," he shouted out to Mimi. "You need to do the honors. To be sure, that vomit is contaminated. She Chinese or what?"

"Japanese," I said. "Look, maybe I can help you find Albie."

Mimi ripped off some masking tape and put it over Tamakichi's mouth, the older woman flopping back on the sofa like a ragdoll, seeming to almost pass out.

"Um, listen," I said, not willing to give up the fight. "You won't be able to find him without me. I'm your best bet. I...I just spoke to him an hour ago. Someone lent me a phone and I immediately called him," I lied, not having heard from Albie for several weeks now. "If you get my cell phone from your car, I can call him, find out where he is, so you can easily get to him. You have your collateral sitting right here. Please don't hurt her. You want to kill me, fine. You want to find Albie, I can help you."

Tamakichi was slouched down on the sofa, her head sitting on her chest, her mouth gagged. Her eyes shot up, however, locking with mine, communicating her understanding of the charade.

"Fuck you," he said. "No deal."

The doorbell suddenly rang out.

"Get on the fucking floor, both of you. Now!" Zack barked, as he kneeled down to hide himself, pointing the gun at our heads.

I got off the sofa onto the floor, pulling Tamakichi down with me. She seemed woozy, disoriented, as she slipped on the vomit that surrounded the sofa and coffee table.

"Don't say a word or you're both dead," he said.

Mimi's gun was pointed at Tamakichi's face. I wanted to wring Mimi's neck. "Lay the fuck down," Mimi ordered Tamakichi, who was still sliding around, struggling to get her balance back.

The doorbell chimed another three times. Then footsteps were heard descending the front steps. Whoever had been there was now gone.

"Fucking stay down until I say otherwise, or I will pull the trigger," Zachery threatened.

After several minutes of waiting, he said, "Okay Sandy, get back on the settee. Were you expecting someone?"

"No. Maybe it's the kids next door checking to see if I'm home yet. I...I don't know. Please, let me call them on my cell phone like you wanted me to do."

"You're fucking crazy," he replied. Then he looked over at Mimi. "Keep the gun to their heads. I'll tie them up and wrap the masking tape around their mouths."

Chapter Twenty-Nine

The Battle Ensues

In the house next door, Jenny was tired of playing hide-and-seek with her brother. She used up all the usual places, hiding under the bed, in the hall closet, below the stairwell, and in the shower stall, Luke finding her every time. She sat down on Aunt Sylvie's bed, feeling sullen and neglected. Where was her mother? Why didn't she come to pick us up last night? They called her four times last night and two times this morning, but each of their attempts went straight to voicemail. She tried to pretend that she wasn't worried, her thoughts going to the night when her mom passed out at the gas station. Although it was months ago, it felt like just the other night.

Luke came running into the room. "Huh, why aren't you hiding?" he asked. "We're still playing, right?"

"No, I don't want to play anymore."

"Why? Why not? Come on, play."

"No Luke, I'm bored with this game."

Aunt Sylvie called from the kitchen. "Jenny, Luke, I have some Jell-O for dessert, cherry flavor with some Cool Whip."

"I hate cherry," Jenny growled.

"Yeah, but I like it," Luke said, running into the kitchen.

"Geesh Mom, where are you?" Jenny said aloud, following her brother into the kitchen. She didn't want to be rude to Aunt Sylvie, who spent most of her time writing and reading magazines. She liked Aunt Sylvie, especially when she baked chocolate-chip cookies and cinnamon rolls, and read books aloud to them, doing all the voices for the different characters. I guess I'll have some Jell-O, she thought. Anyway, she probably doesn't remember that I don't like cherry.

Aunt Sylvie had two heaping bowls of Jell-O topped with a generous dollop of Cool Whip sitting on the table. Luke was already scooping a spoonful into his mouth.

"This is great," he mumbled.

Just then the doorbell rang.

"I'll get it," Jenny shouted, happy to escape the table. "Thank God Mom is finally here."

"No," Aunt Sylvie objected. "Kids, don't get the door at my house. You never know who's there. I'll get it. An adult needs to answer. Doesn't your mom use that rule at your house? I'm sure she does."

Aunt Sylvie struggled to get up from the chair, wobbling over to the door, using her cane for assistance.

As Aunt Sylvie opened the door, Jenny could see it was her dad standing there.

"Dad! Dad!" she exclaimed, running to him. "You're here. We missed you." She hugged him around the waist. "You've been away for such a long time."

Luke came up from behind, jumping into his dad's arms. Albie swung him in the air.

"Albie," Aunt Sylvie said, disappointment showing on her face. "We thought you were Sandy. We're concerned about her. Have you heard from her?"

Jenny then chimed in, "Dad, did she call you to come and pick us up?"

He shook his head. "No, I haven't heard from your mom. When was she supposed to be here? Is she on a story or something?"

"Well yes," Aunt Sylvie responded tersely, "but that story was yesterday afternoon. She hasn't shown up yet. She said she'd be home late, but well, it's not like her to not show up at all."

She pointed back to the kitchen. "You kids better eat that Jell-O before all of the Cool Whip melts away."

Albie put the boy down, and Luke rushed away to finish his dessert. Jenny stood there glued to her dad, who looked worried.

"Come into the kitchen," Aunt Sylvie said.

Albie and Jenny followed her, joining Luke at the table.

"What's going on?" Albie asked, as he reached inside his jacket, making sure that he had his pistol.

"She might be with Zachery, an Irishman she's been seeing. But I don't know. She told me that she was coming straight back after her TV assignment."

"Irishman? What Irishman? You mean her boyfriend? He's Irish?" Albie asked.

"Yes," answered Aunt Sylvie. "Irish accent and everything."

Albie 's mind veered off in multiple directions, feeling the same panic he felt when he first heard about Manny being murdered by the Irish. Stepping away from the table, he yanked the phone out of his pocket in the foyer and punched in a number.

A monotone voice answered on the other end.

"Emily, it's me, Albie. Look, I know it's the weekend, but listen, I need some information fast, real fast. Can you pull up the Irish file and read me the aliases for Wendall Stuart McKinney?"

He waited and then listened to a string of five or six names. Bingo! The last one on the list included the name Zachery. The full alias was Stuart Michael Zachery, Emily indicating that that one was the most recent alias, added only last month.

"Shit!" Albie said aloud.

Jenny looked up from her Jell-O, registering that her dad didn't usually swear in front of them. Luke ignored the curse word. Aunt Sylvie's two dogs paced in the hallway near the kitchen window, appearing restless.

"Dad, what's wrong? Is it Mom?" Jenny asked, running to him as he tucked the phone back into his jacket. "Did something happen?" She started to bite her lip.

"No...no. Some work thing is happening, that's all." He pulled her to him, reassuring her with a hug. He didn't want to alarm his kids or Aunt

Sylvie, but he had to find his ex-wife. Where was she? Not at home, he just rang the doorbell. Shit, it doesn't mean she's not there. Just pray that she's still alive, he told himself. He looked at his daughter and proceeded to lie. "Um, look, I'm sorry honey, but I've got to take this call from work, so I'll step outside and be in my car. I may need to drive away for awhile, but I'll be back."

"Dad, please don't leave us again," Jenny begged, still clinging to him.

Luke continued digging into his Cool Whip, his aunt having handed him another bowl with plenty of creamy topping.

"I'll be back in no time, pumpkin." He tapped his daughter on the tip of her nose. "Promise, cross my heart."

Smiling back at Luke, he opened the front door, then closed it gently behind him, immediately ducking down out of sight behind the bushes between the two houses.

He's in there, I know it. I can feel his slimy presence. Self-degradation enveloped him. He felt repulsed by his own naiveté. I'm fucking CIA. Why was I convinced that Sandy wasn't home because nobody answered her door? He cursed himself again. Zachery is her boyfriend, the Irishman! CIA, how could I call myself CIA? I should have paid closer attention, investigating who Sandy was spending time with, knowing that the Brethren were out to take my family down.

Had she slept with the swine? Had Wendall Stuart McKinny, alias Zachery, put his hands all over Sandy's body? Was he in bed with her right now? His mind flew to the north and south of his imagination. Stop fucking around, he chided himself. Now's the time to click into your tough-guy operative mode, not act like some mushy, jealous ex-husband.

I love her more than I ever did. I love her, he thought, remembering the day he first saw her, insulated, her emotions in absolute check, under the bright lights of the camera at the Oakland Police Station. She was strikingly beautiful, stopping him in his tracks. Maybe it was the way she brushed the stray hair from her cheek, the way she twirled her pen as she asked the Police Chief incisive questions from her clipboard. Sandy was still the only woman he'd ever want.

Keeping low to the ground, he hurdled over the lowest point of the fence between the houses at the back near the tree house he had built only weeks ago for Luke. He could hear Aunt Sylvie's two Huskies barking in the background, wishing they'd shut up.

Deciding whether or not to rush in and perform a raid-style take-down, he was seized by ambivalence. If Sandy was inside and held captive, and he stormed in, then Wendall might instantly pull the trigger, committing the ultimate in revenge, killing her right before his eyes. But the house seemed deserted, not a sound, nor any movement, that he could see or hear. The slime ball probably had Sandy somewhere else. I better get his mountain house address from my car and get my ass over there, he thought.

◆　◆　◆

"Stop moving, you bitch," Mimi ordered as she zip-tied my wrists.

I was suddenly dizzy. My ankle was oozing blood again, the rope digging into the wound. I noticed that the cut had opened again, a trickle of blood sliding down toward my slipper.

Tamakichi sat beside me in her pool of vomit, her body erect, a distinct defiance in the small woman's posture. Splashes of vomit were drizzled across Luke and Jenny's pile of toys that sat adjacent to the sofa on Tamakichi's right.

The whole scene was disgusting, without a doubt, but I realized that this frail, unassuming woman had managed to successfully delay our death. I had to admit that I was scared, as my life was about to end for the second time in twenty-four hours, yet I couldn't help the smirk that crept across my face.

Tamakichi looked over at me. Was that a grin? Then turning her head to her right, the small woman caught sight of the stack of toys. An electronic robot...she recognized it as a very popular toy in Japan. Set on its side close to the pile of other toys, the gold and silver object appeared to be damaged. Without further thought, Tamakichi slid down off the soiled sofa, into the puddle of her own vomit, digging her heels into the throw rug, swiftly edging herself over to the robot.

Hitting the large button on its head, she caused a loud, shrill noise to blare out, like a siren, and then the staccato words: "I am at your com-mand, at your com-mand. I am at your com-mand!" The toy's siren went off again, the shrieking sound reverberating through the house. Then the robot spoke again: "Tell me to bring you my zap gun! Tell me to bring you my zap gun!"

Albie's eyes widened, acknowledging the familiar sound of Luke's ro-bot. He remembered that Sandy wanted to throw out that robot because of the violent language, but he was happy she hadn't followed through. She's in there, he realized, relieved and terrified at the same time. Then he heard a man's voice shouting, "Shut that fucking thing up. Mimi, turn it off!"

Wendall Stuart McKinney, alias Zachery, it's him! Mimi? Wait, wait... isn't that Luke's teacher? That high-and-mighty know-it-all?

"Keep your knickers on," Mimi replied.

"Dammit," Albie said, touching the gun to his head, "she's in cahoots with that schmuck." He cocked his gun. Edging quickly toward the patio door, closing in on the wooden picnic table, he hid behind the heap of backyard toys and bicycles, stretching his neck to peer inside the house without being seen.

Nobody was in the kitchen, but the space between the kitchen coun-ters and the tall stools gave him a narrow line of sight into the living room. He spotted legs, two pairs of legs sitting on the sofa. Sandy's white ter-rycloth robe was visible hanging down to her fuzzy white slippers. She's there! Another pair of legs, wearing black pants, small feet, flat black shoes. Shit, he boiled inside, seeing that their ankles were zip-tied.

With a single move, he kicked the kitchen door open, his pistol point-ed, and took a clean shot at the tall Irishman, and Wendall went down.

Mimi spun around, shooting blindly at the kitchen door. But Albie was already on the floor, crawling for cover behind the counters. Finding him with her eyes, Mimi took another shot, hitting him in his right thigh.

He rolled over out of sight. She had him now, running in for the kill. He grabbed her leg and pulled her down, her gun sliding away on the kitchen tile. She could easily reach for it, take him out, and then finish off the two women on the sofa.

Mimi held the pistol in her hand, ready to take the shot. She felt a hot burning in her chest. A blanket of black was closing in. It was hard for her to breathe. We lost the fucking battle...lost the fucking war. That was Mimi's last coherent thought.

Wendall was still breathing. Albie got on his cell phone to call for an ambulance, but he noticed the Irishman's hand uncurl as he gave the street address to the 911 operator. The thug was gone. A smile crossed Albie's face.

Tamakichi came over to me. Albie put his arm on her shoulder. "You okay, Mrs. Kota?"

Nodding, she reached out to hold my hand. "We beat bad guys, yes?" she said.

I nodded.

"You have good husband, very good husband."

Chapter Thirty

Reunion

Living in a world of snake-charmers and liars for more than a year now, I had successfully hidden behind my mask of mother, victim, journalist, lover, sister, and supposedly jilted wife. But the "real me" was still a skinny little ten-year-old, left orphaned by her two thrill-seeking parents, who went off to Lake Tahoe one morning without a second thought, and were instantly gone forever! My feelings surfaced the day after my near death at the hands of the mad Irishman, suppressed emotions from my childhood seeping out of every cell of my body.

Albie's years of deceit haunted me, his invented corporate private investigations career, his faked infidelity, his desperate attempts to protect his family, memories of my ex-husband forever etched in my consciousness. I love this man. I likely would never stop loving him, but his lies wouldn't leave me.

As I stood in his embrace, gazing over his shoulder, through the sliding glass door to the tree house he built with love for his son, he whispered fresh promises for our future together. He told me how he's given his two-week notice to the CIA as he pulled me closer. I could sense the regrets flooding his heart. But *my* heart wasn't ready to let the hands of time move forward for "us." I yearned to replace the old timepiece with a new one, one that wouldn't include Albie as either my lover or my husband, at least for now.

I want to find love again, I thought, yes, but without filters, without lies. Most importantly, I want to be a good parent to my kids. My career, the one I'm trying to rebuild, is also a priority. The job I've been offered in Sacramento as TV anchor for Channel 6's umbrella station is too good to pass up. It will mean regular daytime hours, including a decent increase in salary. Aunt Sylvie has agreed to come and live with us, bringing her two dogs along. I want her close. Sharing my decisions with Albie, I explained where I stood on the subject of "us" and my planned relocation to Sacramento. I felt ambivalent as I spoke.

"Albie, I just need time to recover," I said. "It's my time to find myself, rediscover my way, get back my equilibrium. And I'll make enough money to buy a bungalow on the Sacramento River with only a ten-minute commute to the television studio. I can't turn this down, Albie, I just can't. You can spend two weekends a month with the kids, if you're open to it."

He nodded, leaning back on the sofa, his hands on top of his head, palms to the ceiling, taking in my words.

It is true, I thought, that life rarely unravels as planned. But this time, this time, I'll be better equipped for the unpredictable twists and turns, stronger from my experiences, wiser from my mistakes. I took his hand in mine and looked deeply into his eyes. He may be in my future someday, but my hunch is that he'll likely change his direction, seduced by some other clandestine adventure, before I ever get to the point of accepting him with all his imperfections.

We sat quietly, my mind wandering to the Japanese marvel that is Tamakichi. I owe my life to her indomitable spirit. If she hadn't thrown up on my sofa that day, if she hadn't jumped on that toy robot, its siren demanding Albie's attention, I'm not sure if we would have all made it through alive. We've both pledged to stay connected.

My thoughts went to Jenny. Upon learning that the Irish family we spent so much time with had been secretly conniving to harm all of us, her reaction was unexpectedly pensive and unemotional. Her obsessive disdain with me seems to have melted away after finding out that her father had never actually committed adultery. She understands why I want to start over without her father, realizes that I need my space in a new setting with her and Luke at my side. She trusts my assurances that she will see him at least two weekends a month, if he lives up to our agreement this time, commits to staying connected to his children. Of course, that's unknown territory at this point.

Albie hugged me close for a quick moment, and then released me, my body already missing his touch. He got up, slipped his hands into his pockets, that signature lazy smile spreading across his face. But his eyes betrayed him, appearing to leave the present to visit how we were as a family before our lives were turned upside down.

We could hear Jenny and Luke upstairs playing, the dice rolling around, clattering on the board, the kids arguing, debating the rules, and then eagerly supporting one another.

"It's your turn, Luke. Come on, get a good roll! Come on, you need a five." Another clatter of dice, one of them seeming to roll off the board onto the carpet. A pause. "Wow Luke, look, you got it! You got a five."

"Yay. I'm gonna win," Luke yelled out.

I grinned, thinking she's been much more patient with Luke over the past few days. I didn't expect it to last for more than another week, but I was grateful for her efforts. "She's growing up," I whispered, getting up and nudging Albie.

He shot me his "proud father" smile. "Yeah, she's a damn good big sister. Hug them goodbye for me, would you?" His eyes moistened. "And listen, you can rely on me to help you make the move up north, if that's what you really want. Just keep me posted on when you'll need me. I'll rent a U-Haul and follow you up there, help you unload everything." He looked like a lost boy for just a moment, then brightened, saying, "Well, I...I guess I'm a free man now...no job, no..." he stopped himself, realizing the unintended bad joke.

Shrugging apologetically, he walked away just a few steps, and then turned back to me, bringing his right index finger up to his right eye, then down to his heart, and then pointed it straight out at me. "I love you, Jelly Bean," he said. "I'm not giving up. That, you can count on."

THE END

About the Author

Linda S. Gunther grew up in New York City and attended Queens College and then Columbia University Graduate School, majoring in Counseling Psychology. She escaped New York City for a different lifestyle on the West Coast. Making a giant leap abroad, she started a new life in London, England, where she studied psychotherapy, taught primary school, counseled parents, and gave birth to her son.

Upon returning to California, she completed her M.B.A. and transitioned into a new career in Human Resources, working for various Silicon Valley companies. She currently lives with her husband Bob on the Santa Cruz coast in Northern California, where she consults corporate clients and writes.

Her passion for travel and continuous learning fuels her fire to create vivid fictional characters and unforgettable storylines. She is also the author of three other romantic suspense novels: **Ten Steps From The Hotel Inglaterra, Endangered Witness**, and **Lost In The Wake**. If you enjoy thrillers with a backdrop of intense family relationships and romance, you will savor every page of this author's novels.

www.ingramcontent.com/pod-product-compliance
Lightning Source LLC
Chambersburg PA
CBHW022103170626
46808CB00002B/568

THE JOHNSON AMULET

AND OTHER SCOTTISH TERRORS